PRAISE FOR

WHEN I WAS ALICE

"Murgia's *When I Was Alice* is a sparkling, suspenseful ode to the Golden Age of Hollywood . . . Murgia weaves a clever, genre-bending whodunnit fleshed out by a cast of quirky characters, a vibrant setting, and a star-crossed romance. I was hooked from the very first page."
—Jenny Adams, author of *A Deadly Endeavor*

"*When I Was Alice* offers masterful prose and an immersive setting, transporting you to the heart of old Hollywood, and wrapping you in an enthralling, time-bending mystery. You won't be able to put this book down until the final, breathtaking reveal."
—Katlyn L. Duncan, author of *Her Buried Lives*

"A haunting thriller of a book—Murgia delivers a timeslip whodunnit, immersing us in old Hollywood's glitter and glamour while exposing its darkest undercurrents."
—Lisa Amowitz, author of *An Island Strange and Wild*

WHEN I WAS ALICE

WHEN I WAS ALICE

JENNIFER MURGIA

CamCat Books

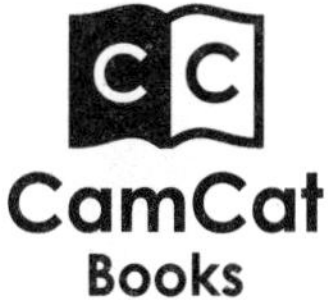

CamCat Publishing, LLC
Fort Collins, Colorado 80524
camcatpublishing.com

This is a work of fiction. Names, characters, places, and incidents are either products of the author's imagination or are used fictitiously.

Hardcover ISBN 9780744310672
Paperback ISBN 9780744310696
Large-Print Paperback ISBN 9780744310719
eBook ISBN 9780744310702
Audiobook ISBN 9780744310726

Library of Congress Control Number: 2023950766

Book and cover design by Maryann Appel
Interior artwork by Alexandr Bakanov, DavidGoh, Pure Imagination

5 3 1 2 4

For my grandmother, the "real" Alice.

And for anyone who needed to fall before they could find themselves.

POLICE REPORT

September 9, 1953

Incident:	Missing Person
Location:	Hollywood, CA
Details:	Alice Montgomery. Actress. Blonde. 5′4″.
Notes:	Do not alert press

CHAPTER ONE

"RYAN?" I LAY MY HAND on the edge of the hospital bed, the cool sheet over my brother's still body barely rumpled. The machine next to me beeps with steady persistence as clear liquid drips into a tube in his arm. I study him in silent expectation because today, more than ever, I need him to hear me—to give some sort of sign that it's going to be all right. But Ryan remains still. I quietly watch my brother's eyelids. Not a single twitch or tremor. No indication that he's aware I am beside him.

My gaze drifts toward the two lumps that are his feet at the end of the bed. I wait for movement but there is none. "I know we planned this months ago. You helped me go over all the lines so I'd nail this, only . . ." My voice snags in my throat, which has suddenly gone dry with the truth: I am going to let him down.

This week my brother was supposed to start his final project at UCLA's School of Theater, Film, and Television. He rented a space downtown to hold auditions for his senior thesis in his major, directing a modernized version of *Rebel Without a Cause*, his favorite movie of all time. When he told me he wanted me to try out for a lead role in his student film—Natalie Wood's character—I pushed for a smaller part. But acting was never for me. In fact, the entire entertainment industry was never for me. It's his thing.

Weighted down with guilt, I know this project is huge, even without the connection to his favorite film. It's his chance to prove he wants to and can direct, therefore breaking into the competitive Hollywood film industry.

Except . . . last week, Ryan went to Lake Hollywood Park, tolerating the tourists, to stare up at the white letters of the Hollywood sign. He often goes there to daydream of one day defying the rules and climbing the infamous letter *H*—carving his name there after his first Hollywood success, signaling to eternity that indeed he is an integral part of the mystique he so adores.

On the way home, Ryan's car spun out of control on Mulholland Highway, busting through the fencing on the other side of the road and down the embankment. An injured coyote was found lying in the middle of the road—apparently the cause of the accident.

That night Mom sat in this very chair next to him, her shoulders shaking with violent sobs. And when the doctors told us Ryan had slipped into a coma, Dad stood so straight, his face pained beyond belief, that he looked as if he were afraid to move. Every day since, we've been keeping a silent vigil, hoping and praying Ryan will wake up.

"You're here early," the morning-shift nurse interrupts as she enters the room, the pants of her navy blue scrubs swishing with each step. She smiles at me and proceeds to assess Ryan's vitals, her quick fingers pressing the confusing buttons on the machine next to his bed.

"I just wanted to check on him," I reply, watching as she loops another bag of IV fluid onto the hooked stand.

The nurse moves to the other side of the room and scribbles the next staff shift on the whiteboard, then gives me a thoughtful look. "He can hear you, you know. He may not be able to show it, but he's in there." She tilts her head, then gives me an encouraging smile before leaving me alone with my brother.

I stand and lean over the bed, gazing down at his inert form beneath the covers. The tiny cuts on his face have already scabbed over and the growth of a thin beard covers his chin. "I hope she's right—that you can hear me." The words are thick in my throat. "And that you know how much we love you and need you to wake up." I squeeze his limp hand and pause, hoping the contact of our skin might trigger something—anything. "I really hope you forgive me," I murmur as everything else I want to say coats my tongue with regret.

IT TAKES TWO loops around the block on Vine Street before I spot an empty space along the curb. The tiny office my brother rented, which is about the size of a storage closet, is still a block away on Yucca Street, and even though my audition time for the student film my brother is supposed to direct is in ten minutes, I can't bring myself to get out of the car.

I should have gone right home after leaving the hospital, but my guilt set me on autopilot, as if I'd find the courage to go through with the audition—to do this one thing for my brother. But as soon as I turn off the engine, it's as if I'm paralyzed.

There's a tug-of-war inside me. I've reasoned with myself that he'll understand why I can't do it—not while he's in the hospital, not while my parents and I are scared to death he isn't going to wake up—that bailing on something so important to him doesn't mean I'm giving up hope. Hope that he'll wake up. Hope that his student film gets made. Hope that he'll graduate. Hope that life will go on as planned, the accident but a little bump in the road.

Even at the library, where I sit at the circulation desk all day and shelve carts of books, Ryan's accident follows me like a shadow. I've overheard patrons between the stacks, people from our neighborhood, kids my brother and I went to school with, ask, "Is Ryan Brighton still in the hospital?"

The conversations are always muffled, yet I zero in on every mention of *accident*, *car wreck*, and *coma*. Their words like knives stab my heart, little by little.

Now, a mere block away from what is supposed to be my brother's future, my brain conjures black tire marks on the road and glass scattered by the bushes. An image of Ryan's too-still body flashes inside my head. He should be here, waiting for me to show up to claim my role in his film, not hooked up to machines, clinging to life. And I should have stayed at the hospital, talking to him like the nurse suggested, encouraging him to wake up.

As if knowing my car is parked in the shadow of the Capitol Records building, my phone pings with a text from my best friend, Beth, who's landed a job there answering phones in one of the offices.

Just wanted to say good luck!

I tuck my chin to my chest and will my heart rate to slow to a normal pace. Only it's not my heart I worry about. I haven't even opened my mouth, but I feel the familiar seizing of my throat. A tightness telling me my vocal cords are gearing up to get stuck on repeat. I had thought my childhood impediment was gone, but it started again when my parents told me Ryan had been airlifted to the hospital.

Changed my mind, I text back. *I'm a terrible person.*

Now listen to me, Grace Brighton. You're not terrible. If it's not what you want, then don't do it. Ryan will understand.

My thumbs hover over my screen, but Beth already knows my reasons—the ones that are warring inside me.

That even though I should help my brother, I'm tired of being Ryan's shadow. Tired of being compared to him. Tired of trying to be what he wants me to be.

That I've chosen to defend my job at the library and not go to college. Tired of living at home when all I want is my own place. Beth and I have talked about renting an apartment together, but I don't have enough money. My high school graduation was at the onset of the pandemic, causing me to lose two years of deciding what I wanted—hence, my reason for still being so dependent on my parents.

I'm already late, I text back. *I'm sure someone better for the role will get it.*

I check the time on my phone. In all honesty, I can haul myself down the street and make it. But the longer I look at the screen, each passing second tells me I'm blowing my chance—perhaps even blowing Ryan's future.

All those weeks of practicing, of getting excited at the smile on his face each time he whipped out a new script for me to practice. Gone. Maybe he'll understand once he wakes up; maybe he won't hate me when I tell him this is something I could only do with him there. If he can't watch me, I can't—won't—perform.

I take a deep breath and type back, *Text you later. Heading home.*

It takes a few minutes for the dots to appear on my screen that mean she's texting back.

Next time you're at the hospital, tell Ryan I'm praying he pulls through.

I toss my phone onto the passenger seat and start my car, wondering what I can possibly do to make this up to him.

CHAPTER TWO

THE SIGHT OF MY PARENTS' cars in the driveway wrenches my stomach. Every free moment they have is spent at the hospital, while I join them after work and in the evenings, so it's no wonder seeing their cars parked side by side, and knowing they are both inside the house, causes my heart to thud faster. I ease my Subaru between the recycling cans against the curb and take a deep breath. They've likely learned I skipped the audition, and their disappointment will bombard me as soon as I open the door.

Or it could be what I've dreaded most these last few days.

The instant I let myself in the front door the back of my neck grows slick and clammy. A terrible feeling crawls over my skin, and just as I am about to brace myself for the worst, my mom pokes her head out from around the corner of the kitchen. She holds a finger to her mouth and nods toward the living room, where my dad sleeps on the couch. I realize now that if something had happened, my parents would be at the hospital, not home. But since they are, the house is too quiet—there are no sounds of crying and anguish. I'm suddenly overwhelmed with guilt over not staying by Ryan's side instead of sitting in my car on Vine, going over all the reasons why I didn't want to audition for his student film.

"Your dad and I came home to get a little rest, but I'm heading over to the hospital shortly. I was just getting a few things to take with me."

"But Ryan . . . he's . . ."

"No change yet, sweetie." My mother looks like she hasn't slept in days. Her eyes are puffy beneath her makeup, and she's hastily twisted her hair into a messy ponytail.

"I'll come with you, just give me a sec."

Mom touches my arm and gives it a soft rub. "I'll take this one. You get some rest." She looks over at my father. "I don't want you to worry more than you already are right now. The doctors told us Ryan's vitals are stable. We just need to wait and see what happens."

I nod, but her words don't convince me.

She shuffles softly back into the kitchen, leaving me alone in the hall, not asking about the audition, sparing me an explanation. Before my brother's accident, my mother was on top of everyone's schedule, but these days home feels like an alien planet. Dad sleeps more than usual, stressed from his busy work schedule he's tried to fit around the hospital's visiting hours, and my mom spends more time by Ryan's bedside than at home—which is how it should be.

But I miss the weekends when we'd all be home together—the smell of popcorn lingering in the air after dinner and the soft strains of vintage music seeping beneath Ryan's door when he would spend weekend nights at home. I'd give anything to hear my family's noises filling one end of the house to the other in our ranch house in Beachwood Canyon—a home my parents could barely afford in the nineties after they got married, until my dad landed a job with a pharmaceutical company, working his way up to executive.

At the end of the hall, Ryan's bedroom door stands open across from mine, the room as quiet as a tomb.

I take a deep breath and slip inside.

The silence is stifling.

I used to drown out the sound of Ryan shuffling around, reciting lines, listening to music, shouting into his PlayStation headset. Now it's as if his room is waiting for his return like the rest of us. His bed is made the way my mom does it, not Ryan's messy excuse of pulling the comforter up over his tangled sheets. His things are untouched yet clean, as if newly dusted—another "unlike Ryan" observation, since my brother thrives in his organized mess.

My eye catches the worn leather jacket hanging over the back of his gaming chair. God, he loves this jacket so much—a replica of one James Dean wore. My mom brought it home from the hospital along with the rest of Ryan's things and painstakingly pulled the glass shards from the sleeve. I place my hand on the supple leather, my fingertips tracing over the jagged rip in the shoulder. The smell of his cologne rises from the collar, causing my breath to hitch in my throat as I realize my brother is the same age as James Dean was when he died.

The microwave beeps down the hall, alerting me that Mom is making another frozen dinner. My stomach rumbles but I ignore it as I stare at the *Rebel Without a Cause* movie poster hanging on the wall above his bed. Even if Ryan wakes up within the next few days it will be a while before he's allowed to come home.

I've never heard of anyone waking from a coma and bouncing back into their life, but I pray with everything I have that Ryan will. Even if he's angry with me for not auditioning today. For jeopardizing his student film, his calling card for getting his foot in the door in Hollywood.

With a heavy heart, I run my finger over the papers scattered across Ryan's desk, touching his future and past as they lie together in a heap. His class schedule sits on top of old play scripts he's never wanted to throw away, insisting I use them to practice my meager acting skills.

Mom is still puttering around the kitchen, allowing me to steal a moment to slide open the drawer of my brother's desk. My breath rushes out of me at the sight of Ryan's phone lying there. The screen is splintered and cracked, and the side of its case is dented. It's gut-wrenching proof of the severity of his accident—the awful reminder that my brother is just as broken and battered, fighting for his life behind the stillness of his eyelids and the silence of our prayers.

Gingerly, I pick up the phone and cradle it in my hands. If Ryan can't be here right now, then this is the closest I can be to him; a glimpse of his life before the accident to manifest that he'll make it.

My finger presses the home button. If the battery hasn't died, then surely the wreck damaged its inner mechanics; but to my amazement, the screen sputters then illuminates as if it's just fine.

I open his camera roll and scroll, and my eyes unexpectedly fill with tears. I'm reminded that Ryan's the smart kid. The Brightons' shining star.

He always has been, while I'm a disappointment.

Ambushed by emotion, I hover my thumb over the screen, ready to swipe away my brother's pre-summer memories when I catch a glimpse of something I've never seen before.

There are a couple of screenshots of Old Hollywood photos—much like the ones my brother found at the flea market at the beginning of summer.

A photo of James Dean stares up at me, his blond hair catching the sunlight and his arm draped around a woman's shoulders. She looks oddly familiar. I enlarge it with my fingers as tiny goose bumps spread over my arms. The young woman in the photo looks like . . . me. A fifties version of me. The same hair color, the same cheekbones, the same eyes. Along the lower portion of the image is a caption that appears to be handwritten in faded pencil: *1953. Hollywood. James Dean and Al* . . . The rest of the name is too faded to read, as if someone's thumb rubbed over it long ago.

I stare at it, puzzled. Ryan had to have noticed the woman's resemblance to me, but then why hadn't he shown it to me?

"I'll be back later," Mom whisper-calls from the hallway, the aroma of lasagna creeping closer.

My brain is still trying to figure out what I'm looking at as I hear the front door open and then close. It's most likely a coincidence that maybe Ryan never noticed, his obsession with James Dean so huge that he mentally cropped out the woman next to him. She's probably not even an actress—just a fan who was lucky enough to have her photo taken with him.

But the more I study it, something about it feels off—something I can't quite put my finger on. In its background is a familiar steel beam and the edge of a white, metal structure. The Hollywood sign. I'd recognize it anywhere.

That's when I notice the sparkle on the woman's wrist. Goose bumps travel from my arms to the back of my neck. I hurry across the hall and into my room, opening my closet for a box of junk I've kept since childhood, and root through it until my fingers touch the bottom. Buried beneath trinkets and knickknacks I haven't touched in years is the bracelet my mom gave me when I was little. I pull it free and hold it up to the photo.

I shake my head. This is impossible.

A bracelet with two charms hangs from the young woman's wrist in Ryan's photo. A race car and a ladybug. I pick through the charms on my bracelet: a four-leaf clover, a silver cat . . . nearly a dozen, all crammed together in a jingly collection—and attached to the links nearest the clasp are a race car and a ladybug.

Just like the bracelet the woman in the picture is wearing.

MY FATHER'S GENTLE snores waft from the living room even though Mom went to bed hours ago after arriving home. I step down the hall and let myself out the kitchen door to the hum of cicadas in the nearby trees and make my way along the side of the house to the front. The street is empty and quiet—it's just past eleven, an hour when most of my neighbors are inside winding down for the rest of the night.

Dressed in black leggings and a hoodie, I feel every bit a criminal for what I'm about to do. I tug my hood over my head as I begin the brisk walk toward the end of my street—to the dead end where the metal gate guards the precarious ascent toward the mountaintop. Clouds thicken overhead and a flash of heat lightning in the distance brightens the sky in shades of a fresh bruise. A rumble of thunder bellows, but it doesn't slow me down.

Just ahead is the door in white stucco—a pedestrian entrance to the packed dirt trail. It looks like an invitation in a fairy tale, even though I know what lies beyond may not have a happily ever after. My chances of getting caught are extremely high, if not by the officers sitting in the cruiser at the mouth of the trail, then surely by the infrared cameras dotting the incline of Mount Lee.

I hang back a little, my entire body like a loose wire as I contemplate turning around. There is another flash of lightning, this time closer and not set so high in the clouds. I'm close enough to hear the scanner through the open window of the cruiser; something about "All units proceed to . . ." and then a garbled address and a crack of thunder so loud it rattles my bones. The officers grumble in annoyance, due to the radio or the storm, I don't know, but they start their engine and leave their post.

A flash of lightning streaks above the houses, followed by another loud boom—this one closer, as if hovering over the intersection of Deronda and Mulholland—and all at once the streetlights blink out and the nearby houses go dark.

I can't believe my luck.

Moments later, the beam of a flashlight zigzags down the hillside, and a ranger emerges from the pedestrian door, locking it behind him. He makes his way to a blue car across from me and starts it. I linger beside the wall lining the street, crouched low near the wheel of a parked car, murmuring to myself that I'm the biggest idiot for thinking this will work.

But it does.

The car K-turns, nearly catching me in the glow of its headlights in the cramped space the street allows, and drives off. The moment the taillights are gone I sprint for the gate, ignoring the posted signs that the park is closed, that there are cameras—that I should leave. If the storm continues, I tell myself, the power might be out long enough for what I'm about to do.

It's dawning on me how stupid this really is. Stupid. Dangerous. Illegal. If Ryan knew, he'd tell me that I have a death wish. But after today . . . what I did—or didn't do—feels like a mistake I need to make right.

Hesitantly, I touch the metal gate, my heart in my throat as I wait for something to happen. Nothing does. I even dare a peek at the small camera near the door, but the red light indicating it's on is completely black. And then I do it. I climb over the metal gate and sprint, keeping to the left side of the trail, avoiding the long erosion crack in the packed dirt so I won't twist an ankle. Several times I nearly trip and fall into the sagebrush and thorns that bank the path, but the fear of encountering a rattlesnake pushes me on, away from the vegetational edge.

I've hiked here many times with my parents and Ryan, but never alone. Never past park hours. Tonight I keep a steady pace, knowing if I think too long about the consequences, my fear will slow me down. Another flash of lightning, and the radio tower is illuminated in the distance. I just need to get to the sign—those white letters urging me to forget I shouldn't be here. That I'm supposed to be the good daughter, the good sister, not some whining child who thinks independence begins with a criminal record.

The dirt trail morphs into a haphazardly paved road and my heart beats wildly as I near the ranger station. The small booth is dark, empty, but I still can't slow my heart. Not until I reach the iconic letters stretching like giants across the dark mountainside, spelling out **H – O – L – L – Y – W – O – O – D.**

Just before the bend in the road leading toward the central communications facility at the summit, I spy a large boulder against the fence, granting me entrance to the wild brush beneath the sign. I go for it. My legs burn with the effort to scale the terrain, my skin scraped and stinging from the tangled brush. At times the hill is so steep I have to lean over my knees to propel myself upward, but it's to my advantage. If the power comes back on, if a helicopter flies overhead, they won't be able to get me until I crest the top.

Only I'm not going to the top.

I set my sights on the white *H* in front of me and trudge on. It stands high and beautiful, encouraging me to reach its base where it's anchored into the earth, even as the storm grows closer, lighting up the sky within the clouds above.

Finally, I reach it. My lungs burn for air and sweat coats my skin beneath my sweatshirt. I'm itching from the shrubs, and I'm scared . . . so scared. But there is no helicopter flying overhead telling me to leave. The cameras hidden on the letters are dark. No one is watching. It's just me and the Hollywood sign, as if the universe has granted me access to this elusive part of the mountain to make amends for what I failed to do today.

This is what Ryan always wanted—to come here and make his mark. But I'm not Ryan. I'm here for something else. If the universe is on my side tonight, then I'm placing my trust in the powers that be to hear what I have to say.

My heart is heavy as I stand at the base of the *H*, and all at once, my emotions crash down on me. My body trembles, unleashing all the tears I've been holding inside.

"Please, whoever is listening, please let my brother be all right," I choke out. "Please let him wake up. I promise I'll . . ." But what promise can I make that's big enough? To be a better sister? One who isn't resentful of living in his shadow all the time. One who's brave enough to be different from my perfect brother—and the expectations of our parents. That doesn't seem good enough, and now that I'm here, I don't know what to promise. What to trade for the biggest wish I could ever make.

I swipe my tears from my cheeks and look up at the letter *H*—this white, gleaming talisman my brother looks to for bigger and brighter things to come—a career that will allow him to live his dream. To him this letter is a beacon of hope, that whatever he wants from life can be his. Even after a horrific accident. Even after cheating death because I know . . . *I know* . . . he's going to make it.

And then something comes over me—a need so fierce to make a wish and really, truly believe in it as he does.

My feet move as if by a gravitational pull toward the maintenance ladder hanging along the side of the *H*. Only it's too high. It hovers about five feet off the ground, so to reach it, I jump and grab onto the first horizontal bar attached to the back of the letter and pull myself up.

Making it to the second bar is just as tricky, but I do it and then inch myself to the end where the bar meets the bottom of the ladder, hoisting myself onto the bottom rung. I focus on the motion of my hands reaching and pulling until I am feet above the ground. Arm over arm, rung after rung, I climb, my eyes scanning the back of the sign and the letter *O* next to me for the little red light of the camera to suddenly blink on. But it's dark, and it's only me and the sign and the stormy sky overhead.

I inch my way toward the very top of the *H* carefully and slowly in the dark. When the ladder ends in open air, I draw in a tremendous breath and gaze down the mountainside at the city toward the sweeping hills of Hollywood, the reservoir glistening in the dark, and far across the flatter landscape at the rising skyscrapers of downtown LA. I know in my heart that this is the perfect place for my wish to take flight—as close to the stars as possible.

"Please, *please* don't let my brother die," I beg. "He's a good person and doesn't deserve this. Please give him that bright future he wants . . . just please . . . let him wake up, let him have that chance."

It doesn't feel like enough, even though the ache of the wish weighs heavily within my bones. I'm scared that my actions today will sabotage him.

If only I could go back and make things right . . .

I will my words to hold importance, imagining them floating high above me toward someone, *something*, that might have the power to make them come true.

If only Ryan were here right now, gazing out at the city below. He would love this, and I vow to myself that I'll bring him here—that I'll tempt fate again to climb this sign with him. Because I know—I just know—that everything has lined up just right for me to be here, to make this wish for him.

I hold on to the thought for another moment, but I am cold and alone at the top of the gargantuan letter. The ground yawns dark and wide below. *Stay calm,* I tell myself. *Just concentrate on making it back down to the ground.* But climbing down seems an impossible feat, let alone getting down the mountain without alerting the police.

A flash of lightning blazes across the sky, even closer now that I'm almost fifty feet above the ground, hanging on to a sheet of metal in the middle of a thunder-and-lightning storm. Oh God, this was stupid. Forget about being arrested—I'll be dead if I don't climb back down.

Thunder follows, deep and menacing, and shakes me enough that my foot slips, leaving my legs to pedal wildly in the air as my hands grasp the top of the *H*. My phone slides from the pocket of my hoodie, pinging loudly against the back of the sign before being swallowed by the darkness below.

Lightning again—this time striking the radio tower behind me. Angry sparks rain toward the ground, caught in a sudden gust of wind and the onset of pelting raindrops. And then I hear it: the rumble of a car between the rolls of thunder and the thuds of my terrified pulse in my ears. Flashing red and blue lights climb the trail to my left, up Mount Lee, closer and closer.

My gaze shifts to the camera on the letter *O*. The light on the camera is flickering red. *No no no . . .*

I have to get down before the power is restored. But the next crack of lightning catches me off guard, causing me to lean over the top rim of the *H* at a frightening angle. And then the rain comes. The deluge causes my grip to lose its hold. My feet lose purchase on the slick ladder beneath me, dangling. The pull is too strong, heaving me over the edge and into the cold, open air . . . and just as another flash of searing lightning grazes the sky, I lose my grip altogether. I plummet past the framework of the sign—falling . . . falling . . .

CHAPTER THREE

I AM DEAD. I AM sure of it—only there is no pain. The light shining against my eyelids is too bright for this time of night. There is no thunder, no violent crack of lightning, no rustling of windblown shrubs in the storm. My body is warm and still, not soaked from the rain . . . and yet there is a wetness on my forehead. I gingerly press my fingertips to it, feeling a damp cloth against my skin, then pull it away and open my eyes.

A song plays in the background, familiar, but static interrupts the smooth chords. Voices whisper, shuffling and pausing as I lift myself up onto my elbows. Around me, a group of unfamiliar faces has crowded, and a pretty woman, her sleek ponytail the color of spun caramel, is seated closest to my elbow.

"Miss Montgomery," she whispers gently. "Are you feeling all right?"

I stare back, my lips forming words stuck somewhere deep in my throat. "Wh . . . what did you call me?"

"Oh—I—err . . ." The woman stammers, then she plucks the cloth from my fingers. "I'll just . . . I'll just freshen this up." She inches away past the wall of people craning to see, and I am left alone with their curious faces.

One by one, the unfamiliar group gathers closer, plumping the pillows nestled beneath me, fretting over every detail. I graze the plush softness beneath my fingers. Didn't I fall? It all happened so fast. I remember plunging into nothingness but have no recollection of impact. Something should have broken . . . I wiggle my fingers, my toes . . . They all seem to be working.

A man with a bright blue handkerchief knotted about his throat pushes forward and offers me a flask. I force a smile. My throat feels like sandpaper, but the noxious fumes swirling up from the flask tell me this is definitely not water. I wave it away.

Their questions bombard me, each as confusing as the next.

"What happened, Alice?"

"Alice, would you like another pillow? A brandy, perhaps?"

I don't understand what they are talking about. *Alice? Why do they keep calling me Alice?*

"It must have been the heat . . ."

"Why is she wearing the same clothes she filmed in last Friday . . ."

"It wasn't the heat. She's been . . ."

"I've been what?"

The shrill tone of my voice silences the onlookers. The woman with the ponytail comes back and stands beside me, carefully placing a fresh washcloth on my forehead.

"Do you remember anything, Miss Montgomery? Anything at all?" she whispers.

Miss Mont . . . Who?

"I . . ." I force my eyes wide open and concentrate on the wall over her shoulder, hoping it will help me remember—anything.

The room is small. Am I in a hospital? It doesn't look like it— not a police station either. Nothing makes sense. All I feel is a vivid panic as it all comes rushing back. *The trip to the sign. I made a wish and . . .*

I fell.

From the Hollywood sign.

The feeling comes back to me of what it felt like to hover atop the *H*, with the wind rushing all around and the city a blanket of diamonds below. I was rushing because I saw the police car drive up the mountain. The rain came. I slipped. That's the logical explanation. And if that was true, then how am I . . . here? It must be a hospital. I'm either injured and can't feel it, or the police escorted me to the psych ward.

"Is Ryan okay? Can I see him?" I sit up too quickly, the blood rushing from my head in a hot wave.

The woman at my side cocks her head and looks at the other concerned faces huddled around us. I follow her gaze to the tall young man standing near the door. He seems to be about my age, and his dark hair and ice-blue eyes make a startling contrast; there is the slightest hint of a shy smile on his lips as he watches with interest.

"Ryan?" she asks, pulling my attention back to her. A deep knot forms between her brows. "I don't know anyone at the studio named Ryan."

"My brother," I answer.

She only looks at me and shakes her head. "I didn't know you had a brother."

It's as if the floor has been pulled out from beneath me, and once again, I am plunging through the empty air.

"Water," I mutter, choking on my confusion. "Does anyone have water? I'm so thirsty."

"Get some water, ice." She snaps her fingers at a dough-faced woman who hovers closely. "But Alice," she continues as she looks at me, her tone gentle as if I am a small, lost child she needs to be very careful with. "You've been gone for days."

Alice? Days?

"Gone where?" I shake my groggy head. My thoughts flow thick as tar, and the bright lights hurt my eyes. "Who's Alice?"

"We've all been worried," the woman prattles on, taking no notice of my confusion. "You've been missing for a whole week, but then you showed up this morning on set and then fainted. Where have you been?"

"Maybe she skipped off for a little rendezvous?" the man with the flask interrupts with a smirk.

The woman returns with a glass of water in time to jab him in the arm.

"What? It happens!" His suggestion gives way to a symphony of agreeable sighs.

I sip the water, grateful for its coolness against my parched throat, but I can't stop my fingers from trembling around the glass. The charm bracelet clinks against it. Only two charms hang from it now—the same charms the young woman in my brother's photo wore. Did the others break off during my fall? A wave of uncomfortable heat sweeps over me. The already tiny room feels smaller by the minute.

"Can I get a little air?" I wave my free hand.

"You heard her," the woman with the swaying ponytail orders. "She's fine now, back to work."

Only I don't feel fine. I feel a little sick. And confused. And . . .

The door swings open, sending a bolt of searing-hot sunshine into the room, and my body bristles with panic.

"Feelin' better, sweetheart?" A man steps into the doorway. His white shirt looks crumpled from the heat, his sleeves rolled up to his elbows. He has a pencil stashed behind an ear, a cigarette balanced between his lips, and a thick stack of pages clutched in his hand, which he waves toward me in a flurry of annoyance. He's obviously upset with me, but I'm relieved he isn't a cop come to reprimand or arrest me for climbing the Hollywood sign.

He nods. "Great! Good to hear it!"

Hear what? I haven't answered him yet. He hasn't let me. He plucks the cigarette from his lips and points it at me. "You have a lot of nerve, holding production up like this. It's your lucky day, I don't have time to hear about your escapades."

"But I . . . I . . ."

The woman who's been speaking to me places herself between me and the man with the jabbing cigarette. "Yes, yes, we'll be right on it. Just give the poor girl a minute to get her bearings."

The whole interaction unfolds as if in slow motion. Whoever this woman is, she holds some control.

"We'll resume when Miss Montgomery is back on set." The man gives me one last look before turning to leave.

The older woman who brought me the glass of water stands next to me. She has streaks of gray in her black hair and wears a smock smeared with crisscrossing shades of red and pink over her doughy figure.

Hairpins spill from her pockets each time she leans over to adjust the blanket someone has draped across my legs.

"Who was that man?" I ask. A deep breath shudders in my chest. "And why did he call me Miss Montgomery?"

"Oh dear." The woman appraises me with concern. "You must have bumped your head hard."

On instinct I press my hand against the back of my head, wincing at the tender flesh beneath my tangled hair.

"Is this your first time working with Mr. Fuss-and-Bother?" she asks. "That's what the studio gets for hiring a new assistant director at the last minute. All pomp and circumstance. No offense, but he rubs people the wrong way around here."

My hand stays glued to my head. The soothing warmth from my palm is the most calming thing in the room, and I really need calming. It keeps me from thinking too hard on the woman's words. Here? Where is *here,* exactly?

The woman hums to herself as she bends to retrieve another handful of fallen hair pins. "If you're feeling better, I'll be back for a redo." She points at the top of my head and twirls her finger in the air. "Not enough hours in the day, I tell you."

The woman with the ponytail stays with me. She studies me for a few moments without saying a word, then she slowly sits on the end of the couch near my feet. "Alice," she says softly, and I detect a hint of caution. "Do you remember anything? Anything at all?"

Of course I do. I made a wish. I fell. I should be in a lot of trouble right now.

"We were filming on location by the Hollywood sign last Friday and, well . . ." she pauses. "You disappeared. You never showed up on set on Monday. We were about to involve the police, but then you appeared this morning, wandering on the hill below the sign. You fainted just as we reached you, but you didn't seem to be hurt. Then we brought you here to the studio." Her voice is slow and steady, but she clenches her fingers in her lap. "Did you get lost? Did something happen out there? Because if anything did, we should report—"

"No," I cut her off. "I don't remember what happened."

"You don't remember *anything*? But you've been gone for an entire week."

I shake my head. "Nothing."

Nothing I can share. These strange people and the fact that I'm not lying in a heap at the bottom of the sign has me completely baffled. I want to replay everything in my head—the wish, the fall—in private. I need to know if Ryan is okay and where I am. If what she says is true, I wandered from the sign and am now in the trailer of some set at some movie studio lot. Alice's trailer, apparently.

Only . . . everyone here believes *I* am Alice. Whoever that is. I don't know what is happening and I suddenly feel dizzy.

"Actually, can I have a minute by myself?"

The woman nods knowingly and rises to her feet, closing the door behind her.

Now that I am alone, I look around, taking it all in. The walls of the tiny room are a serene pale pink. Gossamer curtains sway slowly in the warm breeze from the open window. Part of me wishes for the unfamiliar woman to return, maybe offer me another cool cloth for my head. I want to hide beneath it and shield the burning tears forming beneath my lids as I mull over what she's told me. That I've been missing. No. I was on top of Mount Lee. I remember it clearly.

Alice has been missing. But who is Alice?

I sit up again, my head swimming in a seasick haze.

Panic burns bright and hot in my chest. I need to let my parents know I'm all right. The storm probably woke them, and knowing my mother, if the power went out, she would have gone into my room to check on me and found me missing. Even worse than that thought, could the storm have affected the hospital? I'm sure they have generators, but I'm worried the machines my brother is hooked up to may have lost power. Unless . . . my wish worked and he's no longer in a coma. My wish did *something*, because right now I can't explain where I am or why everyone thinks I'm someone named Alice.

The blanket covering my legs slips to the floor and I let out a gasp. Instead of my leggings, my shins are half covered by the rumpled remains of a soiled dress, my ankles dotted with streaks of dirt and tiny scratches I must have gotten on my way up to the sign. On shaky legs I rise and pad across the floor toward a large arched mirror over a cluttered makeup table. Round bulbs the size of my hand frame the glass, casting a soft light as I peer into it.

A shiver tears down my spine. My face is covered in smears of dirt, but I can see bright makeup beneath it, makeup I never put on.

My hair is curled just so at my temples, falling to subtle waves that rest on my shoulders, not the mess I'd expected from falling fifty feet and rolling down the hill. And the dress: beneath the grit it's the sheerest blush I've ever seen. The fabric is a delicate chiffon, the soft layers of the skirt gliding through my fingers.

I lean closer to the mirror. The hairstyle. The expression in my eyes. Goose bumps dot my arms as disbelief churns through my body.

I look exactly like the girl in Ryan's photo.

CHAPTER FOUR

"OKAY, MAYBE I'M NOT DEAD. I'm dreaming," I whisper, leaning forward and touching my cheek—making sure I can feel it. "When I wake up, I'll still be at the sign, itching and covered in mosquito bites because I was too stupid to walk home." I let out a hopeful sigh. "That's it. Just a dream. Everyone is waiting for me to wake up."

What if I never do wake up?

I think of Ryan lying in the hospital and my parents praying for him night after night. How could I have been so stupid?

To walk out to the sign alone and climb the *H* because I wanted to make a silly wish. Wishes don't fix people. Doctors do. I never even left a note for my parents.

They don't know I left the house, and now I'm . . . I don't even know where I am.

Alarm blooms inside me. "This isn't real," I tell myself out loud. But it feels real. I pinch my arm, my fingernails leaving an imprint, the sting of it drawing tears to my eyes. If this is a dream, I'm not waking up.

"Just calm down, Grace." I cover my eyes with my hands and force myself to be still for a second. "Let's just do things quietly and calmly. Be rational."

I lift a crystal perfume decanter and uncork its triangular top, breathing in the exquisite scent of rose, its fragrance filling the tiny room. Would I even be able to smell in a dream? Beautiful things are everywhere, and they are sparkly and expensive. I look in the mirror. It's all so strange.

Beyond my reflection a spray of roses in a milk-white vase sits on a chrome cart, ablaze in the sun. Beside it, lined in perfect order, are stemmed glasses and an ice bucket, a champagne bottle resting in a pool of melting ice. A tiny envelope peeks out from the bouquet. I turn and pad over to it. With unsteady fingers, I pluck the cream-colored card from the snow-white buds.

For my new leading lady. All my best, James.

I spin around, staring at the interior of the trailer, my brain too full to think, my breath catching in my chest. How is any of this possible? I stop suddenly. How had I not noticed that everything around me isn't just unusual but *outdated*? What looks to be a small radio on a nearby table croons another song. I pick it up—it's just a white box with two brass dials, one larger than the other, but I've never seen anything like it other than in an antique store or as a replica online. I give the larger dial a twist, but each station that comes in clear enough plays something old. Something from another time. I turn the smaller knob, putting a stop to the music, but without it the room falls painfully quiet.

Against the far wall is a closet filled with cream-colored sweaters with tiny embroidered roses—and skirts. Too many skirts. I whip the hangers left and right, but it's all the same. Buttoned linen dresses. A flared skirt with a . . . poodle? Crinoline-layered slips.

Where is the hoodie I was wearing? My sneakers? I drop to my knees and rummage but find only penny loafers and saddle shoes and heels. None of my things are here. Not even my phone.

A yellow rotary phone sits on a small round table between two club chairs. I lift the receiver to my ear, relieved there is a dial tone. But I'm confused as I stare at the numbers arched in circular formation, a finger hole over each one. I poke my finger into the hole above the *0* and spin the dial.

The operator answers.

"Yes," I say, trying to control the trembling in my voice the best I can. "Could I have the number for the Brighton residence? It's on Deronda Drive in Beachwood Canyon."

There is a pause followed by the faint murmur of voices in the background. It makes me think of an old movie I once watched with a line of ladies at a switchboard connecting and listening in on people's conversations.

"Did you say Deronda Drive?"

"Yes."

"I'm sorry. There's no such street." The operator pauses again. "And no listing for Brighton. May I connect you with another residence?"

Something is horribly wrong. I rest my head in my hand and rock back and forth. Maybe I'm in a coma like Ryan. Or worse, losing my mind. Panic flares in my chest until I remember. If my parents aren't home, they might be with him at the hospital. "Could you connect me with the Southern California Hospital at Hollywood? On De Longpre Avenue?" I ask.

It takes a few seconds for the line to connect. A woman answers.

"Registration."

"P-please connect me with Ryan Brighton's room. It's room 213."

"One moment." There is shuffling in the background. Moments later, the woman's voice returns. "Are you looking for Paul Anderson?"

"No. Ryan Brighton." My palms are sweating as I grip the phone.

"A Paul Anderson is in room 213. We don't seem to have a patient named Ryan Brighton."

The room is swimming. "Ryan Brighton. He's twenty-four. He's been there since last week. Car accident?"

"I'm so sorry, miss," the woman says. "Maybe he's at another hospital in the area?"

"No, he's . . ." I close my eyes. My entire world is beginning to crash around me. My parents. Ryan. My house . . . "No," I mutter. "Thank you."

I set the phone down, scrambling for answers, but there are none. My breath comes in short spurts, as if I'm on the verge of hyperventilating. "Mom's cell," I tell myself. But I never bothered to memorize her number, and without my phone, I can't reach her. I drop to the floor and peer beneath the fainting couch, hoping it somehow made its way to this crazy time warp with me and is hiding, but all I see are a few dust bunnies and a box. I reach for it. Inside is a jumble of papers, flyers stamped boldly with an MGM logo, callback sheets, and magazine clippings, carefully trimmed and collage ready.

When I reach the photographs at the bottom, my heart nearly flips out of my chest. It's as if Ryan's collection has made its way into the box. James Dean on his motorcycle. James Dean standing next to a car. James Dean in a fuzzy black sweater, his tousled hair brimming his eyes, a cigarette in his hand. They are identical to the photos in Ryan's phone. What startles me the most is the quality of the pictures. Each one is glossy and new. Even the magazine clippings look as if they are in perfect condition, as if the person who'd painstakingly cut them did so from a current newsstand edition. They aren't old or yellow.

I find the same photo I found on Ryan's phone, of James Dean and the girl who looks like me. Shaking, I pull it free from the stack.

The hairstyle, the makeup. It's like looking in a mirror. And at the bottom of the snapshot is handwriting in pencil like I'd noticed earlier, only it isn't smudged now. In clear, precise penmanship it says James Dean and Alice Montgomery. Goose bumps rise across my arms.

Replacing the lid, I shove the box back under the couch. Sweat courses down my back as I rise to my feet on unsteady legs. I need to get out of this room.

I stomp toward the door but before I even reach it, my gaze lands on a script resting on a stack of books. It's open to its center and flipped over as if someone had been reading it. I skim the first few lines and then thumb through, absorbed in the words before closing it to look at its cover. The bold black heading across the top of the page reads PROPERTY OF FLYNN STUDIOS, then its title: *AMONG THE STARS*, and just below that, a name.

Alice Montgomery.

I set the script down, accidentally disturbing a black datebook that sits askew in the pile. I grab it eagerly. Maybe something inside will me give a clue to what's going on.

The interior is filled with neat, fluid writing. Lunch dates, callback appointments, all clearly planned and scheduled.

A sudden swell of nausea creeps into my throat.

In bold black numbers the date stares back at me.

1953.

CHAPTER FIVE

I QUICKLY CHANGE OUT OF the dirty dress and into a clean skirt and short-sleeved top I find among the clothes on the rack, then peer through the curtain into a courtyard just outside the trailer. Several men carry tall spotlights. A forklift rumbles past.

I need to get out of here and back to the sign. It's the only thing I remember, but more important, I need to make sure I'm not lying dead or in a coma at the bottom of it, because none of this makes any sense.

I touch the doorknob, then crack open the door. Everyone seems occupied as I walk around to the back of the trailer, where a fence separates the busy workers from the street. I lean against it and peer over the top.

Exquisite vintage cars of every shade are parked curbside as traffic streams past. I can barely make out the chrome script across their back ends—Chevy Bel Air and Buick and Chrysler. The fence creaks against my weight as I lean into it, and a board loosens. With a yank, I pry it to one side and squeeze through. Up and down the street, the scene is the same. Vintage. Old. Ridiculously fifties. And while I must be dreaming, it's all so terrifyingly real. On the other side of the street, three young women about my age are walking arm in arm, laughing, their full skirts swaying with each step. My own outfit is reflected in a car's window. I look just like them. A fifties babe.

Bike tires squeal to a stop.

I turn, startled.

A young boy riding a Huffy bicycle stares at me, his eyes wide. "Geez Louise!" A steady blush blooms across his cheeks, trailing back toward his ears. He rights his bike then rides away, all the while peeking back at me over his shoulder.

The street sign on the corner reads Gower and Sunset. But what should be familiar territory looks strange and disorienting. What should be a CVS is now a smaller brick building. A sign that reads Lloyd's Laundromat hangs over the propped-open door, the sweet smell of laundry soap pouring out in a humid cloud. Have I gotten turned around somehow? I spin around and stare at the row of shops across the street, each one eerily unfamiliar. The building on the corner is supposed to be Warm Sugar, a sweet little cupcake boutique, but instead, "Imperial Five and Dime" is painted across its door. Shops I don't recognize line the street the farther I walk.

This is Gower. The sign says so. I push onward, trying to ignore the crowded sidewalk. Women in slim pencil skirts, small children in tow, weave in and out of the crowd. Men in hats and jackets stop for newspapers. I grow dizzy as I tilt my head to read the billboards hovering between the buildings, their broad surfaces painted in a rainbow of enticing slogans.

On one billboard, the overly enhanced face of a man spewing a breath of realistic smoke tells everyone, "I'd walk a mile for a Camel!" Next to it, a larger-than-life movie canvas hangs over an entire corner of a building: "Joan Crawford starring in *Torch Song.* An MGM Cinematic Extravaganza Coming this Fall!"

The world seems to have turned into a giant 1950s movie set. My heart beats wildly in my chest as the buildings close in around me. A man nearly knocks into me as I stand still on the sidewalk, too stunned to move out of his way. He apologizes then hurries along, his nose in the newspaper he carries. I crane my neck, catching a glimpse of the headline: IKE EXPECTED TO WIN PRESIDENCY. Even the newspaper is authentic. I need to get to the Hollywood sign. I need to get to the top of that mountain, where the air is thin and cool, and I'll be able to breathe and wrap my head around things.

I stick my arm out and wave at a yellow checkered cab rumbling down the street. If it, too, is part of a movie set, I'll soon find out.

"Would you mind taking me to the Hollywood sign, please?" I ask as I crawl inside. I want to ask him to drive me home, but if what the telephone operator told me is true, then there won't be anything there.

The driver looks tired, as if he's already put in a long day, but the moment we make eye contact in the rearview mirror, he straightens in his seat. "Beautiful day, isn't it?" He pauses, allowing his gaze to linger in the mirror, his chin lifting as if trying to get a better angle of the back seat.

I swallow hard and try to play it off. "Yes, it is." I shift toward the window and stare out, hoping the driver will take the hint I'm only asking for a ride, not conversation.

The cab sits idling as the traffic passes by and the driver continues to stare at me. He shakes his head. "What's a girl like you going to the sign for? Nothing up there but weeds and sagebrush."

My eyes steal a glance at the mirror, meeting his, which are lifted at the corners with intrigue. It makes my skin crawl for a moment before I answer, "I'm meeting my boyfriend. He has a picnic planned."

It seems to satisfy his interest and he doesn't press for more. Moments later, the cab pulls out into the lane, the buildings rushing past in a colorful blur, a line of tall palms stretching into a wall of green through the window. Each time the cab slows for a traffic light, the scenery out the window is like the street on the other side of the movie lot's fence. The signs, the people, all look outdated yet vibrant and colorful. Alive. Real. They are busy going about their business, all walking and talking just like normal people. And then it strikes me, not a single person is preoccupied with a cell phone. I bite my thumbnail and stare out the glass, torn on whether I should be amazed or worried.

A smattering of Spanish-revival bungalows rises along the hillside in the canyon's relentless heat. They are familiar to me, but they're not as aged or weathered as I remember. And while there's no street sign to mark it, I know when the cab veers onto my street, even if the landscape seems to have changed drastically. We drive past the lot where my house should be as the hole in my heart fills with a rising panic.

The end of the street meets with a dirt incline. There is no metal gate. No police monitoring access to Mount Lee. No threatening signs of surveillance and fines to those who dare venture past this point after dusk. The cab sails along as if the iconic billboard has been expecting me, stopping short of the communications facility, which is no longer caged in by a metal chain-link fence.

"Could you wait here?" I ask the driver, who's just lit a thick cigar, his elbow perched on his open window.

Our eyes meet in the rearview mirror. "Meter's running, kid."

I nod, swallowing my worry about how to pay for the ride, and step out of the cab.

To my surprise, there is no fence prohibiting me from the letters, and I carefully ease my way down to a worn footpath winding through the shrubbery up to the sign. If only it had been this easy last night, even though the terrain seems wilder now and overgrown with shrubs I've never seen before.

I march straight for the giant *H*. Like last night I'm nearly breathless by the time I reach it, but I'm not filled with the fear of being caught or struck by lightning.

The ladder is lower to the ground. I hope that just touching it will jolt me back somehow. But nothing happens. *Did I really climb this thing?* What was I thinking? The letter is enormous and, clearly, I am very stupid. I whack my palm against the metal. All it does is sting my skin.

Maybe whacking my head against it will be more fruitful. I set my foot on the rung and start to climb, making it only a third of the way up before my insides quiver, warning me it's too high. I freeze for a beat, too scared to move. So much for the crazy thought of re-creating last night. I thought climbing it, maybe dangling a little, might trigger things—scare me enough to wake me up from this freaky nightmare.

But all I want is to get my feet back on the ground.

Things are different now, like something is missing—perhaps the desperation and fear from last night. Now this is just a big *H*. Nothing more.

I inch my way back down, sighing with relief the instant my feet touch the lush growth on the hillside. I've only known the dry dusty mountain to be dotted with prickly shrubs, but now there are sage and wildflowers sprouting between the California holly—orange cardinal catchfly and brilliant California bluebells. I sink, folding my legs up to my chest as despair washes over me. Why can't I just go home? It kills me to think my parents probably believe they've lost two children now.

Tears burn the back of my throat as I look down the hillside. Deronda Drive as I know it doesn't exist yet. *My house* doesn't exist. And if my house doesn't exist, my family might not either—like a severed phantom limb I still feel. I rest my forehead on my arms and try to control my breathing. The entire world is spinning.

I don't know how long I've been sitting here, shivering with guilt in the late-day sun. I must have taken longer than the driver ever expected because a horn honks in the distance, pulling me out of my misery and back to my strange reality, where everyone believes I'm a lost woman named Alice.

CHAPTER SIX

WITH NOWHERE TO GO, I ask the cab driver to take me to the first place that pops into my mind. Flynn Studios—the name on the script I found earlier in the trailer. Now, as he pulls alongside the curb on Gower Street, he again glances at me in the mirror over dangling fuzzy yellow dice.

"That'll be a dollar fifteen, miss." The driver turns around, draping his arm across the back of his seat.

"Oh, I . . ." Now what? Forgetting I'm wearing a skirt, I reach for a pocket that's not there, desperate to buy some time. The back of my neck grows hot. "I don't seem to . . . I mean, I, uh . . ."

"Dollar fifteen, you said?" a male voice interrupts from over my shoulder. It's the young man from the trailer earlier, now leaning in through the open window to offer the fare to the driver.

"Thank you. I . . ." I swallow my stammer. "Sorry."

"It's my pleasure, Miss Montgomery," the young man says brightly, ignoring how flustered I am as he holds the door for me.

I step onto the sidewalk, the warm California breeze rustling my hair. The moment I realize he's staring at me, assessing me, he quickly looks down at his shiny dress shoes.

"Yes, well." He smiles and nods. "Happy to have helped."

The cab pulls away as my gaze trails over the young man's shoulder toward the building behind him, the name Flynn Studios arched over a black metal fence.

Maybe I *have* lost my grip on things. This reality means nothing familiar exists. It means I'm alone. I want to go home—only my home isn't there. I should have asked the cabbie to take me to the hospital, but if I walk in and find Ryan's room empty, I think they'll be forced to admit me. An uneasy feeling sweeps over me, leaving me woozy.

Everything becomes a strange, fuzzy shade of gray.

"Whoa there." He reaches out a hand.

With his help, I lower myself to sit on a short concrete wall outside the studio's entrance and focus on the man who's paid my cab fare. He reaches for what looks like a stack of papers and magazines tucked beneath his armpit and produces a rolled-up newspaper. Then he creates a makeshift fan, waving the paper back and forth in a steady rhythm in front of my face.

"Thanks," I murmur, shielding my eyes from the glaring sun. The cool breeze from the newspaper has begun to help clear away the gray tunnel vision. I push myself up from the wall, the dizziness still lingering.

"Hey, are you all right?" The man pauses. "Thought you were a goner. How 'bout you just sit here till you're feelin' better?"

"I'm . . . I'm fine, thanks." It comes out more slurred than I want. "It's just the heat." I swipe my forehead with the back of my hand and sit back down.

He pauses the swaying newspaper and tilts his wrist, stealing a glance at his watch. "Looks like you need to zonk," he says, amused.

Goner? Zonk? I feel my face scrunch in confusion. He quickly fills the silence with, "Rough night or rough morning?"

"Maybe a little of both." I give a tepid smile, then try to stand again.

"Feelin' hungover in the heat of LA never did me any good."

"I'm not hungover. Just very . . ." I sigh. "Never mind." I try to stand again but sway unsteadily.

"Easy there." He sets the newspaper and the stack of papers down, then cups my elbow, holding on to me until I am permanently upright.

I catch his gaze and the pleasant shade of blue beneath his thick, dark lashes, but he quickly looks away. His ebony hair is slicked back, held in place with some sort of touchable-looking gel, styled to the side and swept off his face.

Now that I'm able to get a closer look at him, it's clear he's in his early to midtwenties, but his style makes him look more mature than he probably is.

I've been too occupied with his hair to realize how close I am to the papers he's set down. My leg brushes against them, sending them over the wall and onto the sidewalk between our feet. We both stoop to retrieve them before they blow away in the warm breeze. Then I notice the magazine. It's oversized and vintage. And there is my face. On the cover.

Without asking, I reach for it to get a better look. It's my face, all right, made up to look like a Hollywood starlet. The eyeliner, the pearls, the hair . . . A chill breaks out over my arms.

"If you don't mind my saying," he says in a low whisper as he gathers the rest of the papers, tucking them beneath his arm again. "You look much nicer in person."

I look up to catch the sincere look in his eyes.

He holds his hand out to me. "Dalton Banks. I was in your trailer earlier, but you looked too far out of it to handle pleasantries."

"I'm Gr—"

"It's okay, Miss Montgomery." He gives a nod. "Everyone around here knows who you are. Would you like me to call security to drive you back to your trailer?"

"Oh." Disappointment courses through me. I have nowhere else to go. I need to figure out what's going on, but I can't do that in a trailer full of people. "Is it bad that I don't want to go back yet?"

Dalton gives me a strange little smile that makes me wonder if he truly thinks I'm funny or just plain weird. "But you're mid-filming. It's a crucial time, right?"

I shrug, looking toward the fence that surrounds the "set" he's referred to. On a large building in the distance are the words LOT A. If what the woman in the ponytail said was true, that I—or Alice, rather—was missing and then fainted when they'd found her, would they really expect me to be well enough to be on set in front of a camera? A wave of unease bubbles up inside me.

"Can you keep a secret?" I ask quietly, determined not to sound anxious. "I kind of snuck out."

He looks around uncomfortably, as if the studio has spies that could be listening, ready to drag me back to the pretty pink trailer.

I concentrate on the muscle twitching in his cheek, how it sweeps into the hollows beneath his cheekbones. "I just . . . I just need some time," I admit.

Dalton runs his hand through his hair, mussing it up rather than slicking it down, and takes a deep breath. "They're not too keen on the crew mingling with the stars."

The last thing I want is to get him in trouble. But I just can't go back to the trailer, or to whatever else they expect of me.

"You don't understand," he starts. "I'm just a Foley artist, and—"

"A *what* artist?" I interrupt.

Dalton sets his mouth crooked and sucks in a breath; he stares at the ground as if my question has irritated him. "I'm a sound guy.

I put background noises and whatnot into the film to match the motions on-screen."

"Ohhh." I nod.

"Like I was saying, I'm not the sort of guy you'd want to skip your lines for and, uh . . . sneak out of the studio with."

Oh. A flicker of anger bubbles inside me that he assumes I want that. "I didn't mean that." I turn to walk back to the lot. I don't need any more hints from Mr. Foley Artist.

"Wait, it's just . . ."

"I get it." I spin around. "It's fine. Thanks again for the cab. I'll pay you back."

"It's just that, well . . ." He hurries to catch up to me, holding the magazine out for me to take another look. The bold print states the girl on the cover is Hollywood's Rising Star . . . The "It" Girl . . . The Next Big Thing.

I stare blankly at him.

"No?" His mouth hangs open. "You're pulling my leg. Either you're as humble as apple pie or you don't know what they've been saying about you."

I point at the magazine he's rolled and tucked back beneath his arm. "Oh, I'm sure they're saying quite a lot, but I'm not *that* girl." I feel much better now, enough to notice the curious glances of people passing by, but I can't go back to the trailer.

Not yet. If I have more time, I might be able to figure out how to escape this fifties time warp and get home—back to my family. To Ryan.

Glancing across the lot again, I spot Miss Ponytail. Her head sways from side to side as if searching for something. Or someone. Most likely me. The expression on her face doesn't appear as understanding as earlier. In fact, she looks annoyed. I duck, just as she looks over and begins to head in my direction.

Dalton eyes me like I'm crazy.

"Please, I just can't handle that bossy woman with the clipboard right now."

Dalton rubs his chin, looking at me. "All right," he says. "She'll never find you in here." He shakes his head. "Golly. Alice Montgomery. Who woulda thought?" With another shake of his head, he leads me beneath the arched entrance and up a set of steps, and with the dramatic bow of a gentleman, Dalton Banks pulls on the main door and sweeps me into Flynn Studios.

CHAPTER SEVEN

THE FIRST THING I NOTICE is the noise. Compared to the street outside, this is one hundred times louder. The lobby is abuzz with a flurry of people, all going this way and that. The studio seems to be its own little world—busy and chaotic.

"Are you feelin' better?" Dalton shoves his hands in his trouser pockets and rocks back and forth on his heels. He looks nervous again, but no one seems to notice us.

I nod. I'm grateful to be inside but feel uneasy that the woman from the lot will figure I've gone into the building. That at any moment, she'll walk through the door and drag me back to the trailer. Nervous as I am, my head feels well enough to get a good, solid look at the man who's been kind enough to scrape me off the sidewalk. "You said you were a Foley . . ."

"Foley artist extraordinaire." He tips an invisible hat on his head.

"Sorry, I guess I'm not familiar with the behind-the-scenes lingo yet." I offer a strained smile.

Dalton pauses for a moment, then says, "You look like you could use a little something. Stay here, I'll be right back." He crosses the lobby to the far wall, waits behind a small line of people, then deposits a handful of change into the slots of two vending machines. When he returns, he's carrying a small glass Coca-Cola bottle in one hand and a paper cup in the other. "What's your poison?"

I peer inside the cup. The strong amber liquid reminds me of the drink the man in the trailer had offered. "What is it?" I wrinkle my nose.

"Whiskey."

I make a face but quickly neutralize my expression. I don't want to appear ungrateful but after all that's happened, I really could use a drink.

"Too bad it's not White Claw."

Dalton raises a questioning eyebrow. "I'm guessing your palate is a bit finer than this. A paper cup sure doesn't compare to a champagne flute." He stares at the two drinks for a beat, then he hands me the Coke. "Quenches your thirst better anyhow."

Dalton leads me through maze-like hallways, but I quickly become turned around as he leads me past endless doors, each labeled in bold black lettering: "Special Effects," "Lighting," and "Production." Dalton points out the numerous soundstages, the film lab, screening rooms, costume, and set design facilities. The tour goes on and on, making my head spin that it all fits beneath one roof.

At last, we stop, and my head takes a moment to catch up. "Are those . . . voices?" I ask, leaning closer to the door in front of us. There is a strange hum behind it.

"Casting office." He motions with a jerk of his chin as his eyebrows pinch above his eyes, as if I should already know this. "Busiest place in the house, but I hear MGM gets twelve thousand calls a day. That's twice the volume of Flynn. Even more than Paramount or RKO."

He motions for me to follow him toward the back of the building. A glass door separates us from a massive lot marked with numbered buildings. I immediately notice the one I'd spied over the fence. I mentally trace the enclosure. It stretches farther than I can see, easily taking up several city blocks. Standing sets inside the fencing, complete with building facades and streets, dot the enormous space.

"Holy crap." I stand, staring.

"I . . . uh," Dalton stammers, his cheeks blazing red in the sunlight streaming through the door.

I stare at him nervously until he says, "I've never heard a gal express herself like that."

Of course women didn't speak like that in the fifties, and I'd better adjust, but just as I am about to apologize, he speaks up again. "Impressive, isn't it? I guess this view is much different from the sets you're used to." He points at the bustle behind the glass. "And just think"—Dalton's tone grows low and reflective—"you'll soon be one of the most important people here." Dalton tilts the paper cup and drains the rest of his drink.

Just then, a balding man in wire-rimmed glasses accompanied by an entourage of pencil-skirted beauties rounds the corner behind us, and the mood shifts. The man stops short the moment he sees us. Dalton hurries to straighten the knot of his skinny tie.

"Mr. Banks. I was just looking for you."

Dalton's ears have become a shade that matches his cheeks. "Yes, sir. Sorry, sir. I was uh . . ." The young man next to me becomes visibly nervous and he crumples the paper cup behind his back, hiding it in his fist.

The older man ignores him and, instead, focuses on me, shrinking behind Dalton. A brilliant smile spreads across his lips. "Why, Miss Montgomery," he croons. "Whatever are you doing in here?"

My stomach does a series of flip-flops. Before I can come up with a reason, the man winks at me.

"It's not often our busy halls are graced with the presence of a soon-to-be superstar. I'm sure you remember me." He extends his hand and pulls me from behind Dalton's back. "Mack Flynn. Resident busybody of Flynn Studios." He leans closer to my ear, his warm breath a mix of tobacco and mint. "That's code for chairman. I had the pleasure of meeting you during your screen test."

His gaze gives me a once-over, as if recognition should immediately light up my eyes and I should begin drooling over meeting such an impressive man. I fight to control the squirming feeling growing inside me. "Of course I remember," I lie smoothly, refusing to be noticeably dazzled by his presence. "It's so nice to see you again."

I think I've disappointed him, but nonetheless, he flashes a too-white smile that doesn't quite match the expression in his eyes. "Isn't she a peach?" Mack asks Dalton as he gives me a sly wink.

Dalton jabs his hands in his pockets, paper cup and all, as his color returns to normal and the two banter back and forth. Every so often his eyes shift from Mack to settle on me, and the redness flares up again, heating his cheeks with a blush he can't hide.

"I've got an invoice to sign for those props you ordered." Mack gestures to the stack of papers in his thick hand. "Ten more pairs of women's pumps and a pallet of cabbages?"

Dalton shrugs and opens his mouth to say something as Mack turns his attention back to me and lifts my hand to his lips. "Always a pleasure, Miss Montgomery." His words are kind, but I can't help noticing how his eyes roam from my hair to my toes, as if devouring me for a late-afternoon snack. Then the man pivots on his heels and saunters away, snapping his fingers for the girls to follow.

"Really? He snaps and they follow?" I watch as Mr. Flynn nears the end of the hallway, his pack of pretty dogs at his heels before I shake off the sense of discomfort he's left in me.

Dalton gives me an unreadable look followed by a nervous laugh. "Come on, I'll show you where I hang my hat."

He leads us up a flight of steps and down several hallways before stopping in front of a door marked SOUND in bold black lettering. The room is larger than I expected, and messy.

Dalton watches from the door. "I don't often give classy dames like you the fifty-cent tour, but there's something about you that told me you'd like it."

"It's fascinating," I say with a smile as I take it all in. It's as if an eclectic decorator added a mini home theater and set up a yard sale, all between the four walls of the room.

A jumble of props lies scattered about, and large crates and wooden boxes are stacked alongside one wall. There are bins, barrels, and shelves filled with everything from wineglasses to phone books wrapped in tape, to a ridiculous number of shoes. I walk closer for a better look, amazed at the sight. Women's heels, flats, saddles, and reasonable pumps fill the crate, along with several cabbage heads.

I stare and rub my eyebrow.

"Here," Dalton offers. "Lemme show you." He points toward a large wall and flips a switch behind him. The lights dim, and the whir of a projector fills the room.

I'm mesmerized as the wall fills with light and movement, offering a personal screening just for me.

"Now watch the man in the suspenders."

I keep my eyes on the screen as the man dodges a punch from another character, a beefy gentleman in a sailor's suit, then takes a hefty blow in the cheek seconds later.

It's completely silent.

"Now listen." Behind my back, Dalton moves around. I peek over my shoulder as he chooses a head of cabbage from a nearby bin then sets it on the table near a microphone. He hovers a mallet over it while he waits for the right moment. I turn my attention back to the screen, watching as the man takes a second punch, only this time the sound of a fist meeting his cheek is heard on the film, as well as behind me.

I turn to look at the splattered mess, amused.

Dalton beams. "You should hear it when I use a roasted chicken. Now that's true art." He holds up his fist and squeezes. "It gives it an authentic, juicy smack." In a proud frenzy, he whips around the room, explaining everything from the echo chamber to the cue sheet, to how to synchronize distance and time so it sounds as realistic as possible.

"It may not be a good time to tell you, but I got a C in physics in high school," I admit. I look back at the screen, watching the characters continue their silent argument, finding their mute actions familiar. That was my life back home. I've always been quiet in my brother's zealous shadow.

"Hey there." Dalton edges closer. "You okay?"

The look on his face stirs me, pulling me out of my haze. I nod and busy myself with the props lying about the room. If I barely allowed myself to be seen and heard at home, how can I possibly fit in here? As someone else?

Dalton putters around, and within minutes, I've received the lesson of a lifetime on Foley, but my attention is drawn toward the hallway and a door marked with the words "Greenroom."

It creaks open as I hover near the doorframe.

A head of blond hair emerges from the doorway. Broad shoulders, covered by a jacket of supple brown leather. My breath catches in my throat. *Ryan?* But the jacket's shoulder is smooth, perfect—not a rip in sight. A pair of hands pulls at the collar, popping it so it stands up against his neck, and then he turns, pulling a pack of Chesterfields from the pocket. A match strikes and the snap of sulfur morphs into a cloud of nicotine. His lips slide into an easy, sultry smile.

A piece of my heart splinters. It isn't my brother. It's *him*. And the box of pictures stashed in the trailer doesn't do him justice.

My knees knock together. My throat suddenly goes dry.

"Glad you're back, kid." He reaches out and flicks the charms on my bracelet, his fingers lingering on my wrist, tracing the skin there. And then, with a wink, James Dean saunters down the hall, leaving me in a daze.

"Ahem." Dalton clears his throat.

I spin around, feeling off kilter, and acknowledge poor Dalton, who, for some reason, still holds half a cabbage in his hands. I steady myself against the wall and press a sweaty palm to my head.

"I gotta tell ya, I've seen a lot of swoonin' in my day, but nothing like this. You're positively over the moon."

My thoughts spin in circles, eclipsing Dalton's voice. But I'm not swooning.

The sight of James's jacket has played with my head—and my heart—bringing everything to the surface. Dalton is still speaking, but his voice sounds muffled against the memory of Mom dropping splinters of glass into a bowl, of her cradling the jacket in her arms as if she could comfort it.

"They teach you that somewhere?" Dalton tips his head to the side and an expression of wonder sweeps across his face. "Drama class, maybe?"

"Oh, I . . ." My face feels unusually warm. "Wow." My lips let out a long, silent whistle, as I try to cover my building sorrow. I force myself to remember to breathe, sucking in a choking breath as I stare down the now empty hallway. Maybe Dalton believes I'm reacting to the handsome actor, but seeing that jacket is like seeing my brother alive and well again.

I push away from the comforting support of the wall and let out a small apologetic laugh. "Are you going to hold that cabbage all day?"

"I was thinking about keeping it." He looks down at the vegetable in his hands and affectionately strokes it. "I've grown attached."

I smirk at his humor, but then feel a stab of guilt. I've taken him from his work and am pretty sure babysitting isn't part of his Foley artistry. "Well, I guess I should let you get back to it."

With regret, I look toward the Exit sign at the end of the hall. Dalton has been like a security blanket for the last hour or so, but I don't want to be clingy. If I stay longer, I'll be tempted to tell him the truth—that I'm not a movie star named Alice. That just a few hours ago, I was perched atop the Hollywood sign and fell . . . into 1953.

CHAPTER EIGHT

"I THINK I'VE HAD ENOUGH of cabbages for one day." Dalton breaks my train of thought, and I turn with relief. He steals a glance at his watch and motions for me to follow him back into the sound room. "It's close enough to quitting time anyway."

Dalton crosses the room to a cluttered desk and lifts the phone while I linger near the door. Within seconds he is speaking into it with polite authority.

"Yes, ma'am, that's right . . ." he says to the person on the other end. "Just tell Judy that Miss Montgomery felt faint."

He peers over at me and winks, calming the butterflies in my stomach.

"The Chateau Marmont? Yes, I know where it is." He pauses, listening to a voice that seems to go on with urgency. "Of course. I'll have a car send her there safely."

Dalton sets the phone on the receiver and turns to me with a smile.

"They bought it. Congratulations, doll. You've managed to elude the studio for the remainder of the day."

"Thank you," I whisper with genuine relief, but something about the term *doll* leaves a sour film over my skin.

Apparently, the attentive ponytailed woman is named Judy, and she's also my set handler. She's perfectly fine with my skipping out for the rest of the day, so long as I return to the set first thing in the morning, ready to work.

The truth is, I secretly hope I'll find a way out of here before that. The tight ball inside my chest is growing larger and more painful the longer I am here.

"I don't normally leave before the end of my shift." Dalton grabs his jacket from the coatrack and flings it across a shoulder. "But it's close enough."

"I feel like a bad influence."

"Nonsense," he reassures me as he grabs his hat. "You were pretty green after you got out of that cab. I'll feel better knowing you get back safely. Come on."

When we stop at a time clock on the lower level, Dalton jabs a large, hole-punched card into the machine on the wall. The machine clicks, taking a giant bite out of it.

Unsure whether I'm supposed to do the same, I scan the cards for Alice's name.

"Must be nice to be contracted. No time clock for you." Dalton fishes his keys out of his pocket. "We worker bees have to keep our hours logged at all times." He leans closer and whispers with a grin, "I don't think they trust us all too much."

We cross the large lobby, pausing at the double glass doors. A handful of girls clusters together on the steps outside, as if waiting for a famous somebody to emerge and sign the small notebooks in their hands. Peering in, their excited eyes pass over us, and I have the feeling they don't know who Alice Montgomery is—or perhaps she isn't a big enough star yet to be noticed by giggling fan girls.

As if reading my thoughts, Dalton shoots me a playful look. "I've got an idea," he suggests. Placing his hat on top of my head, he tips it so the brim hangs over my forehead. "There. Perfect. After your film hits the big screen, these girls will be lined up on these steps for days, but let's give them—and you—a taste of what's to come." He gingerly takes my elbow so I can walk closer to him, and then we step out into the warm sunlight.

Sure enough, the girls focus on us, whispering and craning their necks to see my face beneath the hat. Dalton rushes me past them as if I'm a celebrity he has to shelter from the masses as I keep my head tucked, playing my part until we make it safely to the sidewalk and past their giggly group. I admit it's exciting, and I almost feel bad we've duped the girls. Dalton opens the passenger door to a dark blue sedan parked at the curb. The car is huge, with a bulbous hood and a few dings along its side. I scoot myself onto its long seat, feeling for a seat belt, but there isn't one. There's no way to secure myself inside this unfamiliar car with the man I've just met.

Dalton walks around to the other side, gets in, and heaves the driver's door shut with a clang. A sheepish grin curls at his lips.

"It's a tank," he apologizes. "It belonged to my granddad. Passed it down to me once his eyes went."

I lean over to peer into the back seat. "It's big, but I wouldn't call it a tank."

He slips the key into the ignition and the beast rumbles to life.

"She's a Lincoln Cosmopolitan," he says shyly, but there is a proud undercurrent beneath his apology.

"She?"

"Her name's Stella."

"I like her." I reach forward and pat the dash with affection. "S . . . so"—I raise my voice over the car's throaty engine—"the

Chateau Marmont. Thanks for taking me." Funny how this entire time I've been with Dalton, I haven't tripped over a single word—until now. Something about him calms me.

"Sure thing." He turns onto the next street. "Swanky place. Besides, if I remember correctly, you don't have cab fare."

I shrug at the truth and fight off the guilt that he'd unsuspectingly had to take care of me today. "Betcha didn't know you'd be babysitting when you clocked in this morning."

A smile spreads across his mouth. "Well, it made my day. Who comes to work and gets to hang out with a movie star?"

"I'm not a movie star," I object.

"If you say so." Dalton smiles.

We soon ease into a comfortable silence, and I stare out the window, amazed.

1953 Hollywood.

Is it really outside?

I'd only ever pictured it to be old, like a black-and-white version of reality, but this is bright and beautiful. A Technicolor I can touch and smell. A surreal version I can interact with, from an age where there was a mix of wholesomeness and glamour. Eyeing the people on the sidewalk, I notice a startling difference between this world and the one I've known—how they dress, how they carry themselves. And the cars—when did we start thinking sleeker was better? The cars on the street here have a style and uniqueness that should be brought back. Even the corner of Hollywood and Vine isn't nearly as crowded as what I've seen before. It's not filled with tourists purchasing cheap goods for sale every few feet. It's still a bustling downtown, only quieter. But it really hits me when we make a left onto Hollywood and the iconic Capitol Records building isn't out my window, nor the Hollywood Wax Museum—icons in their own right in my time, but too late for the time in which I find myself now.

Dalton makes a left on Laurel, then a right onto Sunset Boulevard before swooping straight onto Marmont Lane, where out my window a castle-like building of white stone pokes out from behind the lush branches, its gray roofline perched high like a tower.

The car slows and comes to a rest beneath a canopy of deep green. Dalton stares in awe at the luxurious hotel looming before us. "Yowza." He bounds from the driver's side and, before I can blink, opens my door and offers his hand. "Your destination, miss."

"But haven't you . . ."

"Been here before?" he finishes for me. "Never. I've only ever driven past it, and you can't really see much from the road." He looks up at the elegant hotel. "Golly. You've sure got it made. Anyone who's anyone stays here."

The sheer size of the hotel is intimidating, but Dalton's reaction makes it feel ten times more so. It's not just a big ritzy hotel. It's a label that says you are important enough, rich enough to set foot inside. My heart pounds as a wave of imposter syndrome sweeps over me. I am just Grace. A woman who's suddenly found herself in a very strange predicament . . . or a dream . . . and waking up this morning as Alice has twisted things into a surreal nightmare, leaving me scared and vulnerable. Having been thrown into Alice's life, I have nowhere else to go besides the studio and now, this fancy hotel.

A valet steps from the booth nearby, but Dalton waves him away.

"You don't want to come in? See it for yourself?"

Dalton shifts uncomfortably. "Nah . . . I don't belong here."

Neither do I, I think to myself.

"Besides, chivalrous or not, if Mr. Flynn found out I escorted you inside, he would fire me in an instant. Well . . ." Dalton rocks back and forth on the balls of his feet, hands shoved into his trouser pockets. "I suppose this is where we part ways, Miss Montgomery. At least for a little while."

"But I still have to repay you for the cab."

Dalton waves his hand. "It's on me."

I nod gratefully. "Thanks again. I mean it."

Dalton jingles his keys in his hand, then tosses them into the air. "See you around the studio."

The moment Dalton drives away, loneliness covers me like a lead blanket. An uncomfortable shiver trails itself up and down my arms as I walk toward the hotel's entrance, knowing I don't belong here. What if someone realizes I'm not Alice Montgomery?

I step into a lobby that steals my breath. Like Dalton moments ago, I am awestruck by the hotel's glitzy atmosphere.

The vast space is adorned with art deco detail. The two-story vaulted ceiling is flanked by opulent carved arches, and the windows, elongated to gothic peaks, stream with light. Fashionable people clink glasses on smooth leather couches, and there are flowers . . . dozens upon dozens of flowers.

A uniformed bellhop tips his hat as he passes me, his shoes tapping across the waxed floor.

A sincere smile here, an eyebrow arched in appreciation there . . . Everyone is so pleasant that my worries of being found out slip away.

As soon as I make eye contact with a motherly-looking woman behind the front desk, she immediately drops what she's been working on and slips around the counter to walk over to me. My pulse races at the notion that she might think I'm Alice—or worse—that someone has tipped her off that I'm an imposter and have no reason to be in such a lovely hotel. I'm startled when she drops a brass key into the palm of my hand.

"I'll escort you to your room, Miss Montgomery," she says urgently, clasping both hands around mine and the key. Then she ushers me into the nearest elevator, and soon we are moving up, up, up toward the floors above.

"You would think, after fifteen years, I'd be used to all this," she tsks. "It's none of my business, but when a young lady disappears for days on end and leaves her purse behind . . ."

"She left her—" I am so surprised I forgot to play my part. "I mean yes, I must have left it behind."

"Well, you can certainly imagine we all thought the worst."

A feeling of unease snakes up my spine. She's right. I don't know of anyone who'd leave behind their personal belongings. Even without my phone I feel like a part of myself is missing. I swallow the notion that perhaps I've stumbled into something far more complicated than a case of mistaken identity, but surely there has to be a reasonable explanation, and so I quickly drum up an apology to comfort the woman.

"I'm sorry to have worried anyone."

The woman looks sincerely distressed and continues like a mother hen. Which makes me think of my mom, and my heart crushes deep within my chest.

"Well, here you are, sweetie." The woman stops in front of a door at the end of the hallway on the top floor. She pats me on the arm. "Judy had some things sent over for you earlier. You'll find them inside."

The key feels strange and heavy in my hand. It's an actual key with a red tassel hanging from the end of it. Not a key card like so many hotels use nowadays.

She must zero in on my hesitancy and asks if I'd like her to see me inside safely. I shake my head and watch her as she pads down the hall, then I insert the key, and close and lock the door behind me.

If I thought I was alone before, the empty space in front of me magnifies it. The curtains are closed, creating a dark hush within the room, and I tiptoe around the furniture to let some light in, which streaks across a pale blue love seat with matching chairs. Against the wall is a long side table adorned with fresh flowers and an impressive collection of vodka, a silver ice bucket, and several long-stemmed glasses. I turn back to the window and look out. The room is located at the back of the hotel and the swimming pool below looks small yet inviting, surrounded by narrow walking paths and lush greenery that lead toward miniature white outbuildings.

I can't shake the uncomfortable feeling inside me. My mind races at the thought that maybe the real Alice is here. In the dark. Hiding. I give a quick sweep of the suite, veering off into the bedroom, the blue-tiled bathroom, the tiny kitchenette, and even the closet. No sign of Alice, or anyone else. Still, I can't calm down.

And then I see it. Alice's discarded purse is on a chair across the room, lying on its side. I immediately go to it. A pair of white sunglasses and a few pennies have toppled out onto the cushion. No wonder that poor woman was worried. The growing mystery of her disappearance makes me worried for Alice too.

Even though it feels wrong to rifle through someone else's handbag, I open it, pulling out its meager contents: a handkerchief, a few dollar bills in a slim red wallet, along with a studio ID card and a gold tube of lipstick. Pink. I study the ID card. Alice looks younger than the glamorous picture on Dalton's magazine cover. It looks like we're the same age. The similarities are uncanny. Freaky, even. If Alice left this room quickly, discarding or forgetting her purse, then this may have been the last place she spent time, other than the location set where everyone thinks she disappeared.

But the purse doesn't offer any explanation for where the real Alice may have gone. She most likely had a second purse and there's no need for all the concern. What is concerning is that I'm stuck here—appearing identical to a woman who probably just wanted to get away for a few days.

I quickly replace Alice's things, set the purse upright on the chair, and look around the room. On another table lies a stack of etiquette books with slips of white papers sticking out from between the pages. There's a note from Judy on top of the pile that says I'm supposed to read the marked chapters. Opening one, I find details on what's expected of a proper woman of this era along with corresponding page numbers. I grimace and place it back on the table.

Along with the reading I'm expected to do I find a script—perhaps the one from the trailer—and a small datebook. My heart pounds as I skim the writing inside. *My* scribbly scrawl litters the margins. Little notes. Rehearsal times. Photo shoots. Shopping lists.

My fingers flip page after page as Alice's life becomes real in *my handwriting*. I shove it aside and sit on the corner of the bed.

None of this makes sense.

I hold my hands to my lips and shake my head.

What I really want is to call home and tell my parents I'm all right, only I'm not sure if I *am*. I am here in a strange place—in what appears to be a totally different time . . . as *someone else*. How is this okay? A disturbing thought nags my brain. If I am here, then where has the real Alice gone? And more so, what if she didn't go anywhere? If I look like Alice Montgomery, write like her—*am* I her?

The hum of the world outside creeps through the window, lulling me into a quiet state of numbness. Every bone in my body suddenly feels achy and tired. But I jolt when the ringing phone splits the silence. I stare at it on the table near the bed, letting it ring once, twice, three times. On the fourth ring, I find the nerve to reach for it.

With trembling fingers, I hold it to my ear. "H-hello?"

No one says a word on the other end. My mouth opens to ask again when I hear the faintest breath. Goose bumps trail along my arms as I listen. The person who's called is listening too. Waiting. As quietly as I can, I set the phone on the receiver, hanging it up.

I bolt to the windows, making sure the latches are secure and the curtains closed. At the door, I double-check the lock, and for good measure, I wedge a chair beneath the handle. Then I turn off all the lights and curl up tight in a corner of the love seat, arming myself with a pillow to hide behind and a heavy bottle of vodka. If someone breaks in, I'm prepared to smash it over their head.

Knees to my chest, I slowly breathe in and out, listening for footsteps. A door slams down the hall, revving my pulse. The scuffling of feet draws closer. But laughter soon follows, along with the voices of a man and a woman who've obviously planned an evening out. I try to let the sound soothe me. I am in a hotel with other people. I am safe here.

Only . . . had Alice been safe? By the looks of it, she'd left in a hurry. In such a hurry that she left her purse behind. Was she running to get away or . . . taken?

Bathed in sudden fear I wonder, *Am I in danger?* The initial fear of being found out as an imposter *if* Alice in fact disappeared overrides what could be rational—that Alice left for her own reasons, that I'm hallucinating after a huge fall. But it's been days and there is still no sign of her. I look like her. I'm staying in her hotel room, her trailer. The fact that this is all so very disorienting might convince whoever is responsible for Alice's disappearance that I've bumped my head and forgotten. And if someone did something to her, later realizing it didn't work . . . what's holding them back from finishing what they started?

"This is just a bad dream," I tell myself. "Tomorrow I'll wake up in my own bed. Everything will be normal."

Because I'm not Alice. I can't be.

CHAPTER NINE

I JOLT AWAKE TO BRIGHT sunshine, disoriented and filled with a strange sense of fear. I barely got any sleep, yet here I am, sprawled on a small sofa, a pillow on my chest, and a toppled, unopened bottle of vodka on the floor beside me. Sometime during the night, I woke to a loud thump. It must have fallen from my death grip when I finally fell asleep.

"No. No. No." Hurtling myself out of bed, I fling the curtain aside and look down onto the grounds of the Chateau Marmont far below.

But I am *still here*.

I return to the sofa and pinch the inside of my arm. Hard. As if the pain were powerful enough to snap me out of this time warp and fling me back to reality. But all it does is bring stinging tears to my eyes and leave a mark on my skin. I sit, listening. The room and even the hall outside are quiet. Until the phone rings.

The sound of it carries the fear of last night, fresh and bright, all over again. I don't want to answer it, but it won't stop ringing.

"Hello?"

"Front desk, Miss Montgomery. Your car will be here in twenty minutes."

I close my eyes, savoring the sound of a normal person on the other end. Someone who doesn't just breathe into the phone.

"Yes . . . thank you."

I fling myself back onto the bed, drag the pillow over my face, and scream into it.

So much for going home.

JUDY IS WAITING beside the studio's main gate as the car pulls up. She looks different today, more professional, and I immediately notice that her hair is soft and shoulder length, free of the ponytail.

She is at my door in seconds. "Where on earth did you disappear to yesterday?"

"I'm really sorry." My words rush out of me in a steady stream. "I didn't feel very good. I . . . I wasn't myself."

One of her eyebrows lifts as she looks me over. "Well, I hope you're much better today. We have a *lot* of work to do."

I dodge an incoming prop as I keep up with her, nearly twisting my ankle. By the time we make it to the trailer, Judy is calmer, and I am out of breath.

"Absolutely no disappearing today," Judy scolds and ushers me inside. "We'll never finish the film otherwise!"

If only I could tell her that I don't care about the film. It's not important compared to everything else. But Judy bustles around the little trailer, ignoring the blank look on my face.

"Did you have a chance to look over your lines last night? The books? I sent a few things over yesterday. Please tell me they were delivered to your room."

"They were," I tell her. "And by books you mean those awful . . ."

She tilts her head and gives a heavy sigh. "Etiquette lessons. You're young, Alice, and young starlets need all the help they can get to make it in this industry." Judy pauses and looks me up and down before settling her gaze on my face. "You're right. You're not acting like yourself. Usually, you're on top of things, Alice. Well, you're just going to have to work extra hard today. Here."

I stiffen at her comment. Not about working extra hard but that I'm not acting like . . . Alice.

Judy grabs me by the shoulders and forces me into the chair in front of the mirror. She hands me an extra script from the pile she's carried into the trailer. "Scene twenty-two. It's important you project the right emotion for this one. Remember, you're falling in love. Show it!"

"Who am I in love with?"

Judy leaves my side to peer out the door, as if waiting for someone. Now, as she turns back to me, she gives me an impatient stare, then marches over to the vase of white roses and makes a grand display with her hands.

I nod. Of course. James. I shake my wrist, listening to the charms jingle against each other.

"Goodness, Alice, you've been so very odd lately." She steps closer and looks down at me. More confusion than warmth shows in her eyes. "Are you sure you can't tell me where you were the entire week you didn't show up for work? I wonder if you bumped your head—maybe have a touch of amnesia. Maybe you should pay a visit to the doctor?"

Everything that's happened in the last twenty-four hours sits on the tip of my tongue, waiting to spill over. I need someone to listen to me—to care, to help—but no matter how rattled and desperate I feel inside, I can't bring myself to tell her the truth. For now, I don't have a choice but to pretend I'm Alice. If Alice is indeed missing and I'm found out, I might become a suspect in her disappearance, because there's no way anyone will buy my excuse that I fell from the Hollywood sign and landed . . . here.

What would that sound like? Time travel? No one would ever believe that. Time traveling is a thing of speculation and quantum physics. Of science fiction. Not a young woman making a wish for her comatose brother.

It's better to play it safe and let Judy think I went MIA for reasons she'll never know.

"Ah, here they come," Judy announces.

The door bursts open, and an entourage of people flows in with a colorful variety of dresses in tow. I recognize a few faces from yesterday, although the minutes after I first woke up are still a bit fuzzy.

A man with suspenders and a skinny mustache deposits two large cases with handles onto a cart. He begins unpacking compacts and soft-bristled brushes, then rolls the cart next to my chair.

"Scene twenty-two is up next, Antonio."

"Ah, yes." The man nods at Judy's reminder.

Apparently, scene twenty-two must be a big deal around here. The flurry within the small space is overpowering. Everyone moves to a rhythm I don't quite understand. Judy perches on the edge of a small sofa, notebook in hand, and begins ticking off the day's agenda. Hands down, she is a walking, talking, super-organized calendar.

"As soon as you're through here we'll get you into costume and on set," she says while flipping through her notes. "I'm afraid to say, no one was pleased that you cut the day short yesterday, but we'll make up for that today."

Judy continues rattling off the day's set schedule while I steal glances at the script in my lap. The lines for the scene I'm to prepare for are super-mushy. The corners of my mouth turn down.

"Oh no, no," Antonio, the makeup artist, says with discouragement from behind me.

I look up, catching a displeased look across his face in the mirror.

"You must keep my canvas smooth, my darling," he tsks. "No funny faces."

"Canvas?" I ask.

"Your face, darling," he croons. "Keep still now so I can work my magic and transform you into a stunning piece of art." Antonio begins lining my eyes then instructs me to hold them open for as long as I can until the lash glue dries to perfection. I watch as he taps a skinny brush into a smear of red glaze on the back of his hand.

"My palette," he whispers.

Finally, Antonio sets his brush aside. I lift my eyes to my reflection and freeze. I look so . . . different. Like a living doll made up to be beautiful and alluring and . . . surreal. I hate it. I want to wash it all off and clear everyone out of the room so I can cry and scream and try to figure things out in private.

I'm practically lifted out of the chair and shoved into a red evening gown, while several costume attendants fluff and primp from all angles. Everyone fusses over me the rest of the morning, while Judy pressures me to go over the lines for a pivotal scene I have yet to memorize. But I can't concentrate.

Between all the fuss, Judy stares at me while she works on whatever is on her clipboard. No smile, no words of encouragement. Just a glance now and then.

Like she is dissecting me.

I get up and pace around the busy room, my body too wired to sit still.

Judy's eyes follow me closely, as if her gaze is my shadow.

If this is Alice's life, then I don't envy her. In fact, I want nothing more than for her to return from wherever she is, so I won't have to be in her shoes any longer. Everything about "being Alice" feels exhausting.

The room starts spinning. The back of my throat tastes sour, as if all of yesterday is now surging up my esophagus. "Can I just sit down for a moment? I feel . . ."

"No!" Judy cries out, mortified. "You'll wrinkle!" She lunges forward, stopping me before I wilt upon the nearest chair. Reproachfully, she shakes her head.

I have the strong feeling I am disappointing her, but this isn't *me*. Any of this. Maybe I wanted it to be a few months ago, when Ryan asked me to be in his film at a time when I wanted to be more like him. When I needed to thwart my parents' concern over what I wanted to do with my life. *You should aim higher, Grace. Be more like Ryan.* Blah, blah, blah . . .

My heart wrenches.

Someone hands me a glass of water as I blink away the tears. If my brother were here right now, he'd tell me to get a grip. I know that's exactly what he would say. And I'd listen. Because ninety-seven percent of the time, he's right.

I swallow my anxiety as Antonio retouches my lips, then I look over the lines of the scene one last time. The words blur together. My stomach is in knots, just like when I contemplated auditioning for Ryan's film. I didn't want to because I wanted to do something for myself instead. If Ryan knew what I was up against now, he'd want me to do this. Maybe the real Alice would too. I would feel terrible, messing things up for her.

A knock comes at the trailer door. "In ten, Miss Montgomery. South set."

Steeling my nerves, I take one last look at my reflection in the mirror and try to convince myself I can be who they want me to be. What other choice do I have? If they learn I'm a fraud, then I'll suffer the consequences. And I can't fathom what those consequences might be.

CHAPTER TEN

"ELEVEN TAKES." I SHAKE MY head. Nothing prepared me for how grueling it was to conduct a single scene on set. I am exhausted.

My feet are swollen, crammed into the pair of silver heels wardrobe gave me. I eagerly kick them off, wriggling the life back into my tender toes.

"That's nothing," remarks Eleanor, who has a small part that singularly consists of waltzing onto the dance floor and smiling seductively into her dance partner's eyes. She leans back and stretches her arms high above her head. "Once they made us redo an entire frame thirty-six times." She plucks a beaded headband from her soft chignon and inspects its sparkle. "I only had to say one teensy line, 'Of course,' and they made me redo it over and over and over. It's not my fault I'm from Brooklyn!"

I listen to her with enthusiasm. She does carry a heavy accent, but I can tell she's exaggerating for the effect.

"My father paid big bucks for speech therapy too," she continues. "Although he wasn't too keen on it at first. He said I was 'denying my background.'" Eleanor emphasizes this with a sharp gesture of her hand. "He'll forget all that when I win an Oscar one day." She fogs the fake gems with her breath and shines them with the hem of her dress.

"Speech therapy, huh?" My own stuttering seems better. It's another perk of the peculiar Alice phenomena. I pull at the side of the dress I wear. The heat has made it itchy and uncomfortable.

A woman from Craft Services makes her rounds with a courtesy basket. Eleanor peers into it and chooses a shiny green apple. She takes a hefty bite. "I may not sound like a New Yorker much, but you'll never take the Big Apple outta me." She emphatically takes another bite and grins, letting the apple's juice dribble down her chin. "Besides, they may need a gal like me. You know, for a gangster movie. I'd be perfect for that."

I like Eleanor. She's my age and the first person I've met this morning who doesn't fuss over me or completely ignore me. She has an easy attitude, which, in a way, reminds me of my best friend, Beth.

Judy has informed me that Eleanor and I will be studying together with an etiquette tutor between set takes.

"So." She takes another bite of her apple and leans over to swap her script for a book titled *Amy Vanderbilt's Complete Book of Etiquette*. "Where were you? Golly, I'm sorry." She rushes to apologize. "I have a terrible habit of being frank. You take a vacation or something? You were gone for a few days."

I poke at my discarded shoe with my toe. "Oh, I was . . . I had a migraine and needed some time off." It's a lie, but I feel a need to cover for Alice. I don't want to be responsible for ruining things for her, and at this point, I have no other choice but to go along with "being" her. Besides, all the rehearsing, the stress—it's enough for anyone's brain to fritz out and need a break. In fact, after just one afternoon, I'm ready to call it quits.

Eleanor shrugs and seems to buy my excuse. She turns her attention back to the book in her lap. Now and then she glances up with a funny expression on her face, as if she's memorizing what's inside it.

The set around us is in constant flow. Props are moved here and there; machines rumble in to haul larger sets away, replacing them with new ones. People are everywhere. I have the nagging suspicion that if I can find out more about Alice—anything about her—it will explain things. But blending into Alice's world is daunting. It's like fitting into a puzzle that has no straight edges or a picture to follow for guidance. And I am the piece that doesn't fit correctly. At home, Ryan is the glue that brings the whole picture together. And if I don't figure out why I am here, or if my wish didn't work and Ryan never wakes up—everything will feel wrong and unfinished.

"Oooh, there he is." Eleanor's voice breaks the silence of my thoughts, and she continues to munch on her apple.

I let out an uncomfortable chuckle, playing along. "Who?"

A spirited grin tugs at her mouth and she shoves my arm with a gentle push. "Oh, come on." I follow her gaze to the edge of the set. Three gentlemen stand close together. Two are producers who've barked at me all day, the other is a handsome man in a suit. He is staring at me. Our eyes make contact the moment I look over—awkward contact that sets off a strange stirring in my chest.

"Him?"

"Mmm-hmm," Eleanor softly teases.

"But he's . . ." I stop, feeling my words tighten. "He's older."

I glance over at the man again. He looks to be in his early thirties, with a chiseled jaw that spreads into a smile as he converses with the others. As if suddenly uncomfortable, his hands reach up to straighten the knot of his shiny black tie, then down again to smooth the front of his suave jacket. Our eyes meet again and his face pales. A strange heat fills my cheeks.

Eleanor hugs her book to her chest and sighs deeply. "And so dreamy. Really, Alice, he's had eyes for you since the first day on set. And my guess is, it's mutual." She nudges me playfully and grins. "Besides, who cares if he's older? You're a woman, he's a man. It works."

"Last take, people!" the director shouts through the megaphone. He looks directly at me as he climbs onto the seat of the dolly, which lifts, allowing him to survey the set from above. The extras take their spots, ready for their cues. I hurry to squeeze my aching feet back into the shoes and stand, forcing myself to forget Eleanor's ridiculous suggestion. It's time to focus. I've made so many mistakes today. Every take until now has ended in an abrupt "CUT!" because of me. From forgetting my lines to forgetting where to stand, it's clear I am a mess, and when the real Alice comes back from wherever she is, I'll be to blame for ruining her career.

The director points toward the far end of the set and tells me to wait for the clapboard to announce the next take. The big, fuzzy boom lowers until it hovers just above my head. I replay the lines over in my mind, but my conversation with Eleanor has set my brain into motion. I wonder who that man is and who he might be to the real Alice. Why did his expression change and his face pale when he spotted me? It isn't my imagination. He looks confused—almost shocked. And it doesn't add up with what Eleanor said. There was no electric romance in that shared moment. None.

Then the clapboard snaps.

I jump.

"Take twelve!"

An arm gently presses along my back, pulling me into an embrace. Before I know it, James's forehead nestles into the hair at my temple, his closeness making me feel swimmy and uncomfortable.

"Why'd you play me like that?" he whispers, as if the words are meant solely for me and not the microphone above us. "Why?" His tone is breathless. Full of angst.

We've run through so many takes that I completely forget my lines for this new scene. His prompts aren't helping me recall what I'm supposed to say. Disoriented, I scramble for the right words, only I can't remember the script. My lines have melted away. They are gone. I am blank. Am I supposed to hold his gaze until the director yells "cut"? It was a smart call to bail on Ryan's film. There's no way I can do this.

"I . . . I'm sorry," I stammer and press my hand to my forehead. The afternoon sun is making me queasy. Grimacing, I seek out the director's annoyed expression. "Can we start again?"

"Take thirteen!"

I can do this. I have to make them believe I'm Alice and capable of acting. I draw up a memory of practicing lines with Ryan, the two of us on the back porch, dog-eared scripts scattered around our feet. Mom coming out with a bowl of popcorn, her expression one of encouragement, as if maybe I'd found my calling and she'd no longer have to put up with the worry of me not finding my way—to finally commit to something long term. Ryan had looked at me, noticing the stiffness in my spine, the sudden tenseness of the moment, and knowing how much I want to call the shots in my own life, he had said quietly, *"Grace will do what's right for her—and she'll rock it."*

I swallow my fear of ruining the scene again and focus on the words I've briefly memorized. My cheek presses against the palm of James's hand, but the gesture feels too tender to be part of the act. Too intimate.

As if something else controls me. James leans closer and presses his forehead to mine, as if feeling it too. From the corner of my eye, the director, Judy, everyone, hunches in anticipation. Dalton stands under a tree; his attention fully focused on me. The moment our eyes meet, he smiles, as if the simple gesture will offer me the encouragement I need.

"You're like a dream," James says softly. "A beautiful dream. Ready to slip from my grasp as if you were never here at all."

And suddenly, his lines trigger something in me.

The words bubble forth as if I've practiced them for days, feeling them rather than saying them. "Even if I wasn't, I would be your dream. Yours alone."

"CUT!" The stinging sound of the clapboard interrupts the moment, and James and I slowly back away from one another. "That's a wrap!"

"We're finished?" Disbelief coats my voice. Have I done something right, after all?

James nods, smiling with approval. "Took us a while, but you nailed it, sweetheart." He pats me on the back, the romantic tension between us suddenly extinguished as he turns and walks off set to light a cigarette. His endearment makes me feel like I'm nothing more than a pretty prop.

If anyone wants my opinion, I think the line was total cheese. When I read it this morning, I was mortified about acting it out, but the moment I turn toward the others, I know I've finally delivered exactly what they wanted.

Judy rushes to my side. Unlike earlier in the trailer, she is beaming. "That was stunning! Truly stunning!" she gushes. "Your eyes! Your expression!" Judy fans herself with her hand.

The director joins us. "Nice job." He wipes his brow with his sleeve and nods. "Just like this tomorrow. Got it?"

"Sure." I force a smile as a small crowd—the extras, the crew—presses closer, congratulating me. I scan the perimeter of the set for Dalton, eager to share the end of the take.

But he isn't beneath the tree.

He's next to a set prop, walking away from Eleanor with a scowl on his face.

And Eleanor is laughing, with a huge, flirty grin on her face. Talking to the man in the suit.

CHAPTER ELEVEN

JUDY PLACES BOTH HANDS ON my shoulders and beams. "That's the girl we've been waiting for! Where has she been these last few weeks?"

"I . . . uh . . ."

She shakes her head. "It doesn't matter. Just don't lose her again!"

I barely listen as Judy prattles on. I'm too busy looking for Dalton but have lost track of where he's disappeared to. Tiny pangs of disappointment explode inside me—that neither he nor Eleanor are by my side celebrating the final wrap like everyone else. More than that, what would have made him look so aggravated? And if Eleanor is convinced something is going on between Alice and that man, then why does she seem so . . . flirtatious?

"Come along." Judy motions with her hand in the air. "You need a dress."

I look down at the fancy red gown I'm wearing.

"For your photo shoot, silly."

Exhausted from filming, I obediently follow Judy to the far end of the lot toward a plain gray warehouse. She flicks a switch inside the door and dozens of fluorescent bulbs sizzle to life, illuminating a massive space full of rows of costumes: dresses, hats, parasols—there's even an entire section of uniforms and metal armor and swords for period fighting scenes. I loudly suck in a breath.

"Impressive, isn't it? It's every actor's dream." Judy steps in and wiggles her finger to follow. "You need a publicity outfit. Something glamorous. If you're going to be our next superstar, you'll need to look the part."

My stomach lurches at the idea her words paint in my mind. My feet are killing me, and I've had enough of playing dress-up as Alice for the day.

But the way everyone lit up after that scene just now. The way James held me in his arms. The goose bumps. The thrill. It's the feeling I dreamed of while acting in my room back home. What Ryan feels after every scene he directs in class. What Ryan wanted me to feel when he asked me to be a part of his film.

But today I did it. On my own. And part of me feels guilty I couldn't deliver a scene like that when I was supposed to—when it mattered most, when it mattered to Ryan. Maybe once I get home, I'll ask if it's too late to audition. Maybe not all the parts are taken. The idea gives me a bit of hope. Tonight, I'll find my way back. Even if it kills me.

With new determination, I follow the sound of Judy's clicking heels.

She leads me down a maze of aisles filled with costumes and props. The labyrinth is confusing, and I am sure, if left alone, I'd get lost and never find my way out. Finally, we reach an aisle nestled deep inside the building, completely walled in by evening gowns. In every possible direction, something glistens or looks softly inviting. Sequins. Rhinestones. Silk. Velvet. It takes everything in me not to reach out to touch it all. Tiny yellow tags are pinned to several of the dresses. I read them as I walk past: *Lauren Bacall: 1943. Mary Pickford: 1919. Joan Crawford: 1953 . . .*

"The ones tagged have already been worn, so try to pick one that hasn't. The studio aims to avoid repetition so the tabloids won't call them out on it." Judy seats herself on a small leather stool. "They're sized small to large. Take your time. We want it to be perfect." She adjusts her glasses and whips out her trusty notepad.

I stare blankly at the racks, barely knowing where to start.

"May I suggest silver? And floor length," Judy recommends without looking up. "The directives are for a stunning glamour shot."

"When is this 'stunning glamour shot' supposed to take place?" I ask.

"Bright and early tomorrow morning."

That means another day of waking up as Alice if I can't figure out how to get home tonight. My shoulders lift and fall with a silent groan as I set my focus on the silver gowns, but each one has already been tagged. "Aren't these all . . ." I pause, finding the right words. "I just don't think these are right for me. They seem so . . . sultry."

Judy hops off her stool to join me. "That's the point. We *want* you to look sultry." She lifts a dress from the rack and holds it up. "You have the look to pull it off. Innocent yet mysterious. Naïve yet smoldering. But you're right, maybe silver is too much?"

A brewing anger builds inside my chest that the persona of Alice Montgomery is to be a seductress, that Judy's directives are to shove me into a sexy dress and literally lure the public—mainly the male population—to the film.

But what about the female moviegoers? Is my sex appeal supposed to send the message that this is true glamour? That this is how women should strive to look? Judy hasn't noticed how offended I am as I wander over toward a rack that seems out of place. It's pushed up against a door, separated from the others and concealed with a protective cover.

"What's under here?" I ask.

Judy's heels click quickly across the floor. She unzips the long closure and lets out a satisfying squeal. Beneath is a breathtaking assortment. "I've forgotten all about these! They were sewn a few years ago for a film that never went to screen and have been here ever since."

"So, like, they've never been worn?"

Judy shakes her head, ogling over our find.

My hand reaches out for a dove-gray dress smashed between two brightly colored evening gowns. It isn't silver, but close enough, and it's floor length and soft. The waist is cinched, threaded with delicate strands of silver and black, and the neckline curves just enough that it might not make me feel too exposed.

"It's not quite the look we want, but try it on." Judy nods toward a dressing screen conveniently stowed in the corner, and I step behind it.

A small mirror is propped against the wall behind the screen. Beneath the makeup and the hair, I am still Grace. Not a superstar. Not a doll someone has made up. I quickly shed the constricting dress I've worn for the last five hours and slip the gray gown over my head.

Gliding into it as it settles into place, I find it fits perfectly. I swivel in front of the mirror, captivated at how the silver threads catch the light shining from the fluorescent bulbs overhead. My reflection has morphed into . . . well, a movie star, not a sex symbol.

I step out from behind the screen. Judy hasn't heard me; her attention is on something she's busy writing in her calendar.

"Ahem," I say softly.

Judy looks up. At first, her expression is unreadable, her mouth drawn into a tight little line. But then she softens, hops off the stool, and steps closer, inspecting the lines of the gown. "Of course it fits," Judy mutters under her breath. I must look confused because not a second later she plasters a bright smile on her face, announcing, "Not a single section needs to be taken in." I smile back, acknowledging the compliment, but the tone in her voice sticks with me. Without saying anything else, she grabs a blank tag and scribbles across it. *Alice Montgomery: 1953*.

She motions toward the screen again and I step behind it to undress. When I emerge, I reluctantly hand over the gown, wishing I could take it back to the hotel with me and try it on again.

Judy lays it over her arm. "Every gown needs a bit of sparkle," she says, then whisks me into a tiny closet of a room with little drawers recessed into the walls. She unlocks one with a key from her pocket.

"Aren't they the loveliest?" Judy sounds positively enamored. The jewelry resting inside sparkles beneath the lights like stars. "Each one is handcrafted by the genius himself, Joseff of Hollywood."

I steal a glance at the woman beside me. Her face glows with pure happiness.

"They're beautiful." I lean over the open drawer. The necklaces and earrings inside look priceless and the thought of wearing them for the photo shoot makes me nervous. "I can't wear these. They're expensive."

"Nonsense. They are divine!" She lifts a pair of diamond earrings from the box and holds them up for me, letting out a pleased sigh. "These should do just fine with the dress."

I back away, grimacing. "What if I lose them? I borrowed my grandmother's onyx earrings once, and well . . ."

"Let me guess." Judy inches closer, now holding the matching necklace up to my throat. "You misplaced one and never heard the end of it."

"Worse. It fell into the toilet and got flushed." My cheeks burn with embarrassment.

Judy shrugs it off. "Accidents happen. Besides, you're going to be a star now, and stars *must* sparkle." She holds onto the jewelry chosen for me as she peers back into the box. "These have always been my favorite." She whispers so softly, I almost don't hear her. Her fingertip caresses a green bead set in Egyptian gold filigree encrusted in gems, lingering a little longer than necessary. Then she replaces the drawer back into the wall and is all business again, shuffling me out into the bright sunshine.

Her words, "accidents happen," strike something within me. Was falling into Alice's place an accident? Part of me can't believe that. Everything here seems so real, as if I am meant to be in Alice's shoes, only I don't know why. And I can't shed the overwhelming feeling that I need to be here—to figure out what happened to the real Alice to find my way home.

I KICK OFF the heels the moment I step into the trailer. After we left the wardrobe warehouse, Judy told me I was done for the day. Now I can't wait to get out of this costume and back to the hotel room. All I want is to be alone to close my eyes and think, with no one tugging at my hair or poking at my eyelashes. Just quiet.

But now that I am by myself, I feel antsy. Like my skin is itching for something to do. I've made a promise to myself that I'll get home, but now that I'm alone long enough to actually form a plan, I don't know where to begin.

I reach behind me for the dress's zipper, but it's too difficult without the help of another pair of hands.

A rap sounds at the door. "Miss Montgomery, you in there?" Dalton calls from the outside.

In a flash I am on my feet, nearly tripping over the hem of the ridiculously long gown. I somehow manage to cross the room without falling on my face and open the door. Dalton stares at me, and the sight of him sends butterflies throughout my chest.

"That's some dress, Miss Montgomery." A shy smile slides across his lips.

"You can call me Alice, you know, and . . . um, thank you," I sputter. "I actually can't wait to take it off." In a flash, I squeeze my eyes shut. "Did I really say that out loud?"

Dalton gives an awkward little nod. "Afraid so."

"Great. It's just . . . so uncomfortable." I sigh. "And it's been a long day." A bead of sweat rolls down my back. "Sorry, do you want to come in?"

He shuffles his feet and gives his usual nervous look around. "Nah, I . . . um . . . wanted to ask if you had dinner plans later, but if you're tired . . ."

"Oh." I hadn't realized how hungry I am, but now that he's mentioned it, my stomach is grumbling. I swallow the lump in my throat. "Dalton Banks, are you asking me out on a date?"

He looks around again and shrugs. "Well, I . . . we don't have to call it that. If you don't want to."

"No, I'd like that."

I pause, not sure if I should mention what I saw earlier. Dalton seemed so annoyed walking away from Eleanor, and my first impression was that he didn't like her talking to that man. "I saw you talking to Eleanor earlier and you seemed . . ."

"Oh that." He shakes his head. "That man she was with, Hawkins . . . I guess he just rubs me the wrong way. I need her to do a voice-over for one of her scenes and she wanted to stay and talk with him." Dalton rolls his eyes. "Anyway, that accent of hers . . ."

A breath of relief slips from my lungs that what I saw wasn't jealousy, and I bob my head up and down, agreeing. "It's potent."

Dalton teeters on his heels for a minute, appearing nervous. "I didn't think you'd actually say yes, and I wasn't bold enough to make a reservation ahead of time, so, if you've had enough fancy for one day"—he nods toward the dress again—"I thought maybe you'd like to go to Mel's? They have great burgers."

I can't help the smile that beams on my face at the idea of going someplace familiar. A place Ryan and I used to go to for late-night ice cream and to satisfy our cravings for french fries. "I don't need fancy. A burger sounds like the best thing in the world right now."

"Great!" Dalton tilts his wrist to look at his watch. "I've got some work to finish up, but if you'd like, I'll pick you up at eight. Unless you're still in need of a ride back to the hotel."

I shake my head, smiling. "I'm fine. I'll catch an Ube—I mean, a cab, I'll catch a cab." Thankfully, I had brought the money Alice left in her purse back at the hotel.

"Oh, um . . ." I pause. "I seem to be stuck in this dress. Would you mind helping? I can't reach the top of the zipper." Dalton's face bursts into a shade of red I never knew possible, but he steps inside the trailer. Realizing I've put him in an awkward position, I offer, "I can call for Judy, if you'd rather not, but I'm not sure where she is."

"Uh . . . no, it's fine." I hear a loud gulp in his throat. From the corner of my eye over my shoulder, I see his Adam's apple rise up and down. I turn back around, waiting a few seconds before I feel his fingers at my back. The zipper slides down my dress slowly. Dalton shuffles away and resumes his stance just outside the door.

"Eight it is, then." His voice is strained, as if the color in his cheeks has soaked into his vocal cords.

I nod. "Burgers."

I shut the door and watch from the window as he walks across the lot toward the main building. Dalton Banks just unzipped my dress. A proper woman from this decade would never have asked him to do that, and the embarrassment hits me all at once. And even so, he's asked me to dinner and still wants to go. On a date. Something I don't have a whole lot of experience with. I feel strangely giddy inside—which is an odd feeling, given my world seems irrevocably heavy. Not that finding myself here, in someone else's shoes, is any better than what my parents and I have been dealing with. This is just different. Different in a way that makes me wonder if finding my way home can wait one more night.

CHAPTER TWELVE

HAVING A FIFTIES FANATIC FOR a brother meant my family would sometimes frequent places like Mel's and Café 50s. And as Dalton and I pick our way through the parking lot beneath neon lights that bounce off the brightly colored cars, I miss my brother more than ever.

"Welcome to Mel's," Dalton says brightly as he holds the door open for me. "They make a mean chicken potpie."

"I thought you promised burgers," I tease. In all honesty, I'd be happy if someone set an entire cow in front of me. I'm beginning to have separation anxiety from my mom's meat loaf. And my mom. A wave of homesickness washes over me. I'd do anything to eat dinner with her and my dad right now, even if it means another frozen lasagna or hospital cafeteria food.

The diner is crowded and loud, and while it looks a bit different, it's still Mel's—still a familiar sight with its blaring jukebox at the far end and raucous conversation in the booths. We meander past the counter toward an empty booth near a long row of windows, and I slide onto the cushioned seat, mesmerized by everything. There are girls in poodle skirts and bobby socks. Couples share sundaes at the counter, and the black-and-white tile floor is crowded with swaying bodies as they dance to the music. The scene around me looks like one of Ryan's Google searches come to life.

"Wow. This place is poppin'," I say, staring around in awe. Beth and I usually go to the Viper Room a few times a month, but this . . . this is a completely different vibe, even compared to when Ryan and I would come here.

"I like how you describe things. You're different." Dalton gives me a shy smile, then looks over his shoulder behind him. "Take those cookie cutters over there. They're all the same." He nods toward three young women around my age who've just walked in. "Watch, they'll each order a shake and giggle at the lipstick stains on their straws."

Moments later three milkshakes appear on the countertop, each topped with fluffy whipped cream and a cherry. One by one they take their glasses and sip through their striped straws, then giggle on cue as if they're still teenagers—or younger.

Dalton turns to me with a proud grin.

"How did you . . ."

"Everyone's the same here. Predictable. But not you." His voice comes out in a rush as he shifts in his seat. "That's my whole point."

"You like that I'm *different*?"

"You're not what I expected. Well, I mean, you're . . . I like that you're . . . *you*." He looks back toward the women and their shakes. "And not . . . that."

His compliment makes my stomach flip-flop. Dalton can't see how hard I'm trying to blend in because he believes I'm Alice. He doesn't know that acting like the starlet really *is* an act. And while I need to keep up the charade, a part of me wishes he could see *me*—

the woman I've been striving to become, even if I belong in a time decades from now, even if I'm stuck living with my parents and haven't followed a traditional path since graduating high school. I want him to see me as a twenty-first-century woman with opinions and goals and firm beliefs. That I'm not a child. That I'm not Alice and I'm certainly not a pretty doll who cowers in the presence of men like Mack Flynn. I catch his gaze across the table. The way he looks at me while I've been lost in thought suggests he's trying to figure me out, and it spikes my anxiety. Hopefully he's just thinking about unzipping my dress earlier.

"What'll it be?" The waitress appears out of nowhere, flipping open her pad of paper for our order.

"Oh." I suddenly can't focus. The menu is enormous, and all I can think about is the chicken potpie Dalton mentioned, but I hate potpie. I've only had it once and it tasted like peas and carrots and cardboard, and . . .

"You wanted a burger, right?" Dalton smiles.

I press my lips into a thin line and try to get a grip on things. "Right. I'll have a burger. And fries." I mouth a tiny *thank-you* across the table.

"The works?" The waitress wears a silly little white cap on her head. I can't stop staring at it.

"Yes, please. And a vanilla milkshake," I add. I look down and busy myself with the saltshaker.

The waitress turns to Dalton and takes his order: a bison burger with a side of fries and a Coke. Then she tucks her pencil behind her ear and walks away.

I give him a look. "Bison burger?"

Dalton shrugs. "Don't mock it until you try it, doll."

I lean back in my seat and cross my arms over my chest. "Doll?"

Dalton watches the waitress until she disappears through the swinging kitchen doors. When his gaze finds my scowl, there is an instantaneous smile—nervous, perhaps. "You've never heard that expression before? You know . . . *doll.* It's just what guys call gals."

But I stay silent and scowl.

Clearly uncomfortable, he reaches into his pocket and sets a dime on the table, sliding it toward me. "You know what? Why don'tcha pick out a tune?" He nods toward the jukebox.

I slide the coin back to him. "I wouldn't know what to pick."

"You're joshin' me, right? Don't you listen to music?"

"I mean, I do . . . I just . . ." I start to fidget as Dalton bolts out of his seat, urging me to follow him.

"Anything?" Dalton asks moments later, tapping the dime on the glass.

We stare into the window at the choices, but I don't recognize any of the songs like I thought I would. The year 1953 is too early for any of the rock-and-roll tunes I used to hear playing in my brother's room. But I do recognize some of the artists. Doris Day. Perry Como. Maybe if I heard one of their songs, I would know it. I look at Dalton. "Why don't you choose?"

He turns a knob below the window and the tabs flip over, revealing a new set. His thumb presses the dime into the slot, then he pushes the keys G, 12. Without saying a word, he crooks his finger and coaxes me out onto the floor.

"I . . ." I shake my head. "Uh . . . no."

"Let me guess. A gal who can't pick a song probably has two left feet." He takes my hand, pulls me close, and then we start to sway. I'm grateful the song he's chosen is slow and not something that requires spinning and swinging, anything to draw attention to my utter discomfort with adapting to this strange era.

"You're wrong, you know," I whisper, letting my cheek fall against his shoulder. "I have a left and a right." I'm suddenly glad my dad taught me how to dance. All those years of standing on his feet when I was little are paying off.

"And I'm sorry if calling you doll upset you." There is a slight tremor in Dalton's hand that sends a curious flutter to my chest.

I lean against him, a silent acceptance of his apology. Even if he used the term *doll* like any other guy might, he makes me less afraid of being alone.

My insides grow swimmy and warm as we sway to the music. The song fades, replaced by a jazzier one I know—"Crazy Man, Crazy" by Bill Haley—thanks to Ryan's extensive taste in fifties music. Our food has arrived, and I follow Dalton back to the booth. I stare at his plate, watching as he dips a fry into a glob of ketchup.

"Okay, spill it," he blurts out.

I freeze in my seat, suddenly afraid that Dalton knows I'm not the real Alice—that he's asked me who I am, and I'll have to tell him something I'm sure he won't believe. My mouth feels dry, and my heart thumps heavily in my chest.

"Spill . . . what?"

He dips another fry. "How you got into acting."

"Oh." Does he want me to have a heart attack? I take a sip of my shake, hoping it will give me a better answer than the one I have. "I sort of fell into it."

"You just seem . . ."

The burger feels coarse and tasteless against my tongue as I wait for him to finish his sentence, and I quickly swallow it down with another slurp of my shake.

"You just seem like you're from someplace else." He takes another bite.

"Do I?"

Dalton rubs his forehead, leaving behind a red mark, then offers a lopsided grin. "Yeah, not from Los Angeles, I mean. Sorry. It's not my place to ask you, I guess."

"It's okay. What about you?" I strategically avert the topic. "You were carrying a lot of papers the day we met. What were they?"

"Oh, I'm a screenwriter." Dalton's face brightens. "Well, an aspiring screenwriter. I'm working on a science-fiction piece."

I bite into my burger, intrigued. "For a movie?"

"Television, actually. I'm counting the days until I land my script in the right hands. Ever hear of Rod Serling?"

The name sounds familiar. "*Twilight Zone,* right?" I've seen a few episodes but don't follow the series.

Dalton tilts his head. "Nah, doesn't ring a bell. I'll have to check that one out." He finishes chewing and wipes his chin. "Serling's a screenwriter and he's brilliant. He's everything I want to be. In fact, I lived right around the corner from him back in Cincinnati."

I suddenly realize that the television show I mentioned isn't on TV yet. My heart starts to pound; I've just told him something I couldn't possibly know. I cover it up with, "You know him?"

"I wish." He shakes his head thoughtfully. "But if you ask the Cincinnati PD, they'll be happy to tell you I make a better stalker than a neighbor."

I'm about to take another bite of my hamburger when I stop to check if he's joking.

"True story, sister. They caught me trying to slip a script proposal into the mail slot of his front door and called me a criminal. Then I moved here to California, but don't worry, my uncle is with the LAPD, so he'll make sure I stay in line." He gauges my reaction. "I'm *kidding*. I'm not a dangerous stalker." He sips his soda. "Anyway, I'm working on an episode I hope he'll consider for *Tales of Tomorrow*. Ever hear of the show?"

I shake my head.

"What?" Astonishment flashes across his face. "Well, you're missing out, sweetheart. It's the most brilliant example of science fiction ever to make television. 'Plague from Space,' 'Age of Peril,' 'The Invader . . .' and my favorite, 'All the Time in the World.' See," he says while shoving a fry in his mouth, "it's about a woman who has a watch that allows her to jump ahead in time so she can rob an art museum. Oh, you have to try this." Dalton reaches over, grabs a fry from my plate, and dunks it in my milkshake. He holds it out for me as I stare at it.

"You eat fries this way?" I hesitantly reach for the fry, holding it between my fingers while it drips vanilla shake onto my plate.

"Of course. You've never tried this before?"

"But it looks like it'll taste so . . . nasty." I look at the fry, certain it's going to taste disgusting.

"Nah, just a little goopy. Go on, try it." He leans over the table expectantly.

Giving in, I take a delicate bite. It's not gross. Just a soggy fry that tastes like a vanilla milkshake. "Hmm, it's not bad."

"Told ya," he says with a grin that grows wider as I continue to dip fry after fry into my shake. The flavor is growing on me.

Dalton dives into a full description of the entire episode, but it's the mention of jumping through time that catches my attention. If only his enthusiasm for all things sci-fi were enough to send me home—to *his* future.

Suddenly everything feels a bit different.

There is something about him—an easiness—that makes me comfortable. Like a gentle tug to be closer and honest. And not just because he's the only one who sees past the woman everyone believes me to be. But if I tell him, will he accept what's happened? Will he think I'm crazy? Will it scare him away?

But while Dalton is preoccupied with explaining about space and time, I wonder if I *can* possibly tell him, regardless.

The hum of another slow song emerges from the jukebox and Dalton tosses his napkin on the table, rising to his feet. "One last dance?"

I scoot out of the booth and follow him back out to the floor. The chords of the song are familiar, something about believing and going astray, and someone coming to find the way. I realize it's the song that had been playing when I woke in the trailer. Resting my hand in Dalton's, I lean against him, asking, "What's this song called?"

"It's 'I Believe,' by Frankie Laine."

After a few beats of swaying to the song, Dalton whispers against the side of my head. "I have to confess something. You intimidated me when I first met you, but I'm glad you came out with me tonight. I like being around you."

"I like being around you too. I feel like you're my only friend at the studio."

Dalton is different. There is something about him that makes me feel I can still be me and not pretend to be Alice all the time.

Maybe I should be honest and tell him.

I close my eyes, feeling him lean his chin on top of my head. I want this moment to last forever. For all I know, I could wake up tomorrow and be gone. Dalton's arms wrap tighter around me. The song has ended, but we stay, swaying to an invisible rhythm that matches my heart.

CHAPTER THIRTEEN

"WHAT'CHA THINKING ABOUT, DOLLFACE? You're awfully quiet," Dalton asks as we drive down Sunset Boulevard.

The windows are rolled down, letting the night air blow into the car, and for the first time in days, I feel clearheaded. Until Dalton calls me dollface. I bristled the first time he said it, and it still makes me feel like I've been placed in a box—the one where women are often placed.

But the way it slips off Dalton's tongue sends a wave through my chest, as if he and I have crossed some imaginary line, bringing us closer.

"I'm thinking about my brother." Which is half true. I am trying to figure out my feelings for the man next to me, but thoughts of Ryan keep creeping in. He would have loved seeing Mel's the way it was tonight, not the drive-in of our time, trying desperately to hold on to the past.

Not to mention, I think he'd like Dalton.

"Is he an actor too?" He steers the car around a corner and accelerates up the next street. "You asked about him when you woke up in the trailer."

"He used to be, when he was younger." I stare numbly out at the bright city lights, shaking away the possibility that Ryan might never act again—or walk again, or talk, or wake up. My parents and I were told he could have irreparable damage to his brain. But I've prayed every night since his accident that he'll be all right. He'll be himself. He *has to* be. "He wants to direct." I want to tell him that the way Ryan's brain works is brilliant. That while just a student at this point, his films evoke a sort of feeling that could honestly make it big one day—his ingenuity and his eye for detail and emotion and . . .

"He doesn't do it anymore?"

"My brother's been in a coma for a week." And yet it feels like it's been longer since waking in Alice's trailer—that somehow the days have absorbed the distance between here and where I should be. Home.

Dalton looks shocked. "Oh, geez. I . . . I'm so sorry." Concern pinches his brows as he alternates from watching the road to looking over at me.

I nod my thanks as I swallow back fresh tears. "It's been hard for my whole family. Ryan is always so lucky. It's almost impossible to believe that someone like him can get hurt."

My lungs let out the sadness I've been holding inside. "We just don't know what the future holds for him." I swivel on the seat to face Dalton. "Ryan would like you. You remind me of how ambitious he is." I look down at the space between us; the screenplay he's been working on is on the seat in a smooth leather folder.

Dalton offers a soothing smile. "If I may remind you, you're about to see your name in lights on the silver screen. Now that's ambition. Meanwhile, I'm stuck in a studio smashing cabbages, when I'd much rather be writing about worlds no one could possibly imagine."

We pull alongside the curb a few feet from the Chateau Marmont's valet booth. Dalton cuts the engine and turns to face me. "I know we don't know each other well enough, but do you mind if I ask what happened to your brother?"

"It was a car accident. Up on Mullholland leading into Beachwood Canyon. His car struck a coyote, and he flipped over the embankment."

"I'm really sorry," Dalton says softly. "That's an unforgiving road."

"He goes there a lot to daydream—about his future, about one day making it big here and seeing one of his films come to life. He's always seen the Hollywood sign as a beacon of hope, but ever since they cracked down on . . ." I bite my tongue and quickly cover up my slip, forgetting that the Hollywood sign isn't monitored here like it is back home. "Ever since we were young, he just can't stay away from it. In fact, he always jokes that he'll climb it one day."

From the corner of my eye I watch Dalton's reaction, afraid he's noticed that I've almost given myself away. But he hasn't.

A shudder passes through him as he turns the dial on the dash, sending a wave of heat through the vents. "I just can't imagine taking the risk of climbing that thing. You've heard of Peg Entwistle, haven't you? One slip and it's . . ." Dalton's hand slices the air near his neck.

The look I give him stops him cold.

"Geez, Alice. I didn't mean to be so crass. Not while your brother is . . ."

"No, I know what you mean. And you're right. Climbing the sign is dangerous and stupid." I turn away from the concern in his eyes and stare straight ahead. The trees surrounding the front drive of the hotel are tinged golden in the lamppost light. I feel so far away from home, and speaking about Ryan stirs up a new worry in my perpetually tightened chest. One that convinces me that in my absence, my brother has died and is now in purgatory until I can find my way back and beg his soul for forgiveness.

I've slipped into my own thoughts so deeply that it's a shock when I'm suddenly aware of the warm hand covering mine. When I look up, Dalton is watching me with a look in his eyes that nearly breaks me.

The truth shifts the air around us, letting my sadness slip across the seat.

This is the conversation I've been wanting to have. To hear it out loud, in the open, hoping it will make sense. But instead, telling Dalton feels horrible.

"I climbed it to make a wish for my brother—that he'll wake up and that everything in his life will go back to the way it was. That my family's life will go back to normal."

The words inside me are eager to come out, even as Dalton's face watches me in stunned silence. I've held the wish—the one monumental thing I want for Ryan, and what's happened after I made it—inside me for days now. Maybe sending it off to the stars above the sign wasn't enough. Maybe I just need to tell someone. And as uncomfortable as it is, something tells me Dalton might be that person.

I glance down again at the screenplay lying on the seat between us. Beneath the supple leather folder is a world he's built. A world he's painstakingly created—so real he hopes that one day someone will watch it and accept the fact that other realities exist. If anyone is open-minded enough to accept time travel as real, it's him. And I need to tell him what happened after I made the wish.

"Do you really believe those worlds you write about exist?" I ask carefully. "I mean, I'm not sure I believe in little green men, but I do think there are things we can't explain. Other places. Time. Glitches."

Dalton blinks a few times as if snapping out of the strange hold I've held on him. He's no longer gripping the steering wheel, and while he eyes me closely, as if expecting me to confess more, he tells me, "Well, sure. I believe it's possible."

"Say someone has an accident, a jolt, hard enough to push them out of the present and into another time," I whisper. "Does that sound crazy?"

"Are we talking time travel or an out-of-body experience?"

"More like time travel."

"Go on," he says.

"So, let's say a person has an accident, like a fall from something tall. Like a building or . . . uh . . . the Hollywood sign—that's tall enough. The fall could have possibly killed them, but instead they wake to a world that isn't the same. It's like, sixty or seventy years earlier than it should be."

"Whoa, wait a second." Dalton casts me a worried glance. "Does this have anything to do with your brother's accident? Not to disappoint you, but I don't think what happened to him propelled him to a different time. And falling from that sign is sorta like a one-way ticket to—"

"I'm not talking about my brother," I interrupt, wiping my sweating palms on my skirt. "I'm talking about me."

CHAPTER FOURTEEN

"THEY TOLD ME I'D BEEN missing for a whole week." My voice is so low Dalton has to lean closer to hear me. "That I stumbled onto the location set, dirty and confused, without memory of where I'd been."

"When?" His voice sounds strange and detached.

"Two days ago, when I woke up in the trailer at the studio. Judy told me the last time she saw me was just after a scene had wrapped on location at the Hollywood sign. Almost exactly where I fell." I've been avoiding his eyes, but like a magnet, I feel the pull to look up. "She kept calling me Alice."

"But *you are* Alice."

"No." I shake my head. "I'm not. My name is Grace."

The instant the confusion hits his eyes, I want to take back my words and hold them inside my mouth.

"Do you know how high that is?"

Dalton's voice cracks.

He closes his eyes, and he cringes, as if picturing me teetering atop the sign, then falling to the ground below.

"I do now." A dark laugh escapes me. "When I woke up, I was here. In this time. That's when I met Judy and then . . . you."

He doesn't say anything, so I keep going, worried that if I don't get it all out within the next few seconds, I'll lose my nerve.

I close my eyes, take a shuddering breath, then open them. "I don't know how this happened, but now everyone, even you, believes I'm some movie star named Alice Montgomery. I'm not her. I only *look* like her. I'm Grace. Grace Brighton. And since that night at the sign, all I want is to wake up from this nightmare and find myself back home."

I wait for him to say something. Whether Dalton thinks it's the coolest thing ever or I'm 100 percent nuts, I can't tell. He's completely silent, his body still and rigid.

"Do you . . . believe me?"

Dalton looks shell-shocked. His gaze strays from my face to stare at something insignificant out the windshield, but a breath later he looks at me and smiles.

And hope inside me starts to build again.

"I'm trying," he says. "I really want to."

I stare at the dashboard of the car. My brain races for anything I can tell him to prove what I've just told him. I could tell him who the next president will be, who will win the World Series . . . but what if he thinks I'm desperately making things up? No, I need something substantial. Something that is going to happen. Soon.

I remember the newspaper he carried with him the day we met. The one he fanned me with outside the studio. "What's today's date?" I ask.

"September seventeenth."

My mind clicks onto something. The other week at the library I found some encyclopedias in the back storeroom. No one uses encyclopedias anymore. That's what the internet is for. But I'd thumbed through one, and growing up as a baseball fan's daughter, I took note of something my dad would have been interested in. "Ernie Banks."

Dalton turns his head. "Who?"

"Ernie Banks. The Chicago Cubs?" I repeat, nodding. "My dad is a huge baseball fan. Tomorrow's newspaper will mention Ernie Banks being introduced as the first African American player for the Chicago Cubs." There's no way Dalton will miss the headline, he's always carrying a newspaper with him, and more important, there's no way I can possibly know this before anyone else.

I'm smiling like a hopeful lunatic. It's going to happen. It *did* happen.

Dalton rubs the back of his neck. "I'm a little stunned a gal like you knows about baseball."

A gal like me? Dalton doesn't seem to notice my eyes narrowing at his remark. "I happen to know a lot about baseball."

My tone causes him to react, and suddenly he's clamoring for the right words. "I just didn't realize . . . I mean . . . you're so dainty and feminine and—"

"And I have a dad and a brother who like sports, and this dainty woman you're sitting next to climbed the Hollywood sign. In the dark. In a storm. And fell and lived to tell about it."

Knowing he's struck a nerve, Dalton backpedals. "I'm sorry . . . Grace. Really. Just forgive me, okay? This is a lot for a guy to take in. If I don't believe you, it goes against everything I say I do—all that science-fiction mumbo jumbo." He pauses. "If the papers mention this, then maybe you're proof that it's all real. That time travel is possible."

"It is possible. I don't know how, but it is." I push aside my annoyance at being stereotyped and urge my expression to not appear so bitter. I need Dalton to believe what I've told him. Reaching across the space between us, I place my hand over his. "I'm not crazy. I'm just . . . lost."

"Grace Brighton." My name sounds foreign as it rolls off his tongue and then he whistles long and low. He flips his hand over, weaving his fingers between mine until we're connected. Reassuring me. Believing me.

"Boy, I wasn't expecting this. I know when stars get into character, they're all in, but . . . you're not pulling my leg, are you? Grace Brighton?" He gives me a strange look, as if he's waiting for the punch line to be delivered.

"I'm not pulling your leg. Promise."

I want him to say it again. Over and over. If he says my name out loud, then it proves I'm not crazy. I don't have amnesia.

I am Grace. I am *here.* Just once, I need to feel I am no longer alone.

"So here I am." I shrug. "I don't know how to get back."

There is a strange pause between us. Dalton gives my fingers a squeeze, then slips his hand away. He may have told me he believes me but the vibe rolling off him clearly reveals something else. Maybe it's just me, but I swear he's inched a bit closer to his side of the car, placing a little more distance between us.

"Have you tried going back to the sign?" Dalton shifts in his seat. He cracks his knuckles then flexes them against the steering wheel. It's as if he can't get comfortable now that I've told him. Like the space between us is too small.

"That's the first place I went. I was just coming back when you paid my cab fare."

He gives a single nod, remembering. "That's why you looked so upset. Sorry, I thought you were hungover." Dalton gives a half smile, but my confession has changed things between us. It's changed the easiness I felt earlier while we were dancing.

The hole in the pit of my stomach grows larger.

"Dalton." I twist the end of my cardigan sweater sleeve between my fingers. "I know you don't believe me."

He turns in his seat to face me, his eyes unreadable in the dim light. "I want to. But it's kinda . . ."

"Hard."

He nods. "Yeah."

I swipe the corner of my eye with the back of my hand, hiding my tears from him. "I guess I . . . I guess . . ." I inhale deeply. "This went a lot smoother in my head."

He inches a tiny bit closer. "Have you tried clicking your heels three times?"

I let out a laugh that comes out more like a snort.

"Sorry," Dalton whispers, "I couldn't resist."

"No, I haven't. But tell you what, if you believe I'm from the future, maybe you can be my scarecrow." I smile. "And if tomorrow's paper says nothing about baseball, I'll understand if you never want to see me again."

"Deal." He offers a small, hesitant smile, but at least it's something. "Sure looks like a fancy shindig is going on in there." He nods toward the bustle of movement out the window, watching as another car pulls up and parks next to us. We watch as couples make their way up the walkway and into the hotel. Soft music floats out the open doors and into the night.

"I'll bet they're expecting you—I mean, *Alice*—in there tonight. Can't have a star stay at the hotel and not expect her to be at the party."

"I don't think I'm feeling up for that. Judy has me running ragged tomorrow."

"When doesn't she?"

I shrug at the point he's trying to make.

"But I've got a photo shoot, and a scene to rehearse, and . . ."

I stare out at the beautiful people walking into the hotel.

I don't want to set foot inside. I don't want to go to a party or retreat to the room upstairs. I don't want to be alone with my thoughts. And what if I get another creepy phone call? Maybe if I tell Dalton what happened last night, he'll come in with me. But I can't ask that of him. I've given him enough to chew on. Besides, he'll just tell me that the phone call was from some anonymous fan. And maybe it was. But I doubt it. Random fans don't get through to a star's guarded room.

I do my best to calm my nerves, but having let my guard down around Dalton moments ago leaves me feeling conflicted. It felt nice to tell him the truth—to have an ally in my corner, whether he truly believes me or not—but it also leaves me at risk. He might rat me out to Alice's entourage.

They might believe I am crazy and lock me up. They still did that in the 1950s, didn't they? Or worse: what if they believe I have something to do with Alice's disappearance, that I got rid of her so I could step into her shoes? They might call the police and I could end up in prison.

No, if I want to get home, I'll have to figure out how to do this on my own. If Alice is key to my story, I need to learn all I can about her. I need to figure out why she disappeared. And what better way to do that than mingle at a party with those closest to the missing movie star?

BIG BAND MUSIC pulses through the lobby, making my skin tingle. Through the lounge doors I glimpse heavy smoke and evening gowns. Men in tuxedos lean against the bar. I've never seen a party as glamorous as this, and definitely not with such a thick cloud of smoke. I'm so used to smoke-free environments back home that the pungent smell of cigars and cigarettes is overwhelming.

Hollywood's finest are mingling just inside, and any one of them might know what happened to the real Alice. My mind is like a tornado of questions I want answers to. From how everyone acts around me, this must be Alice's first film, so who, then, would walk away from the biggest breakout film of their career? No one. And who would leave their belongings behind . . . like clothes, a purse? The most plausible answer is someone who'd never meant to leave. Was she taken forcibly? Or was she running away from someone or something?

One thing is for sure—she is missing. And whoever called her room last night, mistaking me for her, might have something to do with it. If this person now thinks that a devious plan to get rid of Alice was foiled, I'm in danger too. Getting back to where I belong depends on my finding out what happened to Alice. My life might depend on it.

"Ah, the elusive starlet once again," a familiar voice calls out from behind me.

James sits alone in the lobby, fiddling with a near empty glass of amber liquid. He pats the vacant seat beside him and sloshes his drink in the direction of the lounge. "You're avoiding it too?"

"And why are *you* avoiding it?" I walk over to him, ignoring the empty cushion beside him.

He takes a swig of his drink. "Seen one party, you've seen them all," he slurs slightly, then pauses to inspect the contents of his glass. "Why aren't you in there jazzing it up?"

I look over my shoulder toward the revelry. "Honestly? It's a bit intimidating."

James eyes me with casual curiosity. "Says the gal who's been out and about for hours. Where've ya been? Dinner? Dancing?"

"Both, actually."

"Lucky guy." James tilts the glass to his lips and drains the remaining liquor in one gulp.

"Thanks," I say sheepishly. *Dalton probably doesn't think so. Not after what I just dropped on him.* I study James for a second. It's clear why Ryan admires him so much. James is dynamic and brooding on-screen, and in person. But to see him now . . . here . . . knowing he's yet to reach a level of stardom that will turn him into an icon through tragedy gives me an unsettling feeling. That I know too much.

He stretches his legs out, their length nearly upsetting the floral arrangement on the table in front of him, and looks at me with glassy eyes. Then he runs a hand through his blond hair, letting it hang in front of his face.

"It's the same conversation in there that it always is, sweetheart. The same boring, useless conversation. Everyone wants a piece of you. If you're an actor, they want your soul. And if you're a dame, well . . ." He doesn't finish, waving his hand as if giving flight to the rest of his words.

"See that door over there?" He nods once again toward the laughter and the music. "Walk through it and a dozen others will open for you."

"So, you're saying I *should* go inside? Weren't you just suggesting I don't?"

James reaches into the pocket of his jacket and pulls out a pack of cigarettes, offering one to me.

I wave it off and settle myself beside him.

He taps one out, pulling it from the pack with his lips, and lights it. "I'm saying"—he takes a long drag—"that you should be prepared for anything this world throws at you. Are you a risk-taker, Alice Montgomery?"

"Maybe." I climbed the Hollywood sign. That was risky.

He takes another drag then drops the butt in the remains of his drink. Its embers sizzle at the bottom of his glass. "You should be. It's the only way you'll make it here, but do it carefully. Life is short, and those leeches in there will suck the life from you at the first sign of weakness."

Yes, life *is* short. I should tell him what I know, warn him that something horrific is waiting for him a few years from now. It would be easy to tell him what's happened to me, in his inebriated state, easy to warn him about his Porsche and to stay away from the intersection where he'll slam it into another car, the crash making him a legend.

James leans forward, loosening his tie from around his throat. I could tell him so many things, but it seems I should listen to what he's trying to tell me. A warning, perhaps, that it's so easy to fall prey to the film industry. That no matter what decade, Hollywood holds a dangerous grip on what it wants to keep silent.

"I'm just saying, don't let your guard down." James's soulful blue eyes stare into mine. "Even if you do seem more street-wary since you skipped out while we were on location. You also nailed that scene we just did, by the way."

"Thanks." I let his words sink in. It's the sort of advice Ryan would give me—take a chance but be careful—and James's words resonate deeply. So much so that it's almost as if I'm sitting in this lobby talking with Ryan.

James faces me again and gives me a long stare. "You've got a haunted sorta look about you."

"Haunted?" What do my eyes give away? I wonder if it's obvious I'm carrying the weight of worry over my brother. Or the yearning for my old life since plunging off the sign. Could I be haunted by a woman who has disappeared? I don't want to think what the word haunted implies. *I'm not dead. I'm stuck.*

James lifts a finger and twirls it, inching it closer to my face until I flinch, fearing he's going to poke me in the eye.

"Right . . . in . . . there." His index finger stops short of my lashes. "Something abowchoo . . ." he slurs.

I reach up and steer his finger away from my face. Whatever was in that glass is beginning to hit him. "Do I seem different?" I inch a little closer. "I mean, did I seem *haunted* before I disappeared?"

James's sleepy eyes have trouble focusing on my face. He blinks and then shakes his head. "Kind of. I just can't put my finger on it, Alishh."

Oh geez. Maybe this conversation should wait until he can give me a straight answer. James stands and wobbles a bit.

"Oh," I say. "I wanted to thank you for the charm bracelet."

He gives me a quizzical look.

I hold my wrist up letting the charms jingle together.

"Wasn't me, kid."

"But . . ." I thought for sure it was from him; he had touched it coming out of the greenroom.

CHAPTER FIFTEEN

I STEP THROUGH THE FRENCH doors and my heart stills. Ryan's obsession with James Dean has painted a vivid picture for me of what Hollywood's Golden Era looked like, and this is it. I've looked through enough websites and memorabilia of Ryan's to recognize that Tinseltown is sparkling in this very room, sipping champagne and rubbing elbows with one another.

John Wayne is leaning against the end of the bar, swirling his drink. Rock Hudson is grinning, while a small group of women gushes in his presence. Lana Turner, Barbara Stanwyck, Susan Heyward . . . It's all mind-blowing and surreal and I'm suddenly glad I had the foresight to ransack Alice's closet upstairs after James left. I fit into Alice's clothes as if they were my own, and the black beaded dress was the right choice.

Bits of conversation float toward me, snippets of studio secrets, scandals, and contracts, while waiters work the room, passing trays of hors d'oeuvres.

A trio of gentlemen stands at the long, lacquered bar, engaged in conversation. One snaps his fingers in time with the beat. "Gotta love this town."

"Gotta love the dames," his friend chimes, and his gaze follows a red-haired beauty as she walks past.

His comment makes me cringe, so I focus my imagination on how Dalton would look dressed to the nines, his hair slicked back, bow tie at his throat. The idea forms a pleasant warmth inside me. The man at the bar catches me staring and winks, sending prickles of gooseflesh across my arms. I step away and search the crowd for a familiar face from the studio.

"Alice," a masculine voice says from behind me.

I hadn't heard him approach, but when I turn, I am face-to-face with the man who'd stared at me the other day on set. Eleanor was right to gush over him. He is gorgeous, but as debonair as he looks tonight, his hands tremble, causing the ice cubes to clink against the side of his glass. His gaze darts about the room before settling back on me, and then he takes my elbow and steers me toward an unoccupied corner. "Alice," he says again.

I open my mouth, pulling away from him, but he stops me.

"How is it possible? I . . . I mean, how did you . . ." He pulls a handkerchief from his pocket and swipes at his forehead.

I study him closely. The way he looks at me is so odd, so full of disturbed surprise, as if he hasn't seen me in a long while. It's the same way he'd stared at me while I waited with Eleanor for my next set take. "How did I what?" I had planned to be a super sleuth about this, but instead, I blurt out, "Does this have anything to do with my disappearing from the set?"

His handsome face blanches as he pulls at his bow tie, wriggling his fingers between the tie's knot and his shirt collar. But before he answers me, another man approaches us, his voice jubilant and loud.

"There you are!" A stocky, bald man lumbers toward us, out of breath and perspiring along his forehead. He presses his hand against the small of my back, and I stiffen. "You sure know how to make an entrance. Makes me the proudest manager in all of Hollywood!"

The man from the set the other day downs the rest of his glass, never taking his gaze from me, then lifts his index finger, signaling to a nearby waiter, who rushes over with a tray of champagne. "For the lady," he says quietly, then chooses a flute of golden liquid and presents it to me. He stops the waiter from offering him the other glass on the tray. "I'll take something stronger, good man. An old-fashioned. Double. Goodness knows I need it tonight," he mumbles beneath his breath.

"The point of a party is to see and be seen, not to hide in corners." A petite, much older woman sneaks up on us. She has short bobbed hair in the blackest shade I've ever seen. Her palms smooth the bald man's lapels, each finger adorned with a different glittering gemstone. It's an intimate gesture that gives the impression she is with him.

"Mr. Hawkins," the bald man addresses the handsome, pale man who hasn't stopped staring at me. "Of course, you remember my wife, Isadora."

She holds her hand out to him, palm down as if she expects him to kiss it. "Charmed, I'm sure."

Their interaction unfolds as the questions in my head multiply. Which one of them knows where Alice is? Which one called her room? Which one is hiding something?

The bald man diverts his wife's attention to me. "And this lovely ray of sunshine is Miss Alice Montgomery."

Isadora turns her full attention on me, and her eyes sparkle with intrigue. "We *finally* meet!" she croons. "My Geoffrey has told me positut-ely *everything* there is to know about you! Oh, darling, you're simply stunning!" the woman gushes. "But you, Mr. Hawkins, you look like you've seen a ghost!"

The man she calls Hawkins smiles behind his visible discomfort and, despite her observation, continues to stare at me with the most peculiar look on his face. I stare back at him, observing each bob of his Adam's apple as he swallows, each twitch at the corners of his mouth. I think back on my conversation with Eleanor. She'd assumed Alice and this man were having an affair. But if the real Alice is still missing and could possibly be in trouble, why does he act so surprised to see me?

If she was his girlfriend, wouldn't he act happy and protective, rather than uncomfortable? My gut tells me that Hawkins should be at the top of my list of people possibly involved with Alice's disappearance.

I'm so lost in my thoughts, trying to figure things out, that I haven't heard what the bubbling woman has said to me. "I'm so sorry." I smile politely. "Um . . . thank you?"

Isadora lets out a hearty giggle. "Oh, you are adorable! Come, come, my dear, let me present you."

She links her arm through mine and leads me away against my will, off into the buzzing crowd. I look back at Hawkins, wishing I had more time to talk to him. He knows something. I'm sure of it. But the mingling crowd has gathered around him, hiding him from my view. I take a gulp of champagne. My head is beginning to feel like a feather, floating somewhere among the shimmering crystal chandeliers.

"Lucky. Just lucky," Isadora croons as I follow her, "to have my Geoffrey represent you."

I'm puzzled. "Represent?"

"Why, yes!" She pauses to turn and whisper behind her hand. "I may be biased, but he truly is the best talent manager in town."

"And what do you think about Hawkins?" I ask.

"Oh, what a catch that man is." She beelines for a small gathering at the other side of the room. "But he's always so mysterious." She drops the subject and her tiny frame bolts forward through the crowd. "Ah, Joanie! Joan!" Isadora waves her sparkly fingers and tugs on my arm. She butts in without a care and plants me directly in front of the most elegant woman I have ever seen.

"Joanie, my dear, may I have the pleasure of introducing Alice Montgomery." A hint of smugness transforms the expression on Isadora's face and her voice turns sweeter than when she'd been speaking to me. "Alice, meet Joan Crawford. You'll walk in her legendary footsteps, no doubt."

A strained vibe surrounds me. I may be wrong, but if Joan Crawford was a caged tiger, then I am a juicy steak. Even so, this is *the* Joan Crawford. I can't believe I am standing face-to-face with a true Hollywood icon. Ryan and I loved to hate her in *Mommie Dearest*, even though it wasn't really her . . .

"Miss Crawford, it's truly a pleasure," I say, trying to contain myself. "I've seen your work and you are just . . ."

A smirk darkens the actress's exquisite features, stopping me cold. She gives me the once-over. "So, you're Geoffrey's newest prodigy?"

The rest of my compliment falls flat, and I try to focus on her heavy, arched brows.

"And Hawkins? Is he here?" She cranes her neck to look over my head. "Someone call the manager. It seems a rat's been let loose at the Marmont."

I open my mouth to ask what she means, but Joan's icy stare returns and lingers on my skin, chilling me to the bone.

"I'm to take you under my wing, am I?" She exhales boredom.

"I, uh . . . don't think that's the intention here. She just wanted me to meet you." I turn to gesture to Isadora, but she has left me to fend for myself.

"Honey, that woman always has a motive up her sleeve. You'll learn that soon enough. And in case you weren't listening, she pretty much called me old and you, the young replacement."

The actress steps closer. She lifts a slender black cigarette holder in the air. As if on cue, the man to her left lights it. A plume of smoke encircles her head. "Thank you, darling."

She tilts her head, assessing me. "You want my advice? Alice, is it? Pack your bags and head straight for the train station. It'll save you a world of heartache in the end."

My frustration bubbles to the surface, and I refuse to hold it down any longer. "I didn't come here for your advice, but since you're willing to give it, that's all you have to tell me? Go home?" If only her advice was that simple.

"That's it, sweetheart." She takes a dainty little puff and taps the ashes onto the beautiful carpet beneath our feet. Somehow the way she calls me sweetheart sounds worse than Dalton calling me doll. "Oh, and one more thing: stay far away from that Hawkins. He's got an extra set of hands and a reputation to boot."

She leaves me stunned and alone.

Then, just when I need her, the ever-smiling Isadora returns to my side. "Oh, honey, I'm such a fool for leaving you alone."

I fight the urge to shoot her a nasty look, but I've had enough. Enough champagne. Enough unwanted advice. It was a terrible idea to come to this party. I should have followed James's example and left, spending the rest of the night in my room figuring out another way to find out about Alice and get home. I scan the room and spot Hawkins standing with a group of people. If I could just break away from Isadora and go speak to him.

"Joanie takes to very few people," Isadora continues talking. Her apology curls around me like a snake. "There must be something about you she finds threatening to her career."

"No, I'm sure she was just being mean."

"Oh, come now, sweet thing. It's my fault for wanting to introduce you." Without waiting for forgiveness, the woman takes me by the arm again and leads me to the bar. "That old bat is hitting her midlife crisis and, by the look of her, she's not aging very well either."

The lighting here is much brighter than the rest of the room, and I now have a better look at the hurricane that is Isadora. Her skin is heavily caked with makeup as if she were a reptile under many, many layers. Her eyes are roughly lined, and her fake lashes have begun to unstick themselves. But beneath the makeup and the years I clearly see that Isadora was quite the beauty. She still is, if she'd let it show rather than cover it up.

She orders a martini. "Three olives this time, Walter. You know I hate stinginess."

Around us the room pulses with the sounds of big band music. Isadora's drink appears on the bar, the requested number of olives on a long toothpick in the glass. She swishes the olives twice then takes a sip. "Let me tell you a thing or two, Alice. Don't ever get old."

There is a hint of sadness in her voice. Pity she can't see what I see. In seconds her demeanor changes and she is once again smiling, scanning the room for someone to introduce me to, proving she knows nearly everyone here.

"What a beauty," she says without warning. "You've certainly caught Hawkins's eye, you lucky girl."

Am I supposed to feel lucky? Something about the way he looks at me feels wrong. And his comment—as if I had done something.

It feels as if the pieces of an enormous puzzle keep surfacing and I just can't figure out how to link them together.

But I can sense it. Something terrible happened to Alice, and I need to find out what.

CHAPTER SIXTEEN

"TELL ME *EVERYTHING*. EVERY LAST detail," Eleanor says again. She's been sitting on the floor next to my makeup table for the last hour, begging me to describe last night's party while I dab my lips with a tissue. I'll never get used to seeing myself in red lipstick.

Eleanor shoves yet another etiquette book aside. "Did you talk to anyone important? Another director to line up your next film? Although I'm certain Mr. Flynn will surely contract you after your debut. You're so talented, Alice."

Before I have the chance to tell her I was practically held hostage by Isadora all evening, Eleanor looks up with a dreamy glimmer in her bright eyes. "Wouldn't it be wonderful to have a love affair with a man already established in the industry?" She pauses to fiddle with the same rhinestone tiara she wore the other day, blowing on the gems, then shining them to a sparkle on her sleeve. "Even if it doesn't last, there are plenty of fine men to fall in love with."

She chatters on and on, barely giving me time to get a word in as I fuss over my appearance in the mirror. Today is the big photo shoot Judy scheduled for me, and I've spent the last half hour being poked and prodded and "dolled up" for the occasion. For some reason Judy is intent on turning me into an alluring mystery. Someone to make heads spin and hearts swoon. The absolute opposite of who I am and ever desire to be.

"I did meet Joan Crawford," I tell her as I toss the tissue into the small trash can.

Eleanor looks at me in the mirror, her eyes huge. "Oh . . . golly, I'd do anything to mingle at a party like that."

"Maybe you can come with me next time?" I offer, although I hope there will never be a next time. After I find out what's happened to Alice, I hope to find my way out of this time warp.

"Really? You'd do that? Gosh, Alice." The look on Eleanor's face is pure bliss. "And I must add, you look stunning!"

I give my new friend a smile, forcing down my disappointment at another day's passing. I woke this morning in another panic, wondering, if I am here, then where do the people back home think I am? My parents must be worried out of their minds. I can't even imagine what Beth must think. We never go a day without talking to one another, and if I'm not at home, I'm working at the library or checking on Ryan at the hospital. I've been counting the hours until I can meet with Dalton and ask him if he has any theories on time travel—anything that might help. But for now, I am stuck recounting my night for Eleanor as if I've had the time of my life.

"What do you know about that man you pointed out yesterday? Hawkins?" I ask carefully. "Other than you think he's handsome and"—I cringe—"has a thing for me?"

Eleanor is all too happy to discard her lesson on decorum. "The other women practically faint when he's around," she sighs. "He's awfully good-looking." Eleanor nods as if I'll nod back in agreement. "I guess I can't help saying that. But you must admit, he's terribly dreamy."

It isn't enough. I need to find out what he is to Alice. What's the connection, and especially, why did he act so strange last night? But Eleanor doesn't seem to offer anything more than his looks. If she saw him last night, all pasty and agitated, I doubt she'd find him so attractive.

"So," I hedge. "You know those days I took a mental health vacation?" I add air quotes. "Was he around the set those days when Judy couldn't find me?"

Eleanor sticks her tongue in her cheek as she thinks. "No, he was at the studio." She thinks a bit more and nods. "Yes, he was. Judy and he were arguing. I don't know what about, but it was pretty heated."

That's interesting. I need to find a way to pick Eleanor's brain again, to fill in the blanks, but I can't let myself seem too eager—or too misinformed about Alice's whereabouts those days she went missing. I have to pretend I'm simply forgetful.

Eleanor says nothing more on the matter and picks up her book on manners again, groaning. "I'll never be able to do this."

I point to the book in her lap. "Ugh. I haven't started that one yet."

Eleanor flips the book over in her hands, staring at the back cover and then the front. "Look at this," she groans as she shows me the smiling woman wearing an apron on the cover. "This is what my father wants me to become. A respectable housewife with offspring to look after. Not an actress, even though it's all I've I ever wanted to be. He thinks it's ridiculous that I even came out here with hopes of being discovered." She huffs loudly and sets the book down with a loud thud, leaving me to ponder the difference between now and the world I'm used to. Women and men my age study their craft, but here, it's all about relying on your looks and if you can read your lines well enough to make it in the industry. "It's bad enough my father wants me to become my mother, but Judy insisting I learn to be proper is too much." Not waiting for me to answer, she launches into it again. "He called the other night insisting I come home. That he knows a *nice man* at the bank, a colleague of his, who'd like to take me to dinner. He's probably my father's age."

"Maybe he *is* nice," I offer.

Eleanor scoffs. "Well, I certainly doubt he's like the men here. And if I even dare mention I'm interested in a Hollywood man, my father gets all red in the face and mutters 'harlot' under his breath. I'm sure the men here don't care if I can't roast a turkey or nail a transatlantic accent."

"Is that what you're studying?" I point to the other book on the floor next to one with the smiling woman in the apron.

"Yes," Eleanor says sourly. "And I'm butchering it."

I swivel in the chair. "Okay, pick a passage, any passage, and read it out loud to me."

Eleanor raises an eyebrow as she picks up the book and flips to a page. She slowly begins reciting, but it doesn't take long before a nervous laugh trickles out of her mouth. "I just murdered the Gettysburg Address!" She looks equally amused and mortified.

I swivel around in the chair to face her, careful not to wrinkle my dress. "It wasn't that bad," I promise. "Read it again. Slower this time. And form your mouth like this." I shape my own mouth into an *O*.

She tries it a second time but gives up, slapping her hand down on the book.

"I keep pushing the words out, but they don't sound as clipped as yours."

"You'll get it!"

Eleanor sways her head back and forth in doubt, but her eyes hold a glimmer nearly as bright as the gems in her headband.

"Thank you for helping me," she whispers. She scrambles to her feet and leans into the mirror over the dressing table. "Just look at me. I don't know what's worse, my upbringing or my hair." She pats the unruly chestnut curls sticking out around her head.

"Try this." I reach my hands around the back of her head but then stop what I'm about to do. "Can I?"

At her nod I sweep her hair into two sections, braiding each side and twisting it around to form a doughnut. It's a long shot that she'll even like this, the Princess Leia style I haven't yet seen here, but Eleanor seems perfect to pull it off.

Maybe I shouldn't introduce it, but Eleanor needs a boost, something no one else has. Granted, it's a dated look in my time, but maybe it will set a new trend here.

I secure her hair with a handful of pins and whirl her around to face the mirror.

"Ohhh," she murmurs, touching her hair carefully. "What do you call it?"

"Space buns. And you'll be one of the first to start the trend here in Hollywood."

Eleanor is clearly pleased and continues admiring herself as the door opens and a head pokes through. "Time for the photo shoot, Miss Montgomery."

"Here goes nothing."

I glance in the mirror one last time and press my fingertip to the tiny pin curl at my temple, hoping it will stay tightly wound in the heat. Eleanor smooths the hem of the gray gown I'm wearing, sighing as she rakes her eyes over the dress.

I open the trailer's door and pause to take another look at Eleanor. "Thanks for putting up with all my questions. I'm usually not this scatterbrained."

Eleanor sticks another pin in her hair for good measure and smiles back. "That's what friends are for."

THE PHOTO SHOOT for *Modern Screen* magazine took nearly an hour. Half blinded by the bright lights and the constant flash of the camera, I hurry back to the trailer to change for another day of filming. Dalton appears across the lot, a stack of papers in his hand as he stops to speak to a man I've never been introduced to, but Alice might know him. When their conversation ends, he looks over. I wave, but he continues walking toward the main building, leaving me with a sinking heart. He must have thought over what I told him last night and is now avoiding me. It's a terrible feeling and it sticks with me.

As a result, today's set takes are disastrous. It seems no matter how well I think I know the lines or the direction, something goes catastrophically wrong. I've forgotten where to step on a platform and lose my balance, which sends half the background tumbling down. I bump into Eleanor twice. And I trip on the hem of my dress, delaying the scene while the wardrobe girl stitches it.

I keep getting distracted by what is happening off set rather than on set. At one point, I see an extra off to the side taking swigs from a bottle wrapped in a brown bag. No one seems to care that he is drinking on the job, not even when he stumbles worse than I did, obviously intoxicated.

And then a girl rushes up to Mack Flynn, who stopped in to speak to one of the producers. She is practically hysterical, and her voice echoes across the lot as she begs him for a part in the film. Mack's face has gone red. His hand shoots out and he pushes her away, then yells for security, all the while telling her she'll never work at this studio or any other.

Shocked that Mack has been so cruel, my heart goes out to her. All she wants is a chance, and here I am, stuck playing out someone else's big dream. The whole thing is distracting and upsetting.

My brain echoes the words "CUT!" over and over. But I push through, hoping the day will soon be over so I can find Dalton and talk to him. Aside from that, I have to convince everyone I *am* Alice. If I keep at it, then maybe the charade will pay off, and I'll uncover why I've switched places with her—and find my way out of here.

The last scene finally wraps, and everyone makes their way off set, leaving me behind with a bizarre sensation of being watched. That creepy-crawly feeling, as if someone is eyeing my every move.

I nervously begin the walk to my trailer when I recognize the rumble of a forklift behind me. I turn to look over my shoulder, my eyes widening. It's barreling straight for me, and the width of the walking space between the set façades is entirely too narrow for me to step aside and let it pass. It's when I pause to flag down the driver to tell them to slow down, I realize no one is driving it.

With moments to spare, I leap out of the way, hurling myself onto a stack of wooden pallets pushed up against a building. The forklift continues its track, ramming into a pile of plywood and metal poles the workers have left at the end of the lane.

With a pounding heart, I scramble down from the pallets and stare at the unmanned forklift, its engine still grumbling as if it insists on pushing through the barrier blocking it. Several workers run to it before it can break past the mess and wreak havoc on the set just a few feet away. I watch, dumbfounded, as one climbs into the cab, turning off the engine before climbing back down and scratching his head in confusion.

"Alice! Are you all right?" Out of breath, Dalton reaches me and stares at the pallets I've knocked over in my descent to the ground, then stares at the now silent forklift. We walk toward it, pushing our way through the small cluster of workers who are puzzled and accusing one another of setting the machinery on its rampage.

Trembling, my eyes take in the damage.

"I'm fine. I . . . what the hell?" Still shaking, I lean over my knees to catch my breath.

Dalton eyes me with concern. "You could have been killed." As the workers begin clearing the wood and metal, Dalton climbs into the forklift's cab to inspect it, then hovers in the open compartment, looking down at me. "You're sure you're not hurt? Wait . . ." He hops down and lifts my arm. "You're bleeding."

I look down at my elbow. Sure enough, a smear of blood oozes from a scrape along with a small splinter protruding from my skin.

"You should get that looked at," Dalton suggests. "At least get some iodine on it."

I shrug it off. "It's only a scratch. Compared to what could have happened, I'm not especially worried about it."

Dalton's expression turns from worry to awe. "Wow, you really are a different breed. Most gals would shed a boatload of tears and insist on plastic surgery over something like this."

"It's really nothing," I stress. I might be able to put on an act for Dalton, but inside I am a mess. What are the odds of an unmanned forklift careening toward me?

"I'm going to report this to Mack. I'm sure he'll find out who's responsible. This could have plowed you down."

Dalton's focus is split between the forklift and my bloody elbow.

I shoot him a look of appreciation. "I was probably just in the wrong place at the wrong time. Not surprising, given the day I've had."

Still rattled, he reaches behind him and pulls out a folded newspaper from his back pocket. "You were right." A tenderness now replaces the stunned look on his face. "This morning's paper. Front page." He holds it out to me. There is the headline in bold, black ink: ERNIE BANKS MAKES CUBS AND WRIGLEY FIELD DEBUT.

I stare at the paper in his hand, then up at him. "I was worried you wouldn't believe me."

"Why wouldn't I?" His voice causes my heart to skip a beat.

"Well, b-because . . ." I stammer. "Last night when I told you I was . . ."

"I believe you . . . *Grace*." His voice sounds as if he's trying my name out for the very first time all over again.

"You do?"

"I do. And I'm going to help you get to the bottom of this. Starting with finding out how this happened." He nods toward the forklift and the wreckage it's left behind. "But listen, if anything else kookie happens, I want you to let me know. Right away. Promise?"

He pulls a pencil from over his ear, scribbles his phone number on the newspaper, and hands it to me. The moment I take it from him, he gives me a serious look and leans closer, pressing his forehead against mine. Through my lashes I peer up into the intensity of his blue eyes.

"I promise," I whisper back.

"Good." His voice is deeper than usual. "And promise me you'll be careful."

"I promise that too."

Dalton rests his hands on my shoulders, and for a moment I don't think he'll ever pull away. I don't want him to. But the moment is over when the space between us grows larger. He gives me a wink, then heads toward the main building to complain to Mack. I stare after him until my knees feel sturdy again. Then I glance back at the forklift, wondering how it could have escaped the constant flurry of set workers and traveled unmanned down the lot. Funny how no one noticed until it nearly ran me down.

Now that the workers have cleared the mess and gone off to resume their work, I am left alone to peer into the cab. A set of keys rests on the seat, and everything else seems normal. Not that I know anything about forklifts. There are bits of splintered wood strewn about on the seat and the floor and . . . I lean in. Set on top of the gas pedal is a brick, positioned just right. In their confusion, the workers must not have noticed.

A cold shiver tears down my spine.

No way did that brick end up on that gas pedal during the accident, accidentally.

I beeline straight for my trailer, keeping to the outskirts of the set props rather than walking in the middle of the lane. My ears are on alert for another rogue forklift, but there are only the usual sounds of the workers milling around between sets.

Just outside the row of trailers, I notice Judy sitting on an overturned crate, rifling through an endless stack of papers pinned to her clipboard. It strikes me as odd that even she hasn't responded to the commotion and come to see what happened.

Ignoring my disheveled appearance, I draw in a deep breath and walk over to her.

"That's quite a stack of papers there," I say to get her attention. "How do you have time for everything?"

Judy shrugs with impatience. "Simple. It's my job."

The vibe rolling off her is uncomfortable. She finally looks up. "What happened to you?"

I hold out my arm for her to see.

"Oh no, no, no. That won't look good for your next shoot. Let's get you cleaned up." Judy hops off the crate and takes hold of my arm. "Is this what that god-awful noise was about? Want to explain what happened?" She almost sounds accusatory. Like nearly getting steamrolled by heavy machinery is my fault.

"I was run down by a wayward forklift."

"Well, let's take care of this right away." Judy grabs her papers and leads me to the trailer. Inside, she pokes around the tiny bathroom, finally emerging with a white metal first aid kit. She orders me to sit on a chair while she plucks the splinter of wood from my elbow with a miniature pair of tweezers.

"Ow!"

"Almost done." Pulling it free without an ounce of sympathy for the crater she's dug to get to it, she then douses a square of gauze in hydrogen peroxide and cleans the bloody mess of my arm. "There. At least the cut is small. Antonio will have to do his best to hide the brush burns you have."

I look at her from the corner of my eye. Judy hasn't asked for details about what's happened. Normally she gives the impression of knowing about everything or at least wanting to know.

"Aren't you curious about what just happened to me?" I ask her, watching carefully for her reaction.

Judy just shrugs and shakes her head. "It's a movie studio. Accidents happen all the time around here." She gives me the once-over. "Besides, it doesn't look bad enough to rush off to the hospital. I'd say you were lucky."

She's acting strange. I try another approach.

"Why weren't you at the cocktail party last night?"

Judy looks up at me. Her expression is blank. Then her eyebrows rise slightly. "Oh that. I decided to turn in early. Did you enjoy yourself?" Her focus is on the first-aid kit again, stuffing the gauze and bandages back in the right order so the lid will close.

"Oh sure," I say, my tone drier than usual. "What's a party without boatloads of champagne and my manager's wife showing me off?"

Judy smirks a bit. "Isadora at her finest, I'm sure. Let me guess, she attempted to rattle the nerves of an A-lister to keep her position as the all-knowing wife of an executive. Who was it this time?" Judy asks.

"Joan Crawford."

Judy swallows hard and then laughs. "She really went for it!"

"It was awkward." I watch Judy's expression closely. "But not as awkward as talking to Hawkins."

Every bone in Judy's body seems to stiffen. There is even a twitch in her lips.

"He seems so . . . evasive." I have to play it off that I know him well enough not to be so in the dark about his ties to the studio. If he and Alice are indeed close, she'll know of such things. "Remind me, please, what exactly are his ties to the studio? It's all so confusing." I ask with caution.

Without a word, Judy rises to her feet to return the first aid kit to the bathroom. When she comes back out, she leans against the doorframe. "He's an independent film scout who rubs elbows with the American Academy of Film's board of VIPs."

"Hmm." I pause. "I suppose he just has an air about him that implies he does more here. If I didn't know him, I would have guessed him to be a producer."

Judy scoffs at my verbal impression of Hawkins, but it's only a momentary thing, and when she opens her mouth to say more, she seems to change her mind. "He just has the right connections with the right people in this town." Her tone is as if she doesn't care much for him, but it doesn't shed light on what Eleanor witnessed or what they'd been arguing about. Then out of nowhere, Judy asks, "Alice, you trust me, don't you?"

I nod.

"Where were you these last few days? It is very unlike you to go off like that without a word." She pauses as voices surface just outside the trailer. Whoever is outside keeps walking. "The studio was worried. *I* was worried."

I keep silent. I have no idea what to tell her. Telling Dalton felt right, but Judy? Something inside me says I shouldn't.

She waits for a beat then gives me a serious look.

"You're different lately. Not quite . . . you." Judy sighs and looks around. "Hawkins has a track record, and scandal always seems to follow him. I just don't want to see you get involved in something that could hurt your career—or you, personally—if you get in too deep."

Her carefully selected words hold an undercurrent of accusation, making me wonder how deeply Alice is involved with Hawkins, and just as Eleanor suspects, I'm sure it isn't strictly professional. What bothers me, though, is that this feels like another warning to stay away from that man.

The voices are back, giggly and loud. Judy opens the door.

"What am I going to do with that woman?" she suddenly fumes.

I rise from the chair, ignoring the sting in my arm, and peer out the door. Across the lot, Eleanor is laughing and twirling her hair. Hawkins is with her, leaning close, smiling. Then he nudges her arm, as if suggesting the two of them move on. The look on his face is completely different from the look he gave me last night.

It is predatory.

CHAPTER SEVENTEEN

BY THE TIME I RETURN to the hotel, I am too exhausted and stressed to worry about someone hiding in the shadows. Still, I make a thorough sweep of the suite. Satisfied I am alone, I kick my loafers off and shove them under the bed, craving sleep—but the way Hawkins looked at Eleanor haunts me.

The idea of him possibly knowing about Alice's disappearance gnaws at my insides.

I wonder if Alice was fed up with everything and simply gave up. It seems everyone here rubs elbows to get what they want. Some are sneakier than others. Maybe she realized becoming a movie star wasn't worth the aggravation. But then why am I here? In her shoes—in her skin? Taking the place of a woman who wants to escape from her life isn't a good enough reason to make me slip out of my own. That is, assuming that there is a reason why this happened to me. But there must be, otherwise none of this makes any sense at all.

There must be something I'm missing—and relying on others to help me piece things together isn't enough. The answers I need can only come from Alice herself.

"All right, Alice. It's time to find out where you went." I look around the room. The hotel's housekeeping staff keeps it shiny and clean. Even though her clothes are still in the closet, there are few items that truly belong to Alice.

The first time I opened the datebook, I was too shocked to see my own handwriting filling the pages to notice anything of importance. To be honest, I hadn't been looking for what might spell out where Alice had gone.

Not until now.

It still gives me chills to see my own writing scribbled on the pages. Page after page is filled with appointments and appearances, much like the calendar Judy always carries around with her. Dress rehearsals, script runs, photo shoots, lunch with so and so . . . Judy kept Alice—and now me—busy enough for three people.

Now focused, and convinced I need to dig deeper for clues on what could have become of the missing starlet, I start on the first page and work my way through. At first glance it all seems too normal to raise suspicion, but I know I need to *really* look.

The dates are jotted with reminders of upcoming interviews with magazine journalists from *Photo Play, Modern Screen,* and *Focus.* Most have to do with the studio: Speech lessons. A screen test on Lot C, Room 4. Lessons. Lessons. Lessons.

I scan the datebook for Hawkins's name—anything that might give proof that Alice met with him regularly, like dinner or lunch, but there is nothing.

Only a reminder about last night's cocktail party and a private wrap party at the end of this week.

I scan the rest of the calendar, flipping ahead to next month, and the months after. They are all blank. Frustrated, I skip to the back of the datebook, hoping she's tucked something away within the blank pages. Like a folded piece of paper. Like a secret.

"Hello, there," I whisper to the scribbles on the second to last page—one that is a blank end page and not part of the year's calendar. The writing is tiny, different from the rest of the datebook, at the bottom of the paper, as if placed there on purpose to *not* be found.

But it doesn't make sense. It's just a bunch of odd numbers and letters: 1132WBS3.

Dalton gave me his number, saying I could call anytime. His shift is over, and he should have left the studio by now.

I grab the newspaper he wrote his number on earlier today, take the phone from the bedside table, and place it in my lap. With hesitant fingers, I dial. He answers on the first ring.

"Al . . . I mean, Grace," he says in a rush. "Are you all right? Is your arm . . ."

A smile tugs at the corners of my mouth. His voice holds genuine worry, and he's remembered to use my real name. "I'm fine, just a little sore. Judy patched me up."

A sigh of what I assume is relief comes through the phone.

"I've been thinking about you," he confesses. "I'm glad you called."

That one sentence finds its way into my veins and fills me with a bright warmth.

"Did you really mean what you said earlier? That you believe me?"

His response comes quickly. "Of course I did. And I do. I believe you." Dalton pauses. "There's something about you, Grace," he says. "Something I don't want to give up on, and if it means pushing aside rational thoughts, well then call me irrational."

I've lost all feeling in my chest; the swelling of my heart is nearly too much to contain. There is so much I want to ask him, so much to tell him.

"Did you find out anything?" he asks, pulling me back to the moment.

"Maybe." The datebook is open on the bed beside me. "You didn't know Alice, right?"

"No, I didn't," Dalton tells me. "Not personally anyway. Our paths never crossed and that's why I introduced myself to you after the cab dropped you off in front of the studio the other day."

"Right. But from afar, would you be able to tell me what she's like, who she hangs around with?" I make myself comfortable on the bed, hoping for a long conversation. "Tell me everything you've heard around the studio from the gossip mill."

"Okay, well . . ." He pauses. "When she first arrived at the studio, she was your typical starlet. Happy. Excited. And the few times I needed to run an errand that led me onto the lot, I was able to catch glimpses of her scenes. She got into character easily, but then after a few weeks she became withdrawn."

"Withdrawn?" I ask. "How so?"

I hear Dalton tapping a pen on a table through the line. "I would overhear things from the crew that she was quiet. It was as if she went through the motions, but that spark she had started out with was gone."

"That's strange." I twirl the phone cord around my finger, wondering what could have happened to make Alice change so drastically. "Did something happen on set? Was there any gossip?"

"I hear things, dollface, but not a whole lot of gossip."

I bite down on my lip. I still don't care for Dalton's nicknames for me, but I can't let my annoyance interfere with the questions I need answered.

"Okay, so who did she hang around with?"

"Judy mostly."

"That's no surprise," I say, rolling my eyes. "Judy's with me all day long."

There's silence on the other end of the phone until Dalton says, "She never used to be."

The tangled phone cord pauses between my fingers. "What do you mean?"

"I don't think Judy spent as much time with Alice when she started filming. Not nearly as much as she does now. With you."

I can't imagine a day without Judy as my shadow—keeping the schedule in line, barking at everyone in my trailer. Judy is on set with me constantly.

As if she doesn't want to let me out of her sight.

"Do you think it's because she's worried Alice will disappear again?" I ask.

"Could be," Dalton replies. "Those days you . . . um, Alice went missing cost the studio a lot of money. I overheard Mack talking about the budget reports."

I twirl the phone cord between my fingers as I mull everything over. "And what about that man, Hawkins? Did Alice spend much time with him?"

"Honestly, I don't know Hawkins at all, haven't even spoken to him, and if she did, I wouldn't know. You're the only one from the 'elite group' I've ever really mingled with. And if you want my opinion," Dalton says in a softer almost warning tone, "I'd stay away from him. Seems like a real heartbreaker, if you ask me."

"How so?" I ask.

"Well, you asked if I've heard any gossip, and there's plenty circulating around him. If what the other guys at the studio say is correct, then that man goes after anything in a skirt. But you know, men will be men, so I just ignore what I hear."

I don't like what Dalton's just revealed. Men will be men. Or as I've always heard the phrase, boys will be boys. It churns my stomach that it's perfectly acceptable here for a man to view a woman as nothing more than a skirt he wants to get under. And equally disgusting is Dalton's nonchalant attitude toward it. Even if Alice *had* gotten close to Hawkins, and then he exploited her in such a way that it broke her heart, forcing her to get as far away as possible, she shouldn't have given up a bright, successful career. Over a man. I sigh into the phone.

"Grace? Are you sure you're all right?" he asks me, his voice low and laced with sweet concern, as if not at all detecting how his words sit with me.

"Not really. I'm not getting any closer to finding out why I'm here. Why I'm Alice." The days have slipped by so quickly, and I can feel despair growing in my heart. I try to push it down and change the subject.

"I found something. A clue, maybe. There are letters and numbers written in the back of Alice's datebook. I don't know what they mean."

Something scrapes in the background as if Dalton is scooting a chair. "Read them off to me."

"1-1-3-2-W-B-S-3."

Dalton is silent on the other end of the phone for a few seconds. "That *is* odd. I wonder what that means."

I let my next thoughts simmer, refusing to share them out loud with Dalton and acknowledging a very real fear. That I need to find out what's happened to Alice. I can't pretend to be her forever . . . I can't be stuck here.

"I need answers, Dalton." My voice creeps higher as the panic settles in. I flip to the back of the datebook again. "I need to find out what these letters and numbers mean."

"I'll see what I can find out from my uncle at the police station. If anyone can get to the bottom of a missing persons case, it's my uncle. He's like a regular Sherlock."

"What about Eleanor?" I question. "Was she close to Alice?" Although Eleanor and I get along easily, she doesn't give me the impression that she knows Alice on a personal level. There was no exclamation of relief that I—or the real Alice, rather—had returned safely after disappearing for days on end. If I had been missing back home and suddenly returned, Beth would be all over me, hugging me and asking a million questions. Eleanor didn't do any of that.

"Eleanor is as normal as they come," Dalton says. "I promise you don't have to worry about her. And no, Eleanor wasn't close to Alice. I only know that because she used to tell me how she wished Alice would talk to her—Eleanor wanted advice from Alice on acting." The tone in Dalton's voice backs up his words. I hope he's right. Especially since I'm not sure if I should tell him I saw Eleanor and Hawkins together. I guess I shouldn't think anything of it. She'd acted the same way with Dalton. And my last conversation with her gave me the impression she's keen on finding a "Hollywood man," the exact opposite of what her father approves of.

"Eleanor told me Hawkins and Alice had a thing going on between them."

There is a moment of silence before Dalton answers me. "That I'm not sure of, but I do know that I don't trust him, Grace. Not one bit."

That's enough for me. My gut tells me not to trust Hawkins either.

"Oh, and Dalton? I don't think the forklift was any ordinary set accident." I chew the bottom of my lip the longer I think back on what happened earlier today. "There was a brick resting on top of the gas pedal."

"What are you saying, Grace?" Dalton has grown eerily quiet.

"I think someone sent that forklift on purpose." I look around the quiet room, then continue: "To get rid of me."

CHAPTER EIGHTEEN

I AM BEGINNING TO SECOND-GUESS the "accidents" that have happened on set before the forklift incident. Was it really because I'm a klutz, or were they all planned to set me up for failure or to be rid of me—the latest attempt being the forklift? One thing is for sure, every day I spend as Alice feels dangerous. And while I don't feel any closer to figuring out where the real Alice is, or why I'm here, I have a suspicious feeling someone wants me to disappear like she has. Maybe even go as far as making who they believe to be Alice disappear for good.

There's one other person I haven't questioned yet, and as I ask the concierge for James's room number, the man behind the front counter lifts his eyebrows suggestively before answering me. "Mr. Dean is in cabana number six. Just near the pool."

The sun is setting as I walk along the heavily shrouded path, but the cool shade of evening does nothing to melt the worry from my thoughts. Small lanterns flick on in the dimming light around the bend, where I spy a set of whitewashed steps leading to the poolside villas. The grounds are beautiful, but everything here feels surrounded in mystery. By the time I find cabana number six, I worry James won't be able to tell me what I need—or help explain the clue I've found in the datebook.

The small outbuilding is the only one without a porch light lit, but soft strums of a guitar drift through the open window, giving proof that someone is inside. If I turn back now, he'll hear my shoes and catch me. I hug Alice's datebook to my chest and rap lightly at the door. There is a shuffle, and then the door opens, revealing the moody actor, bare-chested and hair mussed, in wire-rimmed glasses and a pair of white lounge pants.

"Alice." Surprise imbues his tone. "Come in."

"Um," I start. "I hope I'm not bothering you." I step over the threshold of the doorway into the softly lit room and my gaze settles on the instrument he's just been playing. The room smells of fresh cigarette smoke and cologne.

"Not at all. What brings you to Casa de Dean?" James shuts the door behind me and proceeds to walk across the room to a small kitchenette. "You hungry? Thirsty?"

"No thanks." I join him opposite a tiny counter.

He opens the refrigerator and peers inside, pulling a glass bottle of milk from the otherwise bare shelf, then pops the cap off with his thumb and tilts it to his lips.

"Glad to see you're drinking something healthier," I say with a laugh.

He makes a face over the rim and when he's done drinking, there is a dribble of milk on his bottom lip. He licks it off before the back of his hand swipes at his mouth, then he picks up a pack of cigarettes, pulling one from the box with his lips and lighting it.

"You sure I can't get you anything? I don't have any champagne, but there's gin here somewhere," he says as he turns his bare back to me to rummage through a cabinet next to the refrigerator. "I can make you a sloe gin fizz or a Tom Collins." Bottles clink together as James works his way through his inventory, which holds more alcohol than food. "How 'bout a highball?"

"No really," I insist. "I'm fine, but thanks."

He emerges from the cabinet and leans casually against the counter, exhaling a cloud of smoke.

James is different in person than on set. So much like Ryan—his movements, the same light behind his eyes as if a million thoughts are rushing through his head. And in this exact moment I see the real him.

Not the icon. Not the legend.

But a man who is on the cusp of a bright career, destined for something wonderful. The only problem is I know how it ends for him. And I wish I could tell him, warn him, do anything to prevent this bright light I see before me from becoming extinguished.

"There's something I want to ask you." I settle myself atop an empty stool. "That night at the party, you said I had a haunted look in my eyes. What did you mean by that?"

He pulls long on his cigarette, his brows pinching together over his light blue eyes. "I said that? Wow. I must have had one too many."

"Is there something different about me?" I ask hopefully. "Something different than when filming began?"

James gives me a long, thoughtful look as he taps his ash onto a paper napkin.

I watch, mesmerized and a little frightened that it will ignite and engulf the tiny kitchenette in a full-blown inferno.

"You *are* different, but I can't quite put my finger on it." He finally gives me a crooked smile. "Feeling the pressure of stardom?"

I hug the datebook closer. "Maybe."

"You do seem as if you've changed since I first met you." He rests against the counter, assessing me. "You're not as bright and eager as you were your first day on set. You're guarded and quiet, like you've been through something."

I have been through something. I fell from the future into the past—into Alice's world. Pretending to be her while still being me—while trying to find my way back—is getting complicated. And maybe Alice went through something too. "I don't know who I'm supposed to be anymore." I sigh, searching for a way to lead into why I've come here.

"It's the pressure. Trust me. They want you to be the person onscreen, your character, but they also want you to be the icon they're building in everyone's imagination." James takes another long drag from his Chesterfield. "You'll get used to it. Most of it is hype. Acting brings out the best and the worst in a person."

He leans across the counter, his face incredibly close to mine. "It's an art, really, to be someone purely fictional, yet full of life. With every breath, you add a bit of yourself into that person, fleshing them out, coaxing something substantial into them." He smiles.

"But," he says, "each time you become someone else, you replace your soul with a bit of that character, until you don't know who you are anymore. Does that make sense?"

I look at him and nod slowly. If only he knew.

"What's that?" He gestures to the book I'm clutching.

I set the book on the counter. "It's just Al . . . um, my datebook. There's something in it I don't remember writing. I was hoping you might know what it means. Maybe something to do with the script?" If I could roll my eyes at myself, I would. Of course it's not anything to do with the script, and James might see this as a poor attempt to come to his cabana for another reason. He might take this as me throwing myself at him, which I'm sure many women have already done. I push it across the counter toward him and watch as he opens the cover. "It's on the second-to-last page. See?" I reach out and flip through the pages to the indecipherable letters Alice wrote inside.

James looks at the writing. "I don't know. Looks like you jotted down a secret code or something." He takes one more look before sliding the book across the counter toward me.

That's exactly what I was hoping it could be. A secret code. But for what, I don't know. My heart sinks, knowing he can't help me piece it together. Coming here is just a dead end.

"Could it be a license plate number?" I ask, running my fingertip over the cryptic letters.

"Nah, too long." He stares at the open page upside down. "Not the right sequence of numbers and letters. Unless it's foreign. But that still doesn't look right to me." James pushes his elbows up from the counter. "Sorry I couldn't help."

"It's okay." I tuck the datebook under my arm and stand. If I pass the numbers along to Dalton's uncle, maybe he could run a plate check anyway. "You did help, actually. You remind me of my brother. I haven't been able to talk to him. So . . ." I bite down on the inside of my cheek to stop the tears that are now burning behind my eyes. The last thing I need is for James to see me as a weak woman—and I certainly don't want him to think I'm some meek fifties doll, upset over a bunch of cryptic scribbles I can't decipher. "So this really helped."

James comes around the counter and walks me toward the door. "I didn't know you had a brother."

"I do." I smile sadly. "And you've influenced him so much. He loves your films." I doubt any other person could be a bigger fan. I smile again, but James is staring at me with a strange look on his face—because I just made a huge mistake. None of James's movies have been released yet. It's 1953, and his first film, *East of Eden*, won't hit the screen until 1955. Then *Rebel Without a Cause* later that year, and of course, his last film, *Giant* . . . released posthumously in 1956. Oh God, what did I just say? What did I just do? I scramble for a cover-up but I'm afraid it's too late. "Sorry, I think I must be frazzled from trying to figure this out. Long days on the set. You know how it is . . ."

"Sure," he says. "I have those too." But he's still looking at me like I'm crazy.

"I meant to say, my brother will love your films. He . . . he wants to direct one day."

For a diversion, I look down at a stack of magazines spread out across the coffee table. James is on every cover except one. They still don't do him justice. Just like the box back in the trailer. The other magazine is the issue Dalton had been carrying the day I met him. The one with Alice on the cover. *Why am I here, Alice? And where are* you?

James's words float through my head—about acting bringing out the best and the worst in a person. Alice's expression on the cover looks too cheery to plummet so low during the short period of her new career. She was a starlet with high expectations, her whole life ahead of her. Just like this living, breathing man next to me. But what if all of this had brought the worst out in someone else? What if my suspicions are correct that Alice didn't disappear on purpose?

"You have that haunted look in your eyes again." James reaches out and traces his finger across my eyebrow. It's a subtle gesture, not at all romantic. Like a friend concerned over another. And I'm grateful my mixed-up words are forgotten for the moment. "I feel like we're made of the same fabric, Alice. Don't lose yourself."

I look away from James and back to the cover of the girl I resemble. A chill breaks out over my arms. "I'm afraid I'm already lost."

CHAPTER NINETEEN

I TAKE MY TIME MEANDERING the winding paths of the hotel's grounds. All the while, James's comment strikes like an arrow to my chest. *Don't lose yourself.*

The funny thing is, even though I am *here*, mistaken for someone else, I feel more like me than I have in a long time. Ever since Ryan started excelling at everything. College, filming, his big plans for his future . . . everything. He made my parents so proud that I let myself recede into the shadows. But now I feel . . . alive. Like the mystery of Alice has lit a fire within me, propelling me forward with purpose.

Dusk falls quickly, and even though the grounds are well lit, the path's shadowed curves fill me with anxiety. I hurry back to the main building feeling like I can't get there fast enough. If the idea of being alone in the room had felt terrifying, out here it feels a million times more threatening. The instant the elevator dings at my floor and the door slides open, I speed down the hall and let myself into my suite. My heart is pounding. I flick on every light in every room, but it makes the outside appear darker than ever.

I pull each curtain closed, separating myself from the blackness outside my windows.

Suddenly, my throat seizes at the last set of curtains. There is movement down below.

"Don't be an idiot, Grace. You're in a hotel." Still, the reasoning that anyone staying here wouldn't be confined to just their room doesn't feel so reasonable anymore. Not after what happened today. Especially not since I 100 percent truly believe something fishy surrounds the disappearance of Alice Montgomery.

Inching closer to the glass, I look down at the pool. The water shimmers beneath the glow of the tall lampposts around it. My eyes focus on the surrounding brush and trees, waiting for them to rustle. There is nothing out of the ordinary.

Until my line of vision sweeps across the sidewalk just as I am about to step away.

Out in the open, an unmoving figure stares up at me. Right at me, as if they've been looking at my window this whole time. I can't tell if it's a man or a woman, but the moment our eyes lock, the dark-clad figure turns and bolts away.

I step back, distancing myself from the window and colliding with the bed. I was just down there. Alone. In the dark. James wouldn't have followed me, would he? I quickly dismiss the thought. James is too haunted himself to terrorize me. And if he'd followed me back to make sure I got here safely, he'd at least wave. This has to be the same person who called my room the other night. They know where I'm staying. And unlike James, they know which window to look at.

Grabbing the phone, I bring it down onto the floor with me as I wedge myself between the side of the mattress and the nightstand. I dial Dalton.

Two rings this time, but at last he picks up.

"Hey there. I wasn't expecting you to call again so soon—"

"D-Dalton?" I interrupt him.

There is a pause and then his voice comes through the line. "Grace? What's the matter?"

I can barely get my mouth to form the words.

"Someone's watching me."

A rustling sound comes through the phone along with a quick clang of metal like keys.

"I'll be right there."

The line goes dead. I sit for who knows how long with the phone to my ear, listening to the silence. Only when the phone sequences through a series of clicks and an operator's voice comes on the line do I hang up.

I HEAR THE elevator open and close. After a few seconds, a knock strikes my door.

"Grace? It's me."

I hurry to let him inside.

To my surprise, his arms wrap around me before his body is fully past the doorframe. Leaning into him, I allow my arms to envelop him, clutching him to me.

It's been so long since I've felt another person: a hug from my mom, my dad, holding Ryan's hand in the hospital . . . For a few still moments I feel his heartbeat against my chest. I'm sure he feels mine, beating erratically.

He slowly pulls away, twisting himself free to bring both hands to my cheeks.

"Hey, it's okay now. I'm here."

But it's not okay. Nothing is.

I have my doubts even Dalton can save me from whatever this time warp keeps throwing at me. Especially strangers spying on me, calling me . . . thinking I am Alice.

I give a shaky nod.

"Tell me what happened."

I pull away and pace across the floor as I tell him I visited James to ask him about the cryptic scribble in Alice's datebook. "He wasn't any help with that. He had no idea what it could mean," I tell Dalton. "Then after I came back up to the room, I went to close the curtains, and I saw someone staring up at my room. Like they'd been there all along, watching me."

Dalton raises an eyebrow. I point to the window next to the bed. He immediately walks over and peers out. "No one's there now."

"Whoever it was left as soon as I saw them."

I sit down on the love seat. "The other night, someone called. I picked up, but there was just breathing." I scoot myself into the corner just like I did that night. "Like whoever was on the other end just wanted to listen."

Dalton sits next to me. "Like they were calling just to see who picked up?"

I nod.

He stares off into the room, as if trying to put the pieces together. "Like they wanted to see if it was Alice?"

"I think they wanted to check if she really was back, because . . . because . . . I don't know why, but I think something bad happened to her," I blurt. "Dalton, she's been missing for over a week. Whoever knows what happened is confused because I'm in her place."

"This is too coincidental."

I curl in tighter as I study him. "What is?"

"The accident at the studio. The phone call. Now this." Dalton scrubs a hand over his face and lets out a deep sigh. "I don't like what's going on here," he says, breaking the heavy silence.

"Yeah, neither do I."

"I'm serious, Grace. I want you to be careful. Like really careful." He stands up and starts pacing. He moves to the window to look out again, before coming back to stand in front of me. "If I could afford it, I'd get a room here, just so I can be close by if anything else happens. But I'm afraid that's out of the question," he says sheepishly. "I don't have the dough."

I'm touched at the size of Dalton's heart, but of course this place is too expensive. Even my parents would never be able to afford to stay here.

"No, I totally get it," I say with a bob of my head. "Lifestyles of the rich and famous, right? Trust me, this isn't something I'm used to either," I admit as I rub the palm of my hand over the smooth velvet of the love-seat cushion. "If things were different, I'd enjoy this temporary luxury, courtesy of the studio, but I can't let my guard down."

"I guess I'm beginning to get freaked out over this too." Dalton kneels in front of me and takes my hands in his. "If we stick together on this—if you let me keep an eye on you—I'd feel better knowing you were safe."

There's a twitch in his jaw as he says it, like Dalton is clenching his teeth. I know he means what he says, but I don't want him to think of me as a damsel in distress. Just like I didn't want James to think of me as weak. I can take care of myself. I've wanted to prove my independence from my parents and Ryan for so long, and now that I'm truly 100 percent on my own here, I feel the determination inside me to follow through with it.

But this isn't what I'm used to. This decade. These circumstances I'm finding myself in . . . I'm mistaken for another woman, targeted, stalked . . . this is more than I bargained for.

"Why don't you stay here with me?" I tear my gaze from his and glance around the spacious suite. "It's plenty big enough."

A flash of shock crosses Dalton's face and he rises to his feet, leaving me to look up at him.

"No, I . . ." he stumbles over his words. "I can't do that."

"Why not? You can keep an eye on me, like you said."

Dalton swallows. A gulp loud enough I can hear it. "It's just not right."

I'm puzzled. If I'd asked anyone else to stay a free night in the Chateau Marmont, they'd say yes instantly. And then it hits me. It's the boundaries between here and what I'm used to. The difference between what's considered right and proper between men and women here and in my world.

I chew on the inside of my cheek, feeling the heat of embarrassment. "Sorry," I tell him as I try not to notice how he's stepped away from me and is now lingering halfway between the love seat and the window. "Where I come from this wouldn't be a big deal. I hope you don't think I was suggesting we do anything other than talk and sleep. Not together . . ." I add quickly.

"It's okay, Grace. I want to be here for you but . . . I just can't stay here."

I nod again, understanding.

"Look, if anything else happens, call me. Promise?" There's a look of remorse in his eyes as he pauses then tells me, "There's something I didn't tell you." His hand hovers on the doorknob to the hallway outside my room. "When I shut off the forklift, I saw the brick."

I sit up a little straighter.

"I didn't want to scare you. But I told Mack about it. He's going to look into it. Find out who's responsible."

"You didn't tell me you knew, even after I told you about the brick over the phone."

Dalton's jaw twitches and tightens. "I should have. I guess I wanted to help figure this out for you—on my own. I feel this need to keep you safe, because . . . well, I don't want anything to happen to you. Not if I can help it."

I rise from the love seat, walk the few feet to where he stands at the door, and reach out to touch his stubbly cheek with my palm. God, he looks almost as worried as I feel. And he's adorable. Even if I'm confused and a bit hurt he's kept this information to himself.

"I'm all in to help you figure this out."

"Thank you," I reply softly.

I don't know how it happens, but suddenly Dalton leans closer, as I stretch forward to meet him. His lips press mine. Not hungry but sweet. He opens the door, gives a quick look in both directions before stepping out, then walks swiftly down to the end of the hall that is opposite the elevator. It's when he opens the door to the stairwell that I understand he doesn't want to be seen leaving my room, for the same reason he refused my offer to stay here. A line he doesn't want to cross that is so different from where I come from. And as I consider the respect he's offering me, I wonder if what I felt in the kiss is enough to bridge the gap. Dalton and I are worlds apart. Not just in what the future holds but in what he and I both believe in. And there is a sinking feeling in my gut that tells me how I feel about our kiss just now might come with a higher cost than being in danger or never seeing my family again.

CHAPTER TWENTY

THE NIGHT IS RESTLESS, FILLED with unforgiving dreams of lurking strangers and my own mind circling through the difference between my world and Dalton's. I wake in a tangle of sheets, a sheen of sweat clinging to my skin. All I want is to curl up and not leave the hotel room, but my fear is such that I can't give up the charade and not show up to the studio. There was a stranger beneath my window; someone set a rogue forklift after me . . . but all I can do is keep silent and power through, no matter how scared I am, so I can find out who they are—and if they are responsible for Alice's disappearance.

After a long day of filming and putting up with Judy, I am finally in the cab on my way to the hotel. An hour ago, I asked one of the operators in the main building of the studio to patch a call through to the sound room, and when Dalton answered the phone, over the whirring of a projector in the background, I asked him to meet me this evening. Not challenging the protocols of meeting in my room,

I told him I would be outside and that I would wait for his car. If Dalton is all in like he says he is, then he needs to see where this all started. And hopefully going to the Hollywood sign will create a time line for what happened to both me and Alice.

The hotel is busy tonight. The lobby is full of people checking in, checking out, and the adjacent dining room echoes with the tinkling of glasses and silverware on dinner plates. Everyone appears happy and oblivious to the panic I feel. I envy them.

I wait for Dalton to pull up to the entrance. I insisted that he can park farther away and that I'm perfectly fine walking to the car, but he wouldn't have it.

Not when a strange person is lurking in the dark spying on me. Instead, I stand in the well-lit entryway until the headlights veer around the curved drive. Dalton hops out of the car and opens the passenger door for me.

Even though we are on a mission, I can't stop thinking about the kiss. The way it makes me feel inside, and how I want to feel his lips on mine again. Even as the car rumbles along, I steal a look at him. My gaze immediately falls to his mouth.

As if knowing I am covertly checking him out, Dalton's right hand leaves the steering wheel, and he threads his fingers in mine.

He smiles as he stares straight ahead at the road.

"What?" I ask.

"I keep thinking about it too."

The tone of his voice, the smile, and the sincerity behind it . . . it's almost as good as the kiss itself.

"Are you sure you want to do this now? It's dark out."

"I'm sure," I say as I look out the window. The Hollywood sign is just up ahead. Waiting for me. "It's around the same time of night I made the wish for Ryan. I want it to be as accurate as possible."

James's words echo in my head, his insistence that I look haunted. But I refuse to be haunted by Alice any longer.

We make a left from the hotel and then a right onto Hollywood Boulevard to Franklin, driving along until we reach the turnoff onto Beachwood Drive, which leads into the hills. The car snakes its way up the winding roads, the landscape so different from what I'm used to. Finally, the street that will someday become my neighborhood stretches before us, winding tightly up the side of the mountain. Dalton turns the oversized steering wheel and coaxes the car onto the road.

This is the closest to home I've been in days, and my heart clenches—the ache of it filling me like never before.

"Park down there." I point toward the end of the road. Like the day the cab drove me to the sign, it isn't blocked by the metal gate that's been at the end of my street since I was born. There are no police cars monitoring where the street abruptly cuts off, merging into the side of the mountain. The scraggly bushes edging alongside the pavement look wild and unruly. Stella's headlights cut the encroaching darkness, shining a bright light on the narrow path I know all too well.

Dalton turns the key and Stella's engine grumbles to silence. He stares at the hillside, the formation of white letters looming over us. "I remember when it said 'Hollywoodland'"—he lets out a quick laugh—"and then it was 'ollywoodland' because the *H* had fallen over, and it was restored and shortened to just 'Hollywood.'" He pauses to turn his head and gives me a quick look. "That was a year before I moved from Cincinnati and came here to live near my uncle. I figured my plan of one day being on Rod Serling's radar was a stretch, so I came to Hollywood to find my own way." He glances down at the script that hasn't moved from the seat of his car. "I guess I'm still working on it."

I follow his line of vision from the file he's so passionate about and out the window toward the *H*. That letter and I have history. We've been through something together. And Alice too. I feel it in my bones. I open my door and step out. Dalton follows as I lead the way up the hill, expertly navigating the uneven terrain in the dark once we reach the boulder I climbed over the night I came to the sign. The moon has come out to join us, shedding enough light so we can see.

As we step closer, a sweet sadness sweeps over me. To everyone else, these giant letters are a landmark. To me, they took me away from everyone I love, leaving me here to figure out how to get back to my family.

"Geez, it's huge." Dalton cranes his neck, his gaze trailing the letter all the way to the top. "Good God, Grace, you climbed up there? You're way braver than me."

I don't feel brave. I still feel the rush of wind caressing my skin as I plummeted down, down, down toward the ground.

Dalton looks visibly shaken by my side. His hand slips into mine, his fingers curling, holding on tight. "I can't imagine what it must have been like. You must've been terrified."

I bob my head up and down, nodding. "I was. It was storming that night. Wind, thunder . . . The power was knocked out, and the cops that usually guard the entrance at the street left their post. So did the ranger," I say as I look over my shoulder to where the small station had been. "It gave me an in and I climbed the fence near that boulder over there," I point, "and then I just kept climbing. I guess I pushed aside getting caught, or the consequences. I just had to make it to the sign. I had only Ryan on my mind that night—and the wish I wanted to make for him.

"Alice was filming on location here." I walk farther up the steep slope, inching my way closer to the letter's base. "My brother had a picture of her and James from the location set on his phone. Right about here . . ." I stop and inspect the angle of the metal, remembering how I instantly recognized it in the photo.

"What do you mean 'on his phone'? Like, attached to it?"

Dalton's face is scrunched with confusion as I tell him: "No, it was in his camera roll." I stop and press my lips together. "I don't know how to explain it so you'll understand. There are portable phones, we call them cell phones because they work off cell towers, and they're small enough to hold in one hand, like a little rectangle. But it's basically a miniature computer. You can make calls, text, look things up on the internet, and it has a built-in camera. That's how I saw the picture."

His face shifts from confusion to disbelief as I continue. "She was wearing this in the photo." I hold my arm out and jiggle the charm bracelet.

Dalton lifts my wrist to his face so he can see it better in the dark. "I've noticed this on you. You never take it off."

"That's because it isn't Alice's," I tell him. "This is *my* bracelet. Everything else I wore the night I fell from the sign disappeared when I woke up in the trailer. My phone, my clothes I wore that night . . . all but this bracelet. My mom gave it to me years ago, only mine had more charms on it." I slip my wrist from his grasp and pull it in toward my chest, touching the charms left on it. "When I woke, my charms were missing. All but these." I point out the race car and ladybug hanging from it. "The same two—the only two—that were on the bracelet Alice wore in the photo."

Dalton looks back up at the letter *H* and rubs the back of his head. "So, you think the sign and the bracelet have something to do with why you're here?"

"I don't know. I think so. I hope so." I shrug. "The bracelet is the only thing that keeps me tethered to my life back home *and* the one I'm living here."

"A portal." Dalton looks down at the charms. "The *H* could be a portal. And the bracelet could be the trigger."

I start up the path again. The *H* is in arm's reach. "If I can reenact what happened the night I slipped . . ." I reach for the ladder, now much lower than when I'd climbed it before. "Maybe I can go back home."

"Grace, stop." Dalton's voice rings out. Within seconds he's by my side, his hands pulling mine from the metal rungs. "You can't climb this and jump, thinking it will get you back. That's—" He looks up. "Come on, Grace. You don't really believe in malarkey like that, do you?"

"Says the guy who's obsessed with science fiction." But I let him remove my hands. His palms warm the cold away from mine.

"Okay, fine. Maybe it's possible. But I get the feeling there's more to it." He continues rubbing my hands, slower, as if he doesn't want to let me go. "Why did your brother have a photograph of Alice?"

"I don't know." I shrug again, beginning to feel desperate over all the missing pieces. "He obsessively collected James Dean memorabilia. Having the picture could be a fluke, but he *had* it." I take a deep breath, trying to control my frustration. "It's all I have to go on, Dalton. I think Ryan noticed how much she and I resemble one another."

"And you have a bracelet that looks like hers," Dalton adds. "I agree. This doesn't feel coincidental."

I shiver but it isn't from the chill in the air. It's because of what I'm about to do. Despite Dalton's attempt at reasoning, I reach for the ladder and begin to climb.

"Grace, no."

But I ignore him. All at once, the familiar feeling of the night I made the wish for Ryan sets me on autopilot. I climb higher, ignoring Dalton's protests, ignoring the panic in his voice below me. I'm halfway up the ladder when my arms start to shake.

"This is suicide, Grace. Please come down."

I risk a glance below, and in the light of the moon, I see that Dalton is pacing. He stops to place both hands on the top of his head as if he's freaking out, and then he stops, looks up, and places his own hands on the rungs as if to climb up after me.

I wanted a second chance at this. Recreating that night to send me home only . . . Dalton's presence is changing the entire equation, altering the conditions I need to do this. And there is no storm—the only storm is inside me, churning and roiling with desperation to go home.

"I just . . ." And then the tears start to fall. I look up at the top of the *H*, so close, just a few more feet . . . but I feel the tug to look down at the man who is clearly distraught, hovering on the ladder beneath me. The man who is willing to climb up after me out of fear of what I'm doing.

"If you do this . . . if you jump, Grace, it's no guarantee that you'll find your way back home."

I let out my breath, knowing he's right. There is no guarantee.

"And maybe that's not a bad thing," he says softly. "You could live out your life here. Not as Alice—as you. I wouldn't mind that so much."

Something in my chest pinches at what he's saying. I angle my foot, reaching for the rung below me, and when I find it, I step lower onto the one below that. I reach the ground, but my hands are still fisted around the sides of the ladder, not quite willing to let go. Not quite willing to give up what means the world to me.

Dalton's hand reaches out from behind me and covers mine. "You could have a life here. You can choose to stay."

Slowly, I turn and face him. I can't hide my tears, the way my expression crumples in defeat, but he's so relieved, now that I'm back down on solid ground. He immediately wraps his arms around me and holds me close to his chest. I feel his heart beating at a surprisingly fast pace, then I feel him take a deep breath and swallow. "I care about you, Grace. I've never met anyone like you." Dalton shifts his position, his fingers touching my chin, lifting my face upward.

His words curl around my heart . . . even though I'm going to break his.

"I care about you, too, Dalton, and I could stay. I know you want me to. But we're too different. This *time* is too different that . . . I'm not so sure I can stay here for *me*."

A shadow passes over Dalton's face. I know I've hurt him, but he covers it with the smallest hint of a smile and cups my elbow with his hand before taking a step back. I give the *H* one last look before we walk in silence back to the car.

"Are you cold?" Dalton reaches behind us and pulls his coat over the front seat. He drapes it around my shoulders.

It smells like him—the scent I've come to know over these last few days, like an aftershave or cologne that smells of cedar and a hint of mint. A series of quivering waves erupts deep within my chest. I barely know him, yet I'm so comfortable snuggling against the warmth of his jacket, breathing it in.

Dalton fiddles with the dial on the radio, finding a soft tune that floats through the speakers and into the warm space. He cracks his knuckles and pulls at the collar of his shirt. "You scared me," he says in a low whisper. "I truly thought you were going to jump and then . . ." He pauses to look out the window as if he can't look directly at me just yet.

"And then what?" I ask.

He closes his eyes, and I notice how his throat moves with his swallow as he turns to finally face me. "I was afraid I was going to lose you. One way or another. You'd either find some strange miracle to take you back or you'd . . ."

I nod, letting him know I understand what he's saying—what he's feeling.

I have the direst need to get home to the life I've left behind, to find out if Ryan is all right, to let my parents know I, too, am not a big question mark hanging over their heads—that while pretending to be a missing starlet I may be in danger, but at least I'm alive. The worry I must be causing is almost too much for me to bear.

But Dalton . . .

If I stay because I can't bear to lose him too . . .

What does that mean for me?

I clear my throat and draw in a deep breath. "There's a book I read that was later turned into a series on TV. It's called *Outlander,* and as much as I loved the whole theme of it, it's just so ironic that I'm living it. That I've found my way to another time and now have to decide if it's worth staying." I lift my eyes from my lap and silently let Dalton know that I'm at least considering if *he's* worth staying for. "I would have to give up my family. Give up knowing the outcome of Ryan's condition."

Dalton takes my hand and squeezes it gently, but he doesn't take it away, as if he's trying to give me the strength I need to figure this all out.

"I'd have to give up who I am, and I don't know if I can do that. All I've wanted is to break free of my parents' hovering. Sure, they mean well; they love me. But I'm an adult now. I may only be twenty-two, and in their eyes that's still young, but I'm definitely not a child. And I've wanted to be seen differently than my brother. I want them to know I have my own path to follow, but I'm not so sure this is it—the way women are expected to be docile and domestic here. The way men view and objectify us." I look down at our entwined fingers and squeeze back, hoping he knows I'm speaking of men in general, not him. "I'm too different to be here."

"I understand," he says tenderly. "I really do, and I hope you don't include me in that category of men." With a grin Dalton surprises me by saying, "I come from a family of strong women. My mother and my grandmother wore the pants in the family, if you know that expression. But the choice is yours, whether to stay or find another way home. I'll stick to my promise to help you, just . . . promise me you won't throw yourself off the sign. Please don't do that."

I blow out a breath. I want to reassure him I won't do anything drastic, but I can't promise anything. I wanted to come here tonight to see what would happen, but I hadn't thought it through properly. The sky is clear tonight. Dalton is with me. I should have known better that it wouldn't work.

"I promise I won't throw myself off the sign. But I'm not going to promise I won't try this again. Not if there's a chance I can get home."

The wounded look in his eyes is back, so I add, "But I'll consider staying."

There is a moment of silence until Dalton shifts in his seat and looks at me. His eyes are now bright, not filled with worry and sadness.

"What?" I ask.

"Follow me with this, okay? If you're here, then where is Alice? What happened to her?"

I let out a distressed sigh. "I've been asking myself the same question since I woke up here."

Dalton puts his hand over mine. "I know you have. But tell me, why did you climb the sign?"

"I wanted to make a wish for Ryan. That he'd wake up from his coma."

"Exactly. A wish. Because he's in a desperate situation." Dalton's face lights up, becoming more animated as he speaks. "What if Alice had been at the sign making her own wish? What if something desperate was going on in her life just as it was going on in yours—in Ryan's?"

I lean in closer, catching onto what he's saying. "A wish made in the same place, wearing the same bracelet . . ."

"Yes! And maybe at exactly the same time? I mean, obviously a few decades apart, but it happened to be the right timing, the right setup for it to all come together." Dalton rests his back against the driver's-side door, facing me. A curious smile spreads across his lips, as if he's mulling over his words and the possibility of it all.

"Dalton, this is crazy. I mean, things like this don't happen."

He stares at me for a beat. "But it did. Why else would she still be missing? Why else would *you* be here?"

"And if I'm here, is she where I'm supposed to be?" I can't imagine a Hollywood movie star pretending to be me. Assuming she's in my place, my parents will think I've gone off the deep end. And Beth . . . well, Beth will think I'm nuts.

"That's what we have to find out," Dalton says.

I thought I was doing something good by making that wish for Ryan, and it's only now that I see I should have made my wish at his bedside—held his hand while I did it—not on top of a giant letter. I'm afraid I won't ever get back to see him wake up, to see him smile at me in that teasing way of his. Dalton is right. Climbing the sign and expecting to go home is pure madness.

I could have died tonight.

I need to accept the truth that no matter how close I line up the events of the night I made my wish, I may never get back. I might only survive if I stay here.

"I know you miss him."

I look over at the sweet man next to me.

"There's a quietness about you when you think of him. It shows." Dalton reaches over and entwines his fingers with mine. Then he puts his arm around my shoulder, and he pulls me close.

And I stretch forward to meet him.

His lips. My lips. The sweet sensation of his breath on my mouth. The world falls away the instant he pulls me against him and holds me close. I shift in his lap to turn toward him. "I really like you too."

The lips I kiss pull up into a smile. "I've heard starlets usually fall for their leading man, not the sound guy."

I shake my head and rest my forehead on his. "That's just it. I'm not a starlet. And I can fall for whoever I want."

"So, you are falling for me?" Dalton teases gently.

Before I answer, he pulls me close again. "Tell me what happens," he whispers into my hair as I nestle against his shoulder. "What's the future like?"

Breaking it down into a few sentences is impossible, and I consider what is and isn't safe for him to know. Sure, I could give him major facts . . . like names and dates, but something tells me I can't put him at risk by divulging too much.

"Well." I think for a moment. "I mentioned cell phones. You'd love those. They're small enough to carry in your pocket, and besides calling someone, you can send a message as a miniature film called a video, or spell it all out as a text, or simply record your voice. There are small, flat computers called laptops, and games you can play with someone in real time anywhere in the world or look things up on the internet—which is basically a digital encyclopedia but even better and more thorough. There's this amazing thing called FaceTime, where you can hold a conversation with a person and see them on your phone even though you are miles apart."

"Face time?" Dalton asks, intrigued. "What else?"

I am dying to tell him about big news, but I figure that isn't a good idea. After all, what if Dalton knows the right people who can alter history? I don't want either of us to be responsible for anything like that. Not to mention, if I tell him something and he tells the wrong person, that might jeopardize his own future.

It's best to stick with things he's interested in, like technology.

"Well, one cool thing is in about fifteen years or so, NASA will send a rocket into space and the first man will walk on the moon. Oh, remember I mentioned *The Twilight Zone* during our conversation about Rod Serling? He's going to create it as a television series and it's going to be so huge, they'll show reruns decades later. And the movies! Just wait until you see *Avatar*. They've come a long way with sound and visual effects. So much so that they've developed AI . . ." I pause, "that's artificial intelligence, but it's creating such an uproar because it's literally replacing real people and artists, and everyone is worried about their jobs."

There's a gleam in his eyes, and I know I've pushed the right buttons. I'm sure he's skeptical, but he seems fascinated. I snuggle in closer, making myself comfortable, ready to tell him more. Only . . .

He must feel me tense in his arms because he asks, "What is it?"

"There's some pretty terrible stuff too," I tell him.

Dalton shifts me back against him, his breath warm on my hair. "Like what?"

Again, I find myself wanting to tell him about things he *shouldn't* know. Like what will happen on 9/11 and politics and climate change. But how will he ever explain any of that if he's forced to, years from now? I decide instead to stick with circumstances that will unfold sooner than later.

"A man named Charles Manson will have a cult of followers in the late sixties and go on a killing spree in the Hollywood Hills. A director and his wife will be murdered. And . . ." I can't do it. I can't tell Dalton what will happen to James. It's bad enough that, earlier with James, I let it slip that Ryan loves his films, but if I tell Dalton now that James will die early, the risk involved if he knows and wants to warn him . . .

"Never mind," I tell him as I trace his jaw with my fingertips. "Some things are better left unsaid."

He plays with my hair as if trying to soothe away the horrible facts that I know will come true. "It's okay, Grace. You don't have to tell me. The future can't be changed, but you and I . . . we could have a future."

I close my eyes. "That means I'll have to stay."

"Then stay," Dalton whispers.

What would it cost me to fall for Dalton? To be in love for the very first time—with someone I'll have to leave behind the moment I find my way back home? I miss my family. My friends. My life. Everything inside me aches to know if Ryan is all right. But now, feelings for Dalton have slipped into my heart.

"I can't. You know I can't."

"I know," he whispers sadly. "I know I shouldn't be selfish. Just . . . think about it."

"It's not that I don't want to be with you." I like what's happening between us. I want more of it. But how can I trade one life for another? "If I stay, I'd either have to keep on pretending that I am Alice, or go completely off the grid to be myself, or at least move to another state."

Puzzled, Dalton asks, "What's 'off the grid'?"

"Oh, it just means being away from everyone and everything. Like isolating yourself."

"I'm sure it would be a relief to not have to pretend you're someone else anymore," Dalton tells me.

I notice how his body shifts against mine and I wonder if he's pretending too. That his dream of writing science fiction for television feels buried beneath his job at the studio. And I totally sympathize. I still want to be independent—to choose my own path and do what I want.

Now that I'm here, yes, I'm on my own, but it's not my life here, and being Alice is wearing me down. Not to mention it feels dangerous each and every day I put on the act.

"Being Alice right now scares me," I admit. Wasn't it enough to be in the wrong place at the wrong time? Now I constantly look over my shoulder. And the more that surfaces about what sort of trouble Alice may be in, the more anxious I become that whoever is responsible for her disappearance will target me next. Especially if they believe the first job wasn't successful.

"Yeah, I get that you're scared. I wish there was a way I could help keep a closer eye on things." Dalton's arms around me pull a little tighter. Protective and warm.

"Look, I know a room at the Chateau Marmont is out of the question. It's too expensive, but please think about staying in mine. It's a suite with plenty of room for the both of us." I gently add, "It doesn't mean we have to sleep in the same bed."

Dalton tenses beside me.

Damn it. I'm never going to get used to things around here.

"All I mean is that it makes sense, and if someone really is lurking around because they think I'm her—"

Dalton's body relaxes and his arms circle around me again. "No, you're right. It's smart. We'll just . . . well, I'll sleep on the couch because, well . . . you know."

I don't have to look at him to know his cheeks are bright pink. I know exactly what he's implying. Not that I'd mind; plenty of people share a bed and don't do anything. But I have to remind myself that things are different here.

"Yeah, that's what I meant. The couch. At least just for a little while until things don't feel so wonky anymore."

His chest trembles with laughter against my back. "Wonky?"

"Wonky. Like weird."

He gives a little laugh. "I think we're going to have to compare notes on what things mean, just so we can keep up with each other."

I snuggle closer, hoping he senses how much he's beginning to mean to me—and how lost I am for the words to explain how I feel. He's the only person right now who understands everything. My quirks, but also my confusion, my pain—my desperation to get home. Being without my parents and Ryan has created an ache in my heart that I've never felt before. I want to rewrite the night of my brother's crash so it never happened. I want to pray to anyone who will hear me and get a text from my mom that he's awake.

I want a miracle.

"Dalton?" I ask as I stare at the letter *H* on the hillside. "Did I ever tell you I'm a terrible person?"

"Grace, you're not terrible." He tilts my chin, forcing me to look into his eyes. "What would make you say that?"

I close my eyes, only because I can't handle the insistence in his that I'm not awful. Because the truth is . . . "The day I made my wish on the sign, I was supposed to audition for a part in Ryan's student film. I was so angry . . . not that I didn't want to do it for him but angry that my life still revolves around his. Like I'm a planet that orbits around him, ever since I was little. His final project is so important. And I chose me over him." Finally, I look at Dalton but instead of judgment, his face reveals an understanding I can't bring myself to agree with.

"I made that wish for him, but I also made a wish for me. That I could do it all over again. Go through with the audition. Make sure his film would be ready when he wakes up . . . if he wakes up."

And then there it is. That glimmer in Dalton's eyes that tells me I am terrible after all. He is silent and stewing over the thoughts I've set into motion in his head. After all my worrying over my brother and wanting to get home, I'm nothing but a selfish . . .

"Grace, what exactly did you wish for?" he whispers.

"That my brother would wake up, that he'll be . . ."

"No," he stops me. "The other wish. The one you *think* you made for yourself."

I pause, not yet grasping what he's saying. "Think I made? I . . . I remember wishing I could go back and make things right."

Dalton is suddenly a ball of energy, like what I have said has latched onto something brewing in his mind, and he can't contain it. He leans forward, causing me to scoot off his lap and back into the passenger seat. He's now facing forward, his thumbs rapidly tapping on the steering wheel.

"If Alice wished as hard as you did, then she must have had nowhere else to turn."

I pull his warm coat tighter around my shoulders.

"She must have needed a miracle . . ."

I finish his train of thought, clearly remembering the words I said on top of the sign. "*If only I could go back and make things right . . .*"

He nods, knowing I finally understand the wish that may have been set in motion to be answered. It wasn't about Ryan.

It was about Alice.

Alice needs me. And in turn, helping Alice is my ticket home.

CHAPTER TWENTY-ONE

DALTON PULLS UP TO A small brown building on Sixth Street, not far from the La Brea Tar Pits. I remember going to the tar pits on a fifth-grade field trip. That was years ago, and now that the landscape is different in this time warp, nothing about the area looks familiar. The buildings are lower, with only a few taller skyscrapers peppered along the streets, allowing an easy view to the next block of Wilshire. I'd always known this section of the city as the Miracle Mile, but instead of the familiar SAG-AFTRA building, the taller structure says "Prudential," although the American flag still waves on top of it. And missing across the street is the Verifi building.

Then I notice where we're parked. "You live above a wig shop."

Dalton stares out the window for a moment and smiles. "The rent's cheap. And besides, if I go bald one day, no one will ever know."

I shrug. Good point.

"I'd invite you up to my pad, but my roommates will razz me for the next decade if I do. I'll be back in a jiffy."

Dalton winks as he leaves me in the car and runs up the steps to the door. Turning back, he gives a little salute, then lets himself in. The traffic on his street is light and I find myself leaning back and closing my eyes as I wait for him. In moments, the driver's-side door opens, and Dalton reaches over the seat to toss a small brown bag into the back.

"Miss me?" he asks as he starts Stella's engine.

I give him a sweet smile and nod, noticing his overly chipper mood must be from anxiety about staying in my hotel room tonight. Peering over my shoulder, I take note of what little he's brought back to the car with him. He certainly isn't planning on staying long.

"I travel light," Dalton says.

WE PULL UP to the hotel, park the car, and head inside. Everyone stares at us the moment we walk in together.

I guess I hadn't fully planned this out. Maybe Dalton would rather take the stairs up to my floor even though I'm prepared to give the excuse that we're studying lines in my room and his bag contains scripts. But no one questions us. The people in the lobby only offer a few passing glances. Despite the magazine cover treatment, Alice isn't a universally recognizable star just yet, and nobody knows Dalton. A few of the staff know I'm filming at the studio, and a bunch of paparazzi would likely recognize me as Alice if they were allowed inside the hotel, but I march across the lobby toward the elevator with my head held high.

Once we are safely inside my suite, Dalton tosses the bag onto the love seat and exhales. "That was easier than I expected."

"Right?" I add, hurrying to turn on a few lights. He follows me around the room. I turn on a lamp, and he looks out the window, presumably to check if anyone is watching. When he closes the curtains, I don't ask if he saw anyone. Then he checks each room. He even looks under the bed and double-checks that I've locked the door.

Satisfied, Dalton stands in front of the long table with the bottles of vodka. He lets out a long, smooth whistle. "Care for a nightcap?"

I shake my head. "No, but you can if you want."

He replaces the bottle he's picked up, then lifts the lid to the ice bucket to peer inside. "I guess it's best to stay alert. Besides, if I'm sloshed, you might take advantage of me."

I laugh. It feels good.

Dalton settles onto the love seat and watches as I wear an invisible path across the room, back and forth. Now that we're in my room together, I don't know what to do. "I checked everything," he reminds me. "You're safe tonight. From whoever is watching Alice."

He's right. I'm safe, at least for tonight. The room is bright, chasing away the shadows, and I shuffle over to him. He removes his bag from the seat next to him and places it on the floor, but I can't bring myself to sit down just yet.

"If it helps calm your nerves, I'm the one who's risking a lot being here. If anyone leaks that I was spotted going into the Chateau Marmont with Alice Montgomery—with an overnight bag—Mack'll have my hide."

"I'm sorry. I know I'm putting you in an awkward position."

"Nah, don't do that to yourself, doll. I offered to keep you safe and that's what I'm going to do." He pats the cushion next to him.

The softness of the love seat only reminds me how weary I am, and soon, my head is resting on Dalton's shoulder, his arm circling me, pulling me into his side.

"Just let anyone try to call or spy on you now," he murmurs, his voice thick with fatigue. "They'll back off when they realize I'm here with you."

I should check the closet for extra blankets for him and retreat to my own bed, but my limbs suddenly feel heavy, and I can't bring myself to lift my head from his shoulder. All I can do is nod and hope he feels it.

Before too long, the soft breaths of sleep slip from Dalton's lips, and I begin to drift off. It's the first undisturbed, heavy sleep I've had since becoming Alice.

SOMETIME DURING THE night, Dalton must have covered me with a blanket. I wake to find myself alone on the love seat, stretched along the length of it. Peeking up from the floor beside me, Dalton smiles at me. "Morning."

"Why are you on the floor?" I sit up and wipe the sleep from my eyes. "Since I hogged the couch, you could have taken the bed."

Dalton lifts himself up onto one elbow and lets out a yawn. "Didn't seem right to take the bed. Besides, I wanted to keep my promise, so I figured it was best to stay in the same room with you. This way if someone broke in, they'd trip over me to get to you."

I wrap the blanket around myself, realizing I'm still in my clothes from the night before and covering up doesn't really matter. "Thank you. But won't you be achy all day from sleeping on the floor?"

"This is a luxury suite. The carpet is very soft." He laughs. "Really, it's not a big deal." Dalton stands and stretches. "Anyway, a gal's gonna need her privacy, so I'm going to head to the studio. If I'm there earlier than you, no one will see us go together. Is that all right?"

I nod. For Dalton's sake I hope no one from the front desk sees him leave. I'm just about to suggest he take the stairs again when he chimes in: "Besides, Mack asked me to come in early today and he'll flip his lid if I'm late, so I'd better goose it."

He retrieves his bag and rummages for a toothbrush before heading into the bathroom. I take the time alone to pat down my bedhead and make sure I don't look as hideous as I imagine I do.

When Dalton emerges from the bathroom, I notice he hasn't brought his toothbrush back out with him.

"Mind if I leave my stuff here? I assume you want me to stay another night. I'm such riveting company, after all." He reaches upward and stretches again.

"You don't mind?" I try not to show my surprise. "I mean, as long as you want to."

"Sure, it might be nice to talk and not fall asleep on each other next time. You must think I'm a wet rag for dozing off like that."

Dalton steps closer and awkwardly hugs me. But the instant I wrap my arms around his waist and thank him for keeping me safe, he relaxes.

"I'll see you later," he says, and then kisses the top of my head and lets himself out into the hallway.

I listen for the elevator to ding, and when it does, I head for the shower, admitting to myself that Dalton staying the night was the best idea in the world.

CHAPTER TWENTY-TWO

Judy breezes into the trailer bright and early, waving a newspaper. She slaps the paper down in front of me onto the makeup table.

"Full front page."

I lean over and look at the picture of myself in the gray dress, then look up into her proud eyes.

"Aren't you excited?" she says as she beams. "I pulled some strings with the *Los Angeles Daily*." She points her finger at the article. "Otherwise, we'd wait a week for this, and I think people should catch a glimpse of you now. Thank goodness your elbow snafu happened after the fact, otherwise you'd have to be facing the other way. I'm not sure your left side is your best," she says snidely.

The headline reads, Alice Montgomery, Hollywood's Next Golden Girl. Sure enough, it's followed by a full-page spread stating that I am the "pride and joy of Flynn Studios," "the next cinematic sensation to grace the silver screen."

I may have posed for the photo, but it's Alice Montgomery who is supposed to be the star. I feel like I've stolen her glory. I'm not golden, and I'm certainly not a sensation. These last few days on set prove that, even though I'm not fully convinced all these mishaps have been my fault.

"You don't seem excited." Judy frowns at my lackluster reaction. She lingers at my side and then casually asks, "Could it be because you had company last night and your mind is elsewhere?"

My head whips up. I don't say anything but narrow my eyes and glare.

"Look, I don't care who you invite back to your hotel room. That's your business. But you're on the precipice of something big here, and I'd advise you to steer clear of the rumor mill." I can't tell if the look on her face is concern for my reputation or a threat. "You never know who's watching, and around here, once word gets out that you're a loose woman, well . . . let's just say word gets out."

I'm not sure what bothers me more . . . that Judy's words hold a hidden meaning, or that someone noticed that Dalton spent the night in my room. Several people saw us last night after we came back from the Hollywood sign. Several more surely saw him this morning.

And while I was perfectly safe last night, I shiver at the idea any one of them could be the mysterious person who'd been lurking outside, staring up at my room.

"It's really no one's business but my own who I choose to spend time with." My tone is salty. Just how I intend it.

There's a flash of shock on Judy's face and her eyes narrow at me. Just as she opens her mouth to challenge me, a commotion outside catches our attention.

Just outside the open window, the director's assistant stands a few feet from the trailer raking his hand through his hair while he mutters loudly to himself.

Judy lets out an exasperated huff, the assistant's loud ranting causing a momentary halt to her reprimand, and stomps to the door. "Is there a problem?" Judy asks from the doorway.

"One of the girls is missing. Never showed up for costume check. Today of all days."

"Who's missing?" I ask.

The man stares out across the lot as if willing her to show up. "The one with the accent. Eleanor." He lets out an irritated grunt. "Just up and gone, and on the last day of filming." He raises his hands in the air, aggressively mimicking his words.

"Eleanor?" My brows knot together. "I just spoke with her yesterday."

"Well, that doesn't help me now, does it?" The man gives me an annoyed scowl. "Do you know where she is?"

"No, I don't." Eleanor doesn't seem like the sort to take off. Not on an important day like today. Not without a good reason. This film means the world to her, even if she only has a tiny role.

Judy interrupts. "Now, now," she says in an appeasing voice that is too sickeningly sweet to be real. "I'm sure Alice knows no more than you do."

I'm too rattled for Judy's sugarcoating. Eleanor is the second woman to go missing—just like Alice. A chill breaks out across my arms as I recall when I last saw her yesterday. Eleanor had been talking to Hawkins.

The director's assistant leaves, and Judy ushers me back inside and closes the door, our tense words with one another now forgotten. "She's going to hold things up if she doesn't get her act together and get here within the next half hour." Judy tilts her wrist and glares at her watch.

A thought ruptures through my head, spraying more goose bumps down my back.

"Maybe Hawkins knows where she is?"

Judy's gaze slides over me. "Why would he know?" Her voice sounds stern.

"Eleanor was talking to him just yesterday, and . . ."

Judy's expression shifts but she doesn't say anything more. She just seethes quietly as if Eleanor's tardiness is only a disruption to today's schedule and not a worry that should cause so much alarm.

Guilt seeps into my bones. Maybe my mentioning the party to Eleanor pushed her to leave, looking for something bigger and better. That's what starlets do in the company of big Hollywood people, don't they? They schmooze. Flirt. Try to get noticed.

But Eleanor is sweet, at least that's the impression she gave me. She even told me that she's only ever wanted to act, even going against her family's wishes to come out to Hollywood. No matter how small her role in this film, she must have a contract with the studio and hopes to have a steady income and lots of roles. That's not the sort of person who would bail on a film.

"Should we worry?" I fidget, retying the belt of the robe I wear over my costume.

"I'm sure she'll show up, although this morning was the final dress rehearsal before her scene," Judy says. "I'm sure she has a valid reason for why she's not here."

I nod but my stomach roils. As soon as I finish my scenes today, I'll ask someone in the main building for Eleanor's address and go there myself if she doesn't show up.

"I don't want it to bother you," Judy urges. "You have more important things to focus on."

But I can't ignore the suffocating feeling in my chest. First Alice and now Eleanor. A deep worry settles in me that their disappearances are connected. And I have a sense that the stranger outside my window or whoever called or sent the forklift my way has something to do with it.

Judy heads for the door. “On set in ten, okay?” She pauses, glancing at Dalton’s borrowed coat draped over the arm of a chair, then steps out onto the lot, closing the door behind her.

I’d borrowed his coat this morning since it looked like rain, but now that Judy’s noticed it, I’m sure it’s another notch in her warning. A man was in my room last night. His coat is in my trailer. She doesn’t have to say it, but the message is loud and clear: I’m creating a questionable reputation for myself, especially if she finds out Dalton will be staying with me again tonight and tomorrow and hopefully every night until I can figure out how to get back home to my century.

I bring the coat to my nose, inhaling Dalton’s scent. I long to speak to him, but Mack has a busy day scheduled for him, so I’ll have to wait to call him and ask if he’s heard anything about Eleanor. Suddenly the flutter of falling paper caresses my ankle—a business card. I bend to pick it up and bring it over to the window, smoothing the crumpled fold at its center.

I nearly choke.

The business card belongs to none other than F. W. Hawkins.

CHAPTER TWENTY-THREE

IT'S THE FINAL SCENE. Before today, I would have been tongue-tied and full of nervous jitters at the thought of James being so close to me. Now, after so many set takes, being near him feels normal. Even though the last scene calls for a passionate kiss between the two of us, I'm not freaking out. He's beautiful and iconic, but only I know about the iconic part. Like any other actor here, James is eager to play his role and make a name for himself. Knowing that he will but won't be around to savor his success fills me with sadness.

James leans closer, his lips brushing mine with a tenderness that I'm sure looks authentic. I peer up at him through my lashes, just like the script says I should, and feel him lean in. My eyes close. His lips press against mine and then . . . "Cut! That's a wrap!" the director calls out, finally. His announcement is met by cheers and applause across the set.

It's pure luck that I've managed to do everything right. My lines were on point and my memorization skills so improved with each round of takes that filming finishes by midday. I let out a sigh of relief and shake hands with the extras and the crew. Inwardly, I'm just grateful nothing terrifying happened.

As soon as I'm back at the trailer and melt into a plush chair, my heart sinks. I read over the datebook Judy has laid out for me. It appears that she's filled in a lot since I studied Alice's comings and goings just a day ago. Besides the wrap studio party at Mr. Flynn's private home at the end of the week, when I flip to the upcoming months, I see there are several press junkets scheduled, as well as the actual premiere. Beyond that, Judy has penciled in enough publicity to take up the rest of the year.

If I'm lucky, I'll be long gone by then.

"Congratulations, Miss Montgomery!" Antonio's makeup assistant, Marlene, pokes her head in the door.

I follow her to the chair at the makeup table, where she proceeds to dismantle my elaborate updo. I've lost track of how many times my face has been powdered and dabbed at since pretending to be Alice—of how many pins have been stuck in my hair—and I barely feel her fingers uncurling the tight twists.

"Wasn't Mr. Dean just dreamy?" she asks as she deposits the pins into a nearby dish. "Weren't you nervous to be so close to him? Golly, I would just *die* to be you! So close to his lips. That hair!"

I nod, fully understanding the allure of James Dean, but to me, he's a surrogate big brother—offering tips and advice on acting. Funny that now I've had the chance to be around him, I haven't once swooned. Instead, my mind seems to be preoccupied with someone else.

My brain runs through all the sensible possibilities as to why Hawkins's card is in Dalton's coat pocket. Dalton said he doesn't like Hawkins, but with both men working in the industry, of course their paths would cross, especially since I've seen Hawkins here at the studio.

The girl grows suddenly quiet and bends closer. "Did you hear about Eleanor?"

My gaze finds hers in the mirror. "I did. She didn't show up today, did she?"

She looks around uneasily. "What do you suppose happened to her?"

"What do you mean?" My stomach clenches. I have a bad feeling in my gut, but I can't say anything. The only person I can voice it to is Dalton, and I still haven't heard from him today. He wasn't even on set during the final scene. And now that Eleanor's dramatic no-show has become instant gossip, the buzz circulating the studio is almost deafening.

I decide to play things down. "She probably wasn't feeling good and forgot to call."

Marlene stops playing with my hair. "I don't think so. Peggy, one of the extras who knows her pretty well, went over to her house this morning. They carpool together. Anyway"—she looks around before continuing even though she and I are alone—"she wasn't there."

The shake of her head makes my stomach feel funny, as if I know what she's going to say next.

"Gone," Marlene continues. "Just up and went. Left her purse, her wallet, her keys."

The picture she paints of Eleanor's disappearance is all too familiar. I'm glad when she finishes with my hair and turns to leave. I suddenly don't feel well.

"Oh, before I forget." Marlene spins around. "Judy wants you to copy some dates into your calendar. She left hers on the table."

The trailer is quiet after Marlene leaves, giving me time to worry about Eleanor. There must be a logical reason why she never showed up today. Her disappearing just like Alice has to be a coincidence.

But I'm afraid it isn't.

My concern eats at me, and then the guilt hits. As if Eleanor's disappearance is somehow my fault.

Judy's datebook waits for me on the table, and as I begin copying the notes, I try to push the disturbing thoughts out of my mind. Her datebook is startlingly organized in neat black pencil. For all the time Judy spends with me, it's a wonder how she manages to keep track of the other actresses I see jotted down in her book. There is a Sandra penciled in for photo shoots on Wednesdays. Someone named Bea has a costume check on Mondays. And there is Eleanor's name, marked down for speech lessons and another screen test. Lot C, room 4.

I flip through Alice's book and find the familiar entry . . . Lot C, room 4. Alice had the same appointment two weeks before Eleanor. I continue searching through the rest of the dates, but it's the only entry listed for lessons of that sort. My finger flips over the pages at the end, and again my gaze settles on those strange, cryptic scribbles. 1132WBS3.

I've seen those numbers before.

I look around the room, biting my fingernail. Then I march over to Dalton's coat on the arm of the chair and fish through the pocket. I read the business card again.

F. W. Hawkins
Publicity
1132 Wilshire Boulevard, Suite 3
Los Angeles, CA 90017

The numbers and first letters of the address match the cryptic scrawl in the datebook. This is the code. It's Hawkins's address.

My hands ransack Dalton's coat, examining all the pockets inside and out, but there is nothing else. Even though I'm upset he's been holding out on me—warning me about Hawkins, claiming he doesn't know him personally, never even spoke to him, yet keeping his business card, giving me reason to believe they conduct business with one another after all—I lift the coat to my chin and nestle into it. I want to forget what I've found and go back to last night—before another girl went missing and I started doubting things.

Then I realize something.

In both Alice's and Judy's datebooks, the days between Alice's disappearance and me showing up are blank. Every other day is penciled in, to the point of insanity.

But those seven days—nine if you count the weekend before anyone realized she was gone—have nothing. Why would Judy have nothing scheduled on exactly those days? It looks so blank. So . . . wrong.

Enough to make me wonder if Judy knew Alice would be gone.

Did Alice want to disappear and confided in Judy? Then why the big fuss over her disappearance? An act to appease the studio?

Was Alice taken against her will, and Judy is involved?

In a frenzy I lay out everything that belongs to Alice. Lined across the chaise longue are the datebooks and the crumpled business card. Next to them are Alice's purse and the script.

I set to exploring the closet, inspecting each item hanging inside and searching the pockets for anything I may have overlooked. There is only a scarf, sunglasses, a stick of Beech-Nut mint chewing gum, and tissue lint. None are extraordinarily helpful.

On my wrist the gold charms jingle, clanging together like the ticking of a clock, as if reminding me that time is running out—that I've been here too long, filling in for a woman who may never come back.

Under the assumption that I'm Alice, only Judy has expressed that I don't seem like myself. To everyone who knows Alice, my act has been seamless enough to not raise suspicion. I'm the only one who suspects something is wrong here. And Dalton, since I've included him.

I need to dig further, harder, into darker, more precarious places. Only Dalton won't like that I'm not going to ask for his help this time. Because the truth is, as much as I hate it, I'm not sure what that little card in his pocket means.

Dalton will be at the studio for another few hours, and what I need to do can be accomplished without his ever knowing.

It's stupid on so many levels—but I know I have to pay a visit to 1132 Wilshire Boulevard, Suite 3.

CHAPTER TWENTY-FOUR

CARS AND BUSES HONK ALONG the busy street as I head downtown toward Wilshire Boulevard. I glance down at the business card in my hand then up at the street sign, making sure I am going the right way. After several blocks, the cracks in the sidewalks become longer and larger. The businesses thin out, morphing into stretches of laundromats, bars, and decaying tenement houses all clustered together in short strips and separated by large-pitted parking lots. The area is visibly run-down. It makes me nervous. I clutch the strap of Alice's purse tighter and wonder why Hawkins chose to set up his office down here.

In a nearby vacant lot, a group of boys chases after a dog behind a chain link fence. Across the street, a woman with a baby on her hip leans against an open doorframe, staring out at a man whose grease-slicked overalls stick out from beneath a jacked-up Chevy. The woman's gaze follows me with suspicion, warning me I've strayed far from my comfort zone.

I walk steadily onward before stopping in front of a white building, gray with age. The neighboring structure looks barren—boarded up, with dried soap smeared across its windows like clouds so passersby can't peer in. The address matches the one on the business card in my hand. I hesitate, wondering if this is a terrible mistake.

But I didn't come this far to chicken out.

I turn the latch on the door and push it open, then climb up one sagging step into a narrow entry with wallpaper so faded it is nearly white.

"May I help you?" A young woman's voice floats down the hall.

I follow her voice, finding myself in a small, stuffy room. There is a desk cluttered with files, papers, and an old black typewriter.

The receptionist behind the desk can't be much older than me, with platinum-blond curls bobbed to her chin. She pauses to rudely snap her gum.

"Do you have an appointment?" she asks, her gaze sweeping over me from head to toe.

"I . . . um. No, but is Mr. Hawkins here?" I lift my chin and look directly into the receptionist's eyes.

She pulls a pencil from behind her ear and scratches her head with it, her curls sprayed in place so stiffly they hardly move.

"He's in a meeting, but feel free to wait over there." Her pencil points the way to the two mismatched chairs lined up against the wall. "Are you a model, honey?"

"Who, me?" No one else is in the room. "No, I'm an actress." There is a modicum of pride in my own words.

Bubble gum snaps again. "Aren't we all."

I pull the scarf into my lap, threading it between my fingers, then fold and unfold it as I take in my surroundings. A single window lets in a dismal amount of sunlight, illuminating a collage of framed photos on the wall. I recognize some of the faces: Marlene Dietrich, Jean Harlow, and a smattering of others whose names I don't know. Mostly blond, like the woman on the opposite side of the cluttered desk.

The tap, tap, tap of her fingernails on the typewriter keys fills the small office. It's annoying but it gives me something to focus on while I rehearse what I've come to say to Hawkins. *I was in the neighborhood and wanted to say hello. God no. Focus, Grace. Why did you act so strange at the cocktail party? Tell me what happened to Alice Montgomery. Now!*

A door to a room I cannot see squeaks open. The receptionist continues typing.

"Just give me a week for those photos, Genevieve." Hawkins's voice drifts closer. "Then we'll set up your screen test."

There is a rustling of paper, of fabric—as if someone is hastily slipping into a coat—and then a sound like keys dropping to the floor. More murmurs, heavy with confusion.

"Bernadette," he calls out. "Would you please see our client to the back door? She's a bit . . ."

Bernadette rolls her eyes and slaps a stack of papers onto the desk. As she hurries toward the back room, my gaze follows her. Floral dress. Thin fabric. Covered buttons. Black hose with distinct seams running up the backs of her shapely calves.

Hawkins appears from around the doorway, straightening his tie. When he notices me, the color drains from his face. "Miss Montgomery," he exclaims. "What are you—?" He seems visibly upset about my appearance but catches himself quickly. "To what do I owe this pleasure?"

I rise to my feet, the scarf now a pile of crumpled silk in my fist. "I . . ." The reason for coming floats out of my head as if it was never there at all.

Hawkins proceeds to walk into the room, pausing at a large filing cabinet behind the desk. He clumsily thumbs his way through the folders poking up above the top of the drawer and pulls one out.

"I . . ." he stammers nervously. "I believe I've got what you're looking for." Without looking at me, he motions for me to follow him down the narrow hall, back to where his receptionist has gone to attend to the woman he'd called Genevieve, then he ushers me into a small office.

It's the size of a closet. Dark and very messy, with papers and publicity photos scattered about. The pictures, from what I can see, are poor quality, as if taken quickly with a cheap camera. They are everywhere. In cardboard boxes stacked along the floor. On the desk. Sticking out of file folders.

Most are headshots of women in their early twenties, some obviously younger. An uncomfortable feeling creeps from the pit of my stomach to my throat as I begin to see other, more suggestive photos in the boxes. These are not headshots. They show women, girls, in provocative poses, completely nude. Some don't even include their faces but focus only on their breasts, their inner thighs. My gaze falls on a photograph of a stomach, a navel, a tuft of hair at the bottom of the frame.

"Have a seat, Miss Montgomery," he says a bit too loud, and then he shuts the door behind us.

Within seconds Hawkins is in front of me, his face the color of chalk like the night of the party. His eyes hold an almost crazed, confused look as he stares at me up and down. "I can't believe it, Alice. I thought for sure you were . . ."

His voice is thick, as if he's on the brink of a breakdown right in front of me. He reaches out and pulls me into his arms.

I stiffen the moment our skin makes contact. "What are you doing?" I push away against his arms that feel reluctant to let me go.

Finally, he loosens his hold and sinks onto the edge of the desk, raking both hands through his hair. With absolute confusion he looks into my eyes. "I thought I was seeing things that night at the Marmont, that maybe I'd had one too many."

I need answers, but I am beginning to regret my decision to come here.

"You have to believe me," he pleads. "I never meant for it to happen, honey."

Honey? Eleanor was right. He and Alice *are* close.

"It was never meant to happen the way it did." He doesn't look up, as if he's ashamed. "That wasn't the plan. I had no idea she . . ."

"She?" I ask. "She who?"

But my question is left hanging in the air.

His thumb nervously flicks the corner of a folder lying on the desk next to him. The top corner of a paper sticks out of the top. The word CONTRACT is stamped across it. The only other word visible from my angle is *Brooklyn*. The rest is covered by a strip of negatives paper clipped to the top. I tilt my head to the side, straining to see more, but Hawkins notices and he lays the neighboring folder on top of it. Something feels wrong. He is covering up something.

"What did you do?" I ask.

I still see the lettering of the word on the file he tried to hide. I swallow hard. "Are you the reason Eleanor didn't show up for work today?"

His back goes rigid. "I don't know what you're talking about."

"Eleanor," I insist. "From the studio. Brown hair. Strong New York accent."

Hawkins stares at me. "I don't know an Eleanor."

"You were talking to her the other day." I narrow my eyes. "On set."

"I talk to lots of women on set. Hundreds." His arm sweeps the span of the shabby room, making it very clear what the boxes all around us contain. "You think I have time to remember each and every name?"

"Maybe not." I grip the arms of the chair. "But maybe you'll remember what happened a few weeks ago. When Al . . . when *I* went missing. Surely you remember that."

The air in the room seems to shift. The veins in Hawkins's neck pulsate as he nods, as if understanding why I'm here. "Things are different now that you're back, aren't they? A little fuzzy, maybe?"

Nervous heat rushes to my face as he leans closer to me, his face inches from my ear. I instinctively lean away.

Hawkins's eyes narrow and he glares at me. "I don't know how you did it, Alice. How you found your way back from the dead, but congratulations. You had me fooled."

"What are you talking about?" I press my back into the chair, willing it to bend so it lets me further distance myself from his incriminating tone. Through the closed door I hear the typewriter keys resume their unsteady tapping. Bernadette is back at her desk. If I call out for help, will she even hear me? More important, will she do anything about it?

"You're an excellent actress, my darling. Our little romance was well played." Hawkins's sharp eyes trail up my chest to my face, meeting my confusion. "But now you're back and you've developed a conscience. Your name will soon be in lights on every theater marquee, and I'm sure you don't want anyone to know how you got there."

He points to the folder taken from the cabinet in the front room. "You seemed very torn about things the first time we met in this office, but go on, take it."

He slides it closer. I flip it open. Inside is a stack of photos. Of Alice. I pull each one free, my hands struggling to keep them steady. The first is an over the shoulder shot where Alice is in nothing but a scrap of fabric so sheer it would have made more sense to not wear anything at all. But the others . . . My entire body shudders as I stare at the photos. Each subsequent photograph reveals more of the stunning young starlet than I ever wished to see. She's nude.

It's chilling to see the remarkable similarity Alice and I share; so convincing that I have to remind myself it's Alice in these prints and not me. We look identical. She even has a mole on her shoulder like I do. A rush of heat spreads from my neck to my ears, stretching to my face. Hawkins surely notices, and my secondhand feeling of violation is so authentic there's no chance he'll believe I'm *not* Alice. Especially as I take in the look in Alice's eyes and wonder if she had willingly agreed to pose for these, or if she'd been coerced—by Hawkins.

"You're very photogenic," Hawkins intervenes when I thumb through the last set, his voice taking on a huskier tone. When I pause to look up at him, there is a primal glint in his eye, as if he knows which photos I've finally come across. As if his compliment will wipe away the shock on my face.

Back home, photos like these circulate online often. But here in 1953, the exposure would be devastating, especially for a woman. Especially if she hasn't consented and they fall into the wrong hands.

My gaze shifts to the box of photographs nearest the chair. Several of the younger girls don't seem so posed, the camera angle a bit lopsided, their faces never quite looking directly at the lens. My throat is so dry I can barely work up enough saliva to swallow. Even if Alice agreed to pose for the images in my hands, I wonder if the other girls did. And regardless, some are well below the age of consent anyway.

"How did you get these?"

A sly grin draws up the corners of Hawkins' mouth. "Why, you posed for me, Alice darling. How could you forget?"

I shake my head. "No. Those." I nod toward the box closest to me on the floor. "What did you do to get those?"

"Ah," he says with amused understanding and crosses a leg over his knee. "I got them doing what I do best. Promising fame. Their name in lights. Don't play dumb, Alice, it's what you want too. Or are you afraid of the competition?"

"Those girls . . . how many of them are even of age? What are you planning to do with their photos?"

Hawkins uncrosses his leg and sets both of his shiny black shoes on the thin, worn carpet between us. "That's my business, not yours."

"But . . ."

"It's what I do, Alice. I find the talent and I place the talent. I have a . . . *special* relationship with the studio that allows my business to stay afloat."

"A special relationship? You traffic these girls?"

Who is at the receiving end? I do a mental tally of the men I've seen around the studio. Hawkins could be working with any one of them, or several.

"Don't play innocent, Alice. You knew what you were getting into. And the price you paid was worth it, wasn't it? Stardom is just around the corner for you. It's what you wanted. At all costs. And it's precisely what all these other girls are hoping for as well."

Horrified, I clutch Alice's photos protectively to my chest, then open my purse. There is no way I'm leaving them behind for a predator like Hawkins to do who knows what with them. I'll get rid of them.

Burn them, if I have to.

Hawkins's hand shoots out and circles tightly around my wrist. He squeezes, and the pictures fall to the floor, scattering in different directions. "Not so fast, darling. If you want to keep them, I'm sure we can make some sort of arrangement. My bed gets awfully lonely after a long day of work."

I shake my head. Never. This is where I draw the line pretending to be Alice.

"Have it your way then," he says slyly. "But the photos are the property of Hawkins Enterprise, and according to the contract you signed, and your consent for my photographer to take these, so are you."

I narrow my eyes to him. "I'm under contract with Flynn Studios."

"Yes," he agrees, "and how do you think the studio caught wind of a stunning little nobody named Alice Montgomery? Only an agent like me could get you in the door."

The silence in his stuffy little office feels enormous. I watch in quiet horror as he retrieves the snapshots I dropped and clips them back inside the folder. "You're a monster," I manage to whisper through clenched teeth before a glimmer of hope hits me. I can tell Dalton's uncle. I can expose Hawkins for what he's done and prevent it from happening again. "Does Mr. Flynn even know about this?"

Hawkins's eyes flare with intrigue and my threat hangs in the air between us. "You know, it's me you should thank for allowing you to bypass the process I've perfected. I was the one who had a hand in getting you cast . . . the 'right way.' So, you see, doll," Hawkins says with a straight face, "it would be in your best interest to let me hold on to these. You wouldn't want them to get into the wrong hands now, would you?"

"Are you threatening me?" I clutch the arm of the chair.

"Not at all. But I do expect your silence. I believe I now have some insurance that you won't spill what you've learned today. Don't forget, you're the one who came to see me. Remind me, what exactly dragged you out to this part of town?" His lips ease into a dark smirk. "You wanted your hands on the photos, didn't you? You want to pretend they don't exist."

My mind is reeling. I came here to find out how he and Alice were connected. I only wanted proof. Damn those letters and numbers in her datebook.

"For the record, I'm not buying your excuse that you don't remember what happened the night you disappeared, and I'm certainly not going to let you drag me down. I have a business to run."

It's almost impossible to tear my gaze from the folder of photos. I don't want to leave them behind, but I have to get out of here. If I go to Mack about this, Hawkins will leak Alice's photos.

The click-clack of the typewriter in the front room sounds like a bomb ready to annihilate Alice's world. And when it does, pieces of Alice will be everywhere—Alice's life in ruins. And if I remain stuck in this time, it will be *my* life on the line, *my* reputation.

Hawkins rises to his feet and rounds the edge of his desk, placing it between us. "I hear the film has wrapped. Congratulations."

I nod numbly, keeping a close watch on him, waiting for him to pull out another folder with threatening photos.

"And now your face will be everywhere—magazines, billboards. It's all very exciting," he goads.

I hope he's not implying I should thank him. He's a snake; I know that now. I just wish the girls in the photographs knew it too. All these girls . . . it makes me feel sick. My fingers itch to grab every photo, look up who they are and get them far away from Hawkins and whoever else is in on this at the studio, but Hawkins is too close, about to steer me to the door that leads back out into the lobby.

He leans next to my ear as I try not let him see me tremble. "Just so you know," he whispers, "you disappeared once before, it can happen again."

Out . . . out . . . let me out.

I push past Hawkins to get out of the stifling little room. One last glance at the file on the desk reveals the folder has shifted since Hawkins got up to let me out, and I now see a picture that has been hiding inside. Bare, luminescent skin. A shoulder, half a breast. A tender ear weighed down by the shimmer of an exquisite Egyptian earring. That earring looks familiar, but it's the face that grips me.

The brown eyes. The thin lips.

Eleanor.

CHAPTER TWENTY-FIVE

MY HEART HAMMERS BEHIND MY ribs as I hurry out of Hawkins's office and down the sidewalk. His threatening words stick in my head like blackened tar I'll never be rid of—Alice disappeared before; she can disappear again. *I can disappear.* I still feel his tight embrace on my skin—how suffocating it felt as he pulled me close to his chest.

The pungent smell of his aftershave lingering in my nose and on my face. Since waking up as Alice, this is the first time the danger to me has become palpable. The accidents on set, the forklift . . . all could be explained away. But Hawkins's threat—that is unmistakably directed at me.

I reach the busy intersection and frantically wave my arm in the air for a taxi. I don't know where Alice Montgomery disappeared to or if she is ever coming back, but I hope that Eleanor has at least made it back to the studio to film her final scene. I need to convince her that getting involved with Hawkins will ruin her.

A FILM PROJECTOR hums from inside the Sound department. The moment I reach the door, I lean my forehead against it, catching my breath. At my knock, the projector stops, the film flaps around the reel. Shoes step closer and then the door opens.

Dalton takes one look at me and pulls me into his arms. "What happened?"

The entire way back to the studio I steeled myself, working through the panic, working up the words that will make Dalton tell me why Hawkins's business card was in his coat pocket. I pictured him breaking down and telling me he knows about the pictures I've just seen.

But as soon as Dalton pulls me into his warm arms, I melt. Seeing those photos of Alice and Eleanor feels like a weight I can't bear alone. I can't imagine someone as nice as Dalton being okay with what Hawkins is doing behind closed doors.

I close my eyes and wrap my arms around his waist, linking my fingers behind his back, letting this moment still the uneasiness in my heart.

"Grace?" he asks.

I free myself and step back, pushing my hair out of my eyes; my set curls unfurling in the midday humidity. "Eleanor is missing."

"Yes, I know. I heard someone talking about it earlier. She's still a no-show. Is that why you look upset?"

I stifle a shiver. "It's just like Alice." All I want is to snuggle deeper into Dalton's familiar warmth, but the chill inside me won't go away. I draw in a breath that feels too thin. When I exhale, it's as if I was never breathing. "Please tell me how you know F. W. Hawkins," I blurt out. "You told me you don't know him, haven't spoken to him, but that you don't trust him and I should steer clear of him, but please . . . I'm just asking for your honesty."

Dalton is quiet, then pulls away to look at me with a confused expression. "I don't understand what you're asking, Grace. I know who he is from around the studio, and yes, I've heard the rumors that circulate and think he's a sleezy womanizer, but I don't *know* him."

"His business card fell out of your coat pocket." I fish for the crumpled card in Alice's purse and hold it out to him. "Please tell me the truth."

He looks at it as if he's never seen it before. "I swear. I didn't know this was in my coat. I forgot that he gave me his card once and said to send beautiful girls his way. I never did. It's why I can't stand him, but I threw that business card away long ago. Grace, what's going on?"

My heartbeat stammers as I inhale another shaky breath. "The numbers and letters in Alice's datebook . . . it's code for Hawkins's address," I tell him. "I pieced it together after I saw this business card. This card that was in *your* pocket."

"I told you." Dalton's hands move to my shoulders. There's a pleading look in his eyes. "I don't know how it got there."

"I went to visit Hawkins today," I blurt out.

Dalton's brows pinch together and the muscle in his jaw twitches. The change in his expression makes me cringe.

"You went alone?" he says as he bends closer. "Why would you do that?"

The tips of his fingers tense on my shoulders. I know he's upset, but his hands feel too much like Hawkins's grip. I back away, putting some distance between us.

"Did he . . . touch you?"

I look at him skeptically. "Why would that be the first thing you ask me?"

Dalton shakes his head, but his eyes bore deeply into mine. "Because he's slimy. And I know how men in this business act toward women. I wouldn't put it past him."

"No, he didn't," I say. "Well, he hugged me, but only because he thought I was Alice—and then he . . . never mind. I handled it. I was fine."

Dalton's gaze darkens. He looks away toward the empty projector screen. "I'm sorry. I'm still trying to wrap my head around the fact that you went to see him—alone." He pauses for a moment and shakes his head again as if he's trying to rid himself of the image of me and Hawkins alone in his office.

I reach for his arm. "I don't know how that card got into your pocket, but I believe you. Hawkins is an awful man. He has photos."

Dalton stiffens. "What kind of photos?"

Heat creeps up the back of my neck. "Seductive photos. Nudes." I watch the expression in Dalton's eyes turn grim. He opens his mouth, but no sound comes out. "He has boxes full of them," I say. "All of actresses, some underage. He's working with someone here at the studio, sending girls, casting them. And he . . ." Dalton's workspace suddenly feels as claustrophobic as Hawkins's office. My forehead and upper lip bead with perspiration, and my limbs feel heavy even as I'm held in Dalton's arms.

Dalton begins to gently rub my back. "It's all right, Grace. He what?"

Breathing in through my nose, I let the air out of my mouth. "He threatened me. He said Alice disappeared once before—that it can happen again. I know he tried to do something to her, and Eleanor's picture is in a file on his desk, and now she's missing."

I pause to catch my breath. "Those blank pages in Alice's datebook . . . I think she may have met with Hawkins—or *someone*—on those dates." I hesitate, then add, "Could we speak to your uncle? I have a bad feeling about this."

Dalton nods. He offers a weak smile, but it looks forced, and I know he's still seething over the danger I put myself in. "I'll call my uncle today. We'll get to the bottom of this, I promise." He looks at the business card I hold out to him and takes it. "And I want you to believe me. I swear I didn't know this was in my pocket."

I bob my head up and down, reassuring him I believe that he's telling me the truth.

Eager to distract myself from what just happened, I motion toward the stack of scripts on the table. The pile is much higher than the last time I was here, reminding me I've interrupted his work. "Looks like you've got your work cut out for you."

"Yeah, they've got me pretty busy since the film wrapped." He nods, but I don't miss how his shoulders slouch at the work I'm keeping him from. "Actually, about that . . . I may have to work well into the night, so I think I should head home to sleep. That is, if you think you'll be all right without me bunking on your couch tonight?"

My stomach sinks as I untangle myself from Dalton's arms. Hawkins's threat over my knowledge of his very serious crimes feels like a hand wrapped around my throat, and Dalton won't stay with me tonight.

"Isn't there any way you can leave early? I really don't want to be alone tonight, Dalton. I don't think I can, not after everything that's happened."

"I don't know what time I'll get out of here, and it might not look good for me to let myself into your room in the middle of the night. This town's got eyes."

His words mirror Judy's earlier.

I nod that it's fine, only because the look on his face tells me he's sincerely sorry about it. But it doesn't help my nerves. After all that's happened, today and the other days before this, it's Dalton's presence that chases away my fear. I'm disappointed that when I need him most, he leaves me on my own.

"I'm sorry," he says as he threads a new reel of film onto the projector wheel.

"No, it's fine." I handled Hawkins earlier—barely. I can handle being alone tonight.

I inch my way toward the door, but my heart wants to stay. Everything makes sense when I'm with Dalton. But even I have to admit that his behavior feels strange. After learning that Hawkins relies on someone here to funnel his "talent" to . . . After learning he gave Dalton his business card for that very purpose, shouldn't he be more upset, more concerned about me?

A shiver tears down my spine. I watch Dalton, his back turned to me, busy setting up the projector, and wonder, despite his words and kisses, how deep his loyalty to me lies. I wonder if he's even considering asking his uncle to help me or if it's a fake promise.

"New shipment?" I motion toward the open crate of sound props next to the door.

He turns around with what I believe is a look of surprise registering across his features that I'm still here. His expression brightens slightly. "Mack fulfilled my purchase order. Lots of new props to play with."

I peer inside, halfheartedly marveling at all the junk he gets paid to play with. Just beneath the wooden sound props and men's size-eleven shoes is a hint of sparkle. I reach for it and pull the object free. An uneasy feeling trails across my entire body.

I look up, speechless, but Dalton hasn't noticed. He's gone back to his work. I lift the headband, fashioned to look like a tiny tiara. Traces of sticky mud are encrusted around a few of the rhinestones.

"Really, I can come over tonight. I'll get what needs to be done out of the way."

His voice startles me, causing me to drop the tiara back into the crate.

"You shouldn't be alone, Grace."

I edge my way toward the door. Slowly. I want to run, but I don't want him to see how my nerves have become so frayed that I can't stay in this room any longer. "It's okay. Get your work done." I nod adamantly, plastering a smile on my face.

I can't get out of the sound room fast enough. The man inside has suddenly become a stranger as I process what lies in the crate.

Because I'd recognize this headband anywhere. It is identical to the one Eleanor wears at every rehearsal.

The one she refuses to let go of.

CHAPTER TWENTY-SIX

I PULL THE SOUND-ROOM DOOR shut behind me and lean against the wall, my heart hammering against my ribs, my lungs trying to find air. I should have asked who delivered the new shipment of Dalton's props, but something inside me didn't want to draw attention to it.

Why? Why does Dalton have it? Why did he act so strangely just now?

Eleanor was the only extra assigned to wear that silly tiara. It's a costume, not a prop. And she never lets it out of her sight. Even rationalizing that Eleanor returned it with her costume, that it got placed in the wrong box, doesn't sit well with me because I know how much she loves that stupid tiara. In my gut, I know that something terrible has happened to Eleanor. And threatening to rear its ugly head is the idea that Dalton might know exactly what that is.

I push myself off the wall and rush down the stairs toward the casting office to ask for Eleanor's address. There is no sense in waiting around the studio to see if she shows up. Just like my decision to go to Hawkins's office, I am prepared to take matters into my own hands. To do this alone, especially now that I don't trust Dalton.

"Alice, darling!" Isadora, the woman who'd introduced me to Joan Crawford during the cocktail party the other night, stops short of being trampled on the steps and looks up at me. "Funny running into you here. I'm on my way to grab Geoffrey for dinner." The name rings a bell, and I scramble to attach a face to it as she takes another step up to join me. Yes, Geoffrey, her husband. My manager, although I've barely seen him since the party at the hotel. "That man has been spending too much time cooped up in his office. It's time he and I go out on the town for a drink!"

"How are you?" I ask, steadying my voice so it isn't strained. I hope she doesn't spend a long time answering me. I need to get Eleanor's address before the office closes for the day.

Isadora waves her hand, her jeweled rings sparkling beneath the fluorescent lights. "Oh, just fabulous!" she croons. "Although I admit I'm a little bored. Thank goodness Mack has invited everyone to his home for his party tomorrow. I've been counting the days for the film to wrap so I can catch up on my gossip."

For as many times as I've looked in Alice's datebook, I've forgotten about the party. Judy told me it will be at Mr. Flynn's home—a stately mansion in Hollywood Hills. I could ask Isadora about Alice—or Eleanor? But asking her feels awkward. I doubt she'd know anything about Eleanor, who, with a tiny role in the film, probably isn't even on her radar. Besides, it will likely be turned around and blabbed to someone else. And I want real answers, not rumors.

I restlessly tap my fingers on the railing.

Isadora's gaze sweeps over me. "Goodness, are you in a hurry?"

"Sorry," I apologize, giving her a forced smile. "I want to get downstairs to the casting office before it closes."

"Well, I'm afraid you're too late. Those ladies like to leave as soon as the studio packs up for the day. If it's something important, then why don't you just ask Geoffrey? Those old birds downstairs are so scatterbrained." Isadora links her arm in mine as if I've agreed to go along with her to the executive suite upstairs.

I give her a little tug and stop her. "I'm actually looking for the address of a girl I've become friends with on set."

Isadora purses her lips. "Well then, I suppose you'll have to take your chances with those hens in the office tomorrow." Then her face lights up with an unusual warmth, and she cups my chin, turning it left and right as if inspecting me. "Such a pretty face—so youthful! My Geoffrey was right about you," she says. "Why, I must admit, when he showed me your screen test stills, I wasn't sure you'd make it, but I was wrong about you. You have all the makings of a star."

"My screen test stills?" Sweat beads along my back. I know the difference between screen stills and what Hawkins has in his files, but the mere mention of photographs sets me on edge.

"Oh, yes." Isadora reaches down and plucks an invisible speck of lint off her black pant leg. "The photos from your first on-screen test."

"I didn't realize you saw them." I force my heart to stop racing. As long as those other photos don't fall into the hands of anyone as loose-lipped as Isadora, I'll be fine.

"Why, of course I have." She smiles, her red lips parting to reveal a mouthful of white teeth. "I make Geoffrey's business *my* business."

I feel the tug to get downstairs to the office as if it's physically yanking on my arm, but I can't pass up the opportunity Isadora has just presented me. "You know, I never had the chance to see my own screen test," I say seriously, with a hint of regret. "Even if I only see the stills you've just mentioned, I'd be so grateful."

Isadora's face lights up at my request. "Why of course, dear. If I remember correctly, they're stored in the file room in the costume warehouse on Lot C." She pauses to shake her head, causing her short black bob to swing from side to side. "I know, I know . . . it's a ridiculous place to keep them when they could easily be filed away here in the main building. Geoffrey's always complaining about the lack of storage space and had them moved until he can find a better place. There's a little room in the back, just behind the evening-gown aisle." She leans closer as if telling a secret. "My favorite part of the whole studio if you ask me. Anyway, I think you'll find what you're looking for there."

The entry in the datebook flashes in my head. Lot C, room 4. It's where Alice and Eleanor have speech lessons and had their screen tests. Only Judy hasn't scheduled more lessons for Alice since I got here so I've never had the chance to go.

I take a moment to wonder if that room is anywhere near where Isadora is sending me, and even though she's explained the need for storage space, it doesn't make sense for it to be tucked behind rows and rows of costumes. I swallow the terrible taste that suddenly coats my mouth.

"Isadora?" I ask just as she's reached the landing, about to disappear from my sight. "Have you heard anything about a girl named Eleanor? She didn't show up for the last set take today."

Isadora's lips spread into a frown. "Of course I did. In fact, I'm dropping in on Mr. Banks now. I want to suggest that he finds a voice-over for that girl's part," she huffs. "That accent of hers makes my hair stand on end." She reaches up and smooths her jet-black hair with her hand. "I slipped Mr. Hawkins's card to Mr. Banks, but he never called."

"You . . . Did you put it in his coat pocket?"

Isadora cocks her head. "Why yes, dear. I didn't want it to get lost in that mess he calls a studio. Hawkins will find a suitable replacement, I'm sure."

Of course he will. I cringe.

My chest feels like a balloon that has held a year's worth of air. Isadora gave Dalton the card! But it doesn't explain how Eleanor's tiara got into his props—or why it's caked in mud. It doesn't explain Dalton's sudden mood change or the feeling deep in my gut—the one that warns me Dalton is hiding something, that maybe he knows Hawkins better than he's letting on. If Hawkins already asked Dalton to scout for prospects and there's someone here at the studio helping him . . . Oh God, I feel sick.

I should have known better than to place my trust in Dalton. I was desperate, and now he knows too much. He knows nearly everything. What are the chances he won't tell Hawkins? I was stupid, stupid, stupid . . . thinking someone here could help me find my way home, could help me find out what happened to Alice. I may have trusted the one person with a connection to the man who's committed a crime against her.

And to make matters worse, my feelings for Dalton have been building. I even believed he felt the same for me.

By the time I reach the costume warehouse, my heart is in shreds. My mascara is running down my face, blurring my sight so much that I've barely noticed how dark the surrounding lot is. Only a few lights are lit as the workers clean up sets and put equipment away. The distant sound of a hammer echoes across the yard; most likely a worker putting the last touches on something for tomorrow.

A creepy-crawly feeling snakes up my arms, snapping me out of my sorrow, putting my senses on high alert. I whip my head around to see if I can make out anyone in the distance but there is no one. I grab the door handle of the costume warehouse. It doesn't budge. I yank again, but it's useless. The door is locked.

Something sizzles behind me. I turn to see sparks raining on the ground from a tall light. There is a loud pop as the bulb blows out, and the lot is shrouded in sudden darkness. With a pounding heart, I give up on my plan to find the room Isadora told me about and hurry to the brightest area of the lot several feet away. My own footsteps echo, playing with my head, making it seem that someone is tracking me from behind. Finally, at the main gate—and relieved that some lights are still lit in the main building—I look behind me.

A figure seemingly turns toward me, not far from the fence line. I cannot tell if it's a man or a woman, nor can I see their eyes, but they are perfectly still, staring at me.

I run the rest of the way to the street just in time for a yellow checkered cab to stop at the red traffic light. I rap on the window with such force the driver almost spills his coffee.

"Can you take me to the Chateau Marmont?" I ask in a panic. Before he answers, I am already inside the cab, closing the door behind me, staring out the window into the darkened studio lot. There's nothing but darkness now.

CHAPTER TWENTY-SEVEN

MY TRUST IN DALTON IS on shaky ground. I don't know what to think. But still I wait for him to change his mind and call, to tell me he's finished working and is on his way to the hotel. When he does, I'll figure out what to say, how to act around him. Maybe I won't let on that he's high on my suspicion list right now.

But he never calls.

The phone rings several times and each time I lift the receiver to my ear there is silence, a bit of breath. Instead of giving in to the fear I felt the night the first call came, I remain strong. I don't cower. The mystery person on the other end could be anyone, even Hawkins, even Dalton this entire time.

I finally fall asleep with the phone off the hook, putting a stop to the caller's attempts to unnerve me.

The next morning, the costume warehouse is still empty and dark when I arrive at the studio. I've purposely come early to avoid the crowds on the lot, hoping someone will have opened it in preparation for the day. The film I have been working on is wrapped, but there are others still in production that require access to this building.

To my relief the door opens, and I slip inside undetected. I don't dare turn on the lights. I don't want anyone to know I am here and ask why I want to root through the studio's files. I want to get my hands on any photos the studio has of Alice. I want to see if any are like what I found in Hawkins's office and remove them. It might protect Alice when she comes back—if she comes back. If I can't trust Dalton right now, then chances are his promise to ask his uncle to help me was a lie this entire time. There won't be any justice for those women, those girls in the photos, and so I must do what I can to protect Alice.

I make my way toward the back using my memory as a guide. When I first followed Judy through this costumed labyrinth, I was amazed. Now, it's as if the costumes whisper to me as I sneak past them, telling me I will soon stumble upon the secrets they've been hiding.

I reach the last aisle. It's even darker here than up front, and I feel with my hands as I walk along the rows. My fingertips touch the tagged gowns hanging in hushed shadows. I picture the gray dress I chose for the photo shoot and imagine the little tag dangling from its neckline.

Behind a rack of long, scratchy coats there is a door. The knob turns easily when I try it, and I slip inside, feeling for a switch along the wall. A sizzling noise comes from overhead and then the bulb flickers to life, illuminating the room in a sickly yellow glow.

Cardboard file boxes are stacked from floor to ceiling, each marked by year on large, square labels. I lean closer to one, straining to read the date written in faded pencil. It's marked 1931. Looking around, I'm not convinced this is the sort of room anyone goes to for speech lessons. The rest of the boxes are marked by year but also with an actor's name next to it. I lift a dusty lid and peer inside, finding black-and-white photographs of those who starred in earlier movies here at the studio.

The dust tickles my nose, but I keep at it, looking past the boxes to the filing cabinets lining the opposite wall. I yank a drawer open. Inside are files of nearly every actor and crew hand recently and currently employed by the studio. I work my way through them, searching frantically, until my hand stops on a file marked ALICE MONTGOMERY. I pull it out and settle myself on top of a box to read through it.

Inside is a signed three-year contract with Flynn Studios. The other papers don't make much sense to me—they are a jumble of legal documents about clauses and sub-rights. Photographs are clipped together, mostly headshots and a few on-set images taken with a Polaroid, including one startlingly similar to the photograph Ryan has in his room. Others are like the ones in Hawkins's office. Alice's bare skin is luminous beneath the yellow light in the cramped storeroom. I grab each photo that could cause her harm and quickly stash them in the waistband of my skirt.

The very last paper in the pile causes me to do a double take. It's another studio agreement. The addendum states that a "Bernice Brighton, so long as employed by Flynn Studios, and for subsequent publicity hereafter, is to assume the name Alice Montgomery."

I read it again. Bernice Brighton. Alice and I share the same last name. My entire body is shaking. This can't be coincidence; Alice is related to me somehow. Our resemblance now makes perfect sense. I flip back through the pile of papers so quickly it's a wonder I don't rip any. The name is on another one I missed. My heart pounds.

Deep inside the warehouse a door scrapes open, and the lights flick on. Two voices pierce the quiet, echoing throughout the cavernous space. There is a scramble of movement edging closer and a whimper, followed by a full-fledged sob. I spring to my feet and quickly switch off the light, pressing my hand to the door. The racing of my heart feels too quick—sounds too loud—inside me. It's too late to shut the door completely. Whoever is here has already made their way to the back and is standing close by. Yellow light spills through the crack of the door as I peek through, hoping they don't see me.

"I put it right where you asked me to!" a young woman sobs, her cheeks ruddy and tear-stained, her hands clinging to a shredded tissue.

It's too dark to see who is with her, and I've missed what the other person said to make her so upset. A feminine arm sweeps across a shelf full of costume accessories, sending them flying into the air. A horrible clatter fills the room and the young woman recoils.

"I swear, I did," the young woman cries. I don't know her name, but I've seen her around the set from time to time. She cradles her face in her hands and sobs louder.

"Well, it's not there!" The other voice rises over the woman's sniffles.

I freeze and press my palm to my mouth. I'd know that voice anywhere. It's Judy.

I crane my neck to see more, when my elbow jabs a stack of boxes. I scramble to right the top box just in time before it crashes to the floor. My pulse races with fear as the voices grow quiet.

From another direction in the warehouse a door squeaks open, and soon the sound of heavy shoes on the tile floor grows closer.

"What's all this?" Mack Flynn steps around the racks into the light. I can see him from my angle behind the door and it's obvious he's annoyed. "Run along now," he tells the sobbing woman. "I'm sure the belongings were just misplaced."

Still distraught, she sniffles a thank-you and scurries away.

Mack lets out a deep, impatient sigh and toys with something I can't see. "This is twice this week you've allowed yourself to lose your temper over something trivial, Judith. Don't you think you were a tad harsh on the poor woman?"

"But she . . ." Judy's mouth clamps shut as Mack holds up a big, meaty hand.

"I don't want to hear any more of it," he says.

From my vantage point, I can almost hear the gnashing of her teeth as she forces a sweet, conciliatory smile.

"You need to get a grip on yourself," Mack says in an urgent tone. "Ever since Alice came back you've been losing it around too many people and I won't allow any of this to continue."

Judy has stepped closer so that I can now see her. She looks away, as if avoiding Mack's cold stare, and her gaze settles on my hiding spot.

I don't think she's seen me, but I inch away from the door, my heart pounding.

"You're right," Judy agrees with a sigh. "It won't happen again."

I peek again just as Mack pats her on the back.

"That's my girl." He smiles. "Now, Hawkins has a new batch of prospects for me. Let me finish what I'm doing, and I'll meet you in my office later to discuss things."

My heart leaps to my throat. They are in on this? I had considered telling him what Hawkins has been doing, that it's criminal and will eventually soil the name of his studio. Now it looks like he's well aware and doesn't care whether it's criminal or immoral. I can hear him smile and say, "Boys will be boys." And Judy? Is she a willing bystander?

Sweat breaks out across my skin and trickles down my back.

Judy gives a terse nod, her expression unreadable, and heads down the long aisle toward the exit. My entire body shudders with relief, but Mack is still in the building. I watch as he retreats to a door I hadn't noticed before. Inching out, I follow quietly and hide behind a large crate.

Mack opens the door, revealing a long couch covered in red velvet. The lighting in the small room is dim, not fluorescent like the rest of the warehouse. But what gives me pause is the familiarity of it. It's the same background as the photos in Hawkins's office.

"Now, my dear, where were we?" Mack purrs. His voice has taken on a much deeper, huskier tone than when he spoke to Judy. "Ah yes. You were about to let me get to know you better." He loosens his tie. "Why don't we start off with you telling me how much you'd like this role?"

I crane my neck to see who Mack is talking to. Just as he closes the door, a young woman, barely this side of twenty, steps into view. She readjusts her dress and quickens her steps toward the door as if she wants to leave. I glimpse the fear in her eyes just as Mack steps in front of her and pushes the door closed. The sickening sound of it locking soon follows.

The number on the door is four. Speech therapy lessons, my ass.

The woman's scared expression is still in my head. Hawkins told me that Alice had bypassed the process—that she'd been hired "the right way"—even after posing in the nude. If he meant she bypassed the casting couch, then she was lucky, because if I think about it too long, it's *her* terrified face on the other side of the door I'm staring at.

I hope Judy isn't aware of what Mack is doing right now. That she would not play along. That she believes the new prospects Mack spoke of are women auditioning the right way.

Sick to my stomach, I scurry back to the file room. I have to find Eleanor's address. I need to warn her to stay away from these people. It's bad enough Eleanor posed for those photos, but if the next step is to "audition" for Mack, then she needs to know she's better than this—that she'll find another studio, another opportunity that won't take advantage of her.

As I search for Eleanor's file, I can't stop thinking about the exchange between Judy and that woman. What does my showing up have to do with Judy's temper? Even with Alice disappearing for days and causing the studio lost time, Judy's never snapped at me like that. If she's on edge about it, she's kept it to herself around me. And actually, the only time I've seen her stressed was the day Eleanor talked to Hawkins and the day the director told us Eleanor hadn't shown up for her dress rehearsal.

I open the filing cabinet and tear through the rest of the folders. There it is. Eleanor Dunn. I open the file. Eleanor's photograph is tacked to the first page. I flip the paper and find her address, then fold the paper until it's a small square I can hide in my hand. Then I tiptoe out of the closet.

Door number four is still closed when I slip out. The urge to kick it open and help the poor girl behind it is overwhelming. But I can't be caught. Not until I find Eleanor and warn her. Not while Alice is still out there somewhere and finding her might help me get decades away from here.

I hurry down the aisle and leave the costume warehouse, taking the shortest route possible toward the front gate. I still have enough of Alice's money for a bus to take me to Eleanor's house.

I hope she's there.

CHAPTER TWENTY-EIGHT

THE BUS LETS ME OFF at the corner of South Eleventh and Eighty-Eighth in the Morningside neighborhood of Inglewood. I've never ventured this far south before and hastily walk up the street, counting the house numbers. Eleanor's house is a tiny thing. Its weathered white paint has long since chipped away in the California heat, and one of its shutters hangs loose on rusted hinges. Limp petunias grow in a patch near the steps, their exposed roots dry with thirst.

I walk up the narrow path toward the entry, dodging the long, scraggly cracks in the concrete. A yellow paper that reads RENT PAST DUE clings to the door. It was dated two days ago. A nervous tremor is growing in my stomach. Hasn't Eleanor seen the notice? Or has she ignored it?

I pull at the outer screen door, the notice fluttering, and knock twice. Silence.

I try the doorknob, but it's locked.

Back in the trailer, Marlene told me another girl, Peggy, had stopped by. She must have found a way inside since she reported that Eleanor's belongings were still there. I step away from the door and lean over a spindly shrub to peer into a window. The room inside looks dark.

Somewhere, a lawn mower buzzes. A dog barks in the distance. But otherwise, the street seems quiet and vacant. I bite my lower lip, then walk around to the back of the house. Dry laundry hangs stiffly on the line in the yard. A metal garbage can lies tipped on its side, lunch-meat wrapping and an empty egg carton spilled out onto the grass.

The back door looks as neglected as the front. "Eleanor?" I call out, knocking on it. "Are you in there?"

Again, nothing but silence. I try the latch. The door pushes open.

"Eleanor? It's me, Alice." I step into the dim, yellow kitchen. As pitiful as the outside of the house looks, the inside appears tidy. The dishes have been washed and stacked alongside the sink on the counter. A dish towel is folded neatly beside them. A purse sits next to it. A single house key rests on the counter. I shove aside the image of Alice's discarded purse in the hotel room and hope that seeing Eleanor's means she's home. But she hasn't answered my knocks or when I called out to her.

"Eleanor?"

I look around, puzzled. A small slip of paper is taped to the refrigerator, a grocery list written in pencil: eggs, milk, bologna. And next to it, a photo of Eleanor with a couple of girls, friends, or sisters perhaps, since their features are similar. Eleanor never mentioned she had siblings. Her lips are open in a wide smile and her eyes look back at me with their usual gleam—happy and a bit mischievous.

I turn away from the picture and step into the small living room. The sofa has a worn look about it but is pretty in a comfortable sort of way, with large roses printed across the fabric and a pink oval pillow propped in its center. Otherwise, the room is dark and empty. I call out again, projecting my voice up the narrow stairs on the far side of the room. "Eleanor?" Each step creaks as I make my way to the landing at the top. "I'm sorry to barge in on you like this, but I've been worried."

There are only two rooms on the second floor. I open the first door. Blue porcelain-tile walls. White tub. Tiny sink. The door to the other room is closed. It has to be her bedroom. I creep closer just in case Eleanor is sick and taking a nap. "Eleanor?" I whisper softly, rapping my knuckles on the door. "Are you in there?" I take a deep breath and open the door.

Unlike the rest of the tidy house, Eleanor's bedroom is in shambles. Clothes litter the floor. The bed is unmade, the pink sheets haphazardly strewn across it as if they've won the fight against being tucked into place. As I look around the room my heart sinks. She isn't here.

Something is wrong. I look at the bed, wondering if Eleanor has even slept in it. It looks like she has, but the sheets are mussed in such a way that it makes me think she got up in a hurry.

Just like Alice, something or someone forced her to rush off, leaving everything behind.

CHAPTER TWENTY-NINE

SINCE RETURNING ON THE BUS from Eleanor's house, I can't shake the feeling that something has happened to her—just as it had to Alice. They've both vanished in ways that are too similar to believe they aren't connected, leaving me with an eerie, unsettled feeling.

I hurry past the workers dismantling sets. Ever since paying a visit to Hawkins and battling my growing suspicion toward Dalton, everyone I pass is suspect.

I feel their eyes on me as I wonder which of them knows what Mack does in that back room on Lot C. How many of these men who work tirelessly in the heat, building and tearing down sets for just a scene or two, know what Hawkins really does. What kind of man he is.

By the time I round the corner to where the trailers are parked, my unease turns into panic. I only have a day, two at most, to collect my belongings and vacate the trailer before it's assigned to someone else. I wonder how long I can stay at the Chateau Marmont before the studio's generosity runs out.

I try to calm myself down over what's to become of me and unlock the trailer door in such a hurry, I bump into the chair Dalton's coat is draped over, sending it to the floor. I bend down for it, when suddenly I realize something is hidden beneath the chair. It's a pair of men's shoes that look as if they belong with the coat. But I'm sure they aren't Dalton's . . . I've only borrowed the coat, and none of Judy's crew ever left their belongings behind after helping me get ready.

Looking closer I can see there is muck encrusted on the soles. It reminds me of the sealant my dad used to coat the driveway with every summer. It's puzzling for sure, but obviously, someone must have let themselves into the trailer in preparation for the next occupant.

I hurry across the room to the closet to clear it of Alice's belongings. I'll take everything back to the hotel to wait for her to claim them. If she ever comes back. But my mind won't let go of the shoes beneath the chair, how the mud on them is so much like what's caked between the gems of the tiara Eleanor loves so much. That tiara was in Dalton's prop bin. These shoes are near his coat. If anything is going to convince me not to trust Dalton right now, it's what I've found today.

Until I can figure out why the shoes are here, if they indeed belong to the one man I thought I could trust, I want to make sure they don't disappear on me. I grab a black sweater from a hanger and quickly retrieve them from beneath the chair, wrapping the sweater tightly around them. On tiptoe, I reach for the high shelf above the rack of clothes and shove the bulky bundle as far back as it will go. It hits something. My fingers feel around but it's too high, so I grab the stool from the makeup table and climb onto it, staring at the back of the closet. There is a box.

Afraid of losing my balance, I hold the box tightly and climb back down. Inside are papers and newspaper clippings. I scan a newspaper article lying on the top of the pile and instantly my entire body begins to shake. It's a police report about a young man who was in a car accident. *Wesley Brighton, aged eighteen, suffered multiple injuries . . . lost control of the car . . . Mulholland Drive.* I can barely contain the pounding of my heart as I read on. *Taken by ambulance to St. Vincent Hospital . . . remains in critical condition.*

And then it is as if all the air in the room has been sucked out, leaving me without oxygen. The name Brighton. The details of this man's accident eerily parallel Ryan's.

The room spins as I hastily scan the other slips of paper and find an obituary notice.

Wesley Brighton of 3294 Mulholland Drive, Los Angeles, CA. The only words I can see clearly enough through my tears are *short coma* and *succumbed to injuries.*

And . . . Oh my God. I have an address.

I grab the phone and dial zero.

"How may I direct your call?" the operator asks.

My heart is pounding with such fierceness, I barely get the words out. "Brighton residence. 3294 Mulholland Drive, Los Angeles." The seconds tick by like eons as I wait for the response at the other end of the line; my heart full of hope that someone still lives there. That Alice didn't disappear at all—that she went home.

"Would you like me to connect you?" The voice over the phone is suddenly a lifeline. I instantly reply, "Yes."

There is a click. A long pause. Suddenly the phone rings. And rings. And . . .

A man's voice says, "Hello?"

"Yes, hi . . . um . . . Is this the Brighton residence?" My heart is in my throat as I wonder if this man could be Alice's father. Who might he be in my own family tree? For a heartbeat, I realize I might not be alone after all. That down the line, this man who's answered the phone is a relation of mine.

"I'm sorry. They no longer live here."

A crushing weight slams into me, leaving me without words to respond back.

"Hello?" the man asks. "Are you there?"

"I . . . yes, I'm still here."

The man is silent on the other end of the line, waiting for me to speak, but I can't.

"The Brightons used to live here, but that was a while back. I wish I could pass along how to get in touch with them, but . . . well, I'm sorry."

I finally find my voice, although it's trembling, but it's enough to mutter, "I'm sorry to have bothered you."

I hang up the phone, on the brink of caving to the heartache swelling in my chest, but I force myself to remain strong. The Brightons are gone. Alice is gone. Wesley isn't Ryan. I repeat it over and over in my head until I believe that history isn't going to repeat itself, and I lock away my anticipated grief.

I steel myself and reach for the small envelope lying at the bottom of the box. Out slides a tiny gold charm in the shape of a heart, the tag from the St. Vincent Hospital gift shop still attached along with a handwritten note:

Your brother asked me to buy this for him at the hospital's gift shop a few days ago. I am so sorry for your loss.

It's signed by the nursing staff.

I don't remember ever seeing this charm on my bracelet when I was young. With trembling fingers, I clip the charm onto my bracelet with the others. The bracelet must have been from Alice's brother and this little charm is possibly the last gift he gave her. Alice must not have been able to handle putting it on because her brother was . . .

I swipe the tears away with my hand and steady myself. Home feels so far away now. I'm not sure how much longer I can stand being here. I can't bear it if what happened to Wesley happens to Ryan too. I have to make sure it won't. I shove the box back onto the shelf in the closet and turn for the door.

The knock startles me. And when a second knock comes, just as forceful, I back away slowly. A slip of paper emerges beneath the door just as an unfamiliar voice calls out, "Miss Montgomery. There's a message for you."

Moments later the sound of footsteps outside tells me the deliverer has left. I pick up the folded paper: a note from Dalton, asking me to meet him later.

I want to know why Dalton had to ask someone else to deliver the note. What's he busying himself with? And if it's something that might point to where Eleanor has gone, and Alice too.

CHAPTER THIRTY

"HELLO?" I CALL OUT INTO the dark room. "Dalton?"

No one answers. A forlorn feeling trails its way along my skin, reminding me of calling out into Eleanor's empty house. The message slipped beneath my door said to meet Dalton on Lot B, a set recently used to film a restaurant scene. It's scheduled to be dismantled, but for now it still mimics an exclusive restaurant in town called Musso and Frank's.

From what I hear, it's a startlingly accurate resemblance, right down to the leather booths and the mahogany bar fully equipped with rows of glasses and bottles.

It seems an odd place to meet—remote and scheduled for demolition. Just a day ago, if Dalton had found out something about Alice or Eleanor, or even Hawkins, he could have come to me in person. But this . . . the note under my door, the strange meeting place . . . only raises my suspicions about him. Or worse. Maybe Dalton hasn't sent that note at all.

I edge my way onto the darkened set past crates and piles of lumber. A pale light illuminates a long counter where shadows dance between the bottles lined on a shelf behind it. I inch my way toward it, grab one of the bottles, and grip it tightly in my hand, just in case. Around the corner there is a table with a flickering candle in its center.

Footsteps sound from behind me. I raise the bottle over my head and spin around.

"Whoa!" Dalton jumps back, his eyes wide.

Trembling from head to toe as angry tears spring to my eyes, I sweep my gaze over Dalton's face. If there's so much as a touch of malice in his expression, I'll hit him with the bottle and then run out of here as fast as I can.

"I'm sorry. I thought you heard me." He backs away, eyeing my death grip around the neck of the bottle. He lets out an uncomfortable chuckle. "So, you're a bourbon gal, are you?"

I have no choice but to lower my arm, the weight of the liquid pulling it down, but I don't let him take the bottle from my shaking hand. "Never tried it." I watch the shadows play across his face, how he appears confused that I didn't warm to his comment, that I'm not showing relief that it's him and not someone else trying to sneak up on me.

"I'm glad you came," he says with a strained smile. "I had some last-minute things to do so I asked one of the guys from the Grip department to slip a note under your door."

I allow my shoulders to relax, but only for his sake. Inside I'm still wound tight. After everything that has happened, it's no wonder I am on edge all the time. But I think it's wise I don't let Dalton see that right now. It pains me that I no longer trust him, but maybe the best thing to do is to not show it. Stay friendly with him . . . and hope he slips and reveals something about his involvement with Hawkins. With Alice . . . and Eleanor.

"Why are we here?" I ask.

"Let me show you." He peels my grip from the bourbon and sets it on the bar before extending his arm toward the table waiting for us in candle glow. "Shall we?"

I slide onto the seat of the leather booth, which curves around the moon of a white tablecloth. A frosted hurricane lamp glows in the center of the table, sending dancing shimmers of fairy light across the silverware. Dalton situates himself beside me, but he seems off, like something is preoccupying his thoughts. Each time he catches me watching him, he only gives a half smile. Nothing like the Dalton I knew before would do. He leans against the brown leather and stretches his arms across the back as a waiter in a red jacket and bow tie walks out of the shadows. I jump at the sight of him, then recognize him as one of the set crew. He winks at me as he pours champagne into two glasses.

"What is all this?" I stare at the bubbles fizzing in the glasses.

"It's a celebration," Dalton says with a hint of caution. "You've wrapped up your first film. Congrats." Dalton lifts his glass and holds it aloft for me to clink it with mine. "And I wanted to take you someplace nice, only I can't afford the real deal." He takes a sip and looks at me over the rim, his eyes apologetic. I wonder what else he's sorry for.

"It's really sweet that you've arranged all of this," I say tightly. By the time I talk myself into acting more normal, the waiter returns, setting a basket of dinner rolls between us. I wait until Dalton takes one before I reach across and take one for myself. I try to relax against the smooth leather, but I can't stifle the jittery feeling inside me. My stomach is doing somersaults. The tiara, the mud, Eleanor chasing after her feelings—it's as if they are all on a film reel on Dalton's projector spinning around and around, making me dizzy. The tiara was found among his things. Dirty shoes that might fit him were in my trailer. How can I act normally around him if all I can think of is, he might know what's happened to Eleanor? Or worse—be responsible for it.

"Well, you deserve it after all you've been through." He swallows another sip of champagne.

It would be easy to become mesmerized by the candlelight reflecting in Dalton's blue eyes, how it makes his dark hair look sleek and inviting. If I didn't already know he was a Foley artist I would say he could pass for a leading man in one of Mack's films. But I also know not to be so enamored with his looks. I'm not going to fall into that trap.

Still, I have to act appreciative of what he's pulled together here tonight. I can't let him know I suspect anything, at least not until I need to use it against him.

"Hey, are you okay?" I tilt my head, trying to gauge why he's so quiet.

As if suddenly realizing what I've just asked, Dalton gives a tepid smile. "Yeah, I think work is catching up to me."

"Right, you said Mack has been making you work long hours," I say, but I'm not fully convinced that his work has been entirely confined to the sound room.

"The crew did a great job recreating the dining room." I motion around us. "It looks like the real deal."

"Except we're one of the A-listers dining tonight," he says, a smile now pulling at the corners of his lips.

"Oh, well back home, anyone can eat at Musso's. Appearance-wise, it hasn't changed in fifty years, but it's no longer exclusive."

It could be a trick of the candlelight, but I swear I see Dalton's face fall, as if I've stolen his attempt to create something special for us here tonight. Regardless, he raises his glass at my remark and takes another sip. "Just imagine. Mary Pickford, Rudy Valentino, Douglas Fairbanks. You can practically picture them all gussied up, discussing scripts over those famous Musso martinis." He reaches across and plucks another dinner roll from the basket. "And soon, *your* big debut is coming up."

"It is. The premiere is in a few months." I fidget.

"You've got nothing to be nervous about, doll. You're gonna wow them."

I bristle at the way he calls me doll. It's no longer endearing to me but rather presumptuous and creepy. It reminds me of Hawkins calling me honey. "No, I'm not," I reply. "Alice is the star. I'm only filling in."

Out of the blue, his fingers find mine, sending a warning to my head, making me want to pull away. "Who did all the acting these last few days?" He leans closer, his eyebrows shooting up with emphatic urging. "Alice may have worked on the first three-quarters of the film, but you picked up the pieces after she disappeared. It was Grace Brighton . . . a quiet twenty-first-century woman from the future who showed up for takes at the crack of dawn nearly each day, reciting lines, enduring long, grueling hours on set." Dalton points his roll at me. "You, not Alice, stood out in the rain on Thursday and never complained while the crew handled the faulty equipment."

I nod slowly, tracking how closely he's sitting next to me, how he keeps leaning in.

"And . . . may I remind you of the number of takes you've put up with kissing the one man in all of Hollywood nearly every woman who meets him falls in love with."

"I didn't think you saw the last scene. I didn't see you."

"I wanted to be there, but Mack had me working on organizing all the sound for the film." Dalton picks up his knife and I can't help the involuntary flinch. But he's only playing with it, keeping his hands busy, and sets it back down. "I was able to see the reel after they sent it over. In fact, *Among the Stars* is my top priority right now. It's been pushed to the top of the pile, so I get to see all your steamy scenes with Mr. Dean."

The back of the booth wraps around us, enclosing us in a leather embrace that feels too much like the other night in his car. He leans close until his lips hover near mine, but when I don't respond, he pulls away and looks at me. "What's wrong?"

"Nothing . . . I . . . I'm just sorry I had to drag you into all of this," I whisper.

The set hand pretending to be our waiter for the night appears with two plates and clears his throat to get our attention. "Compliments of my wife," he announces as he sets the dishes of fettuccine Alfredo in front of us. He smiles proudly then leaves us again, retreating to the back of the room where the shadows linger.

"By the way, I wanted to tell you . . . I spoke to my uncle." Dalton scoots over, reluctantly allowing a more comfortable distance between us, and forks up a mouthful of pasta. "He said he'll look into Hawkins. It might take some time and he'll have to get a warrant to search his office, but at least it's on his radar." Dalton finishes chewing and brings his napkin to his mouth. "Funny thing is, he didn't seem all that surprised when I brought up Hawkins's name. I'm sure there've been some fishy rumors about him for a while."

I should feel relief that his uncle will check things out, but I'm too skeptical. I nod and mutter thank you anyway.

"So, now that you've met him on his turf, what do you think of the man?" Dalton's eyes watch me closely. I'm scared he wants me to tell him how I really feel, something he can take back to Hawkins. I have to stick to my original suspicions.

"I don't trust him," I say carefully. "Just like you said you didn't." I have no choice but to act as if nothing is wrong between Dalton and me, and to make it believable, I should continue to act like I'm falling in love with him. I'm so afraid that acting different will work against me. Inching closer on the seat until my arm is against his, I rest my head on his shoulder. "I shouldn't have gone to see him by myself. I really should have asked you to go with me." I've been pretending to be someone else for nearly a month now; acting the role of a scared woman hoping my big, strong male will save me could be my ticket to staying alive.

"Oh, I saw Isadora today."

Dalton settles an elbow comfortably upon the table as his other arm slips around my shoulders. "Ah, the infamous Isadora."

"She told me she put the card in your pocket, that she wanted to help with Eleanor's voice-over. I'm sorry I accused you." I stir my fork in the noodles, but I don't have an appetite.

"I don't blame you," Dalton says. "You've had to question everything thrown your way. I'm just glad you trust me, and the mystery of how the card got into my pocket has been solved."

Trust . . . I don't have any of that anymore.

"I found something else." I keep my voice at a level tone. "It turns out Alice Montgomery is a stage name." I gauge Dalton's expression, but he's quiet, waiting for me to go on. "For a woman named Bernice Brighton."

Dalton thinks for a moment. "That's your last name."

"And maybe the connection between me and Alice." My gaze strays into the dark recesses of the studio set. The air feels suddenly heavy. "I've replayed it all in my head, over and over, and not once can I come up with *why*. Why here? Why me?"

"A distant relative." Dalton ponders. "I mean, obviously, the name and all."

"I don't know who she is to me. I don't remember her name ever being brought up." I steal a glance at him from the corner of my eye. From the expression on his face, I can tell he's searching for answers along with me. "Do you believe in coincidence, Dalton?" I say as I watch the three little charms on my wrist sway back and forth. "I don't think I do. I think I was meant to slip from the sign—to make that wish for Ryan because Alice had wished for something about her own brother too."

"Alice has a brother? Grace, how did you find out?"

"*Had* a brother," I emphasize. "I found some newspaper articles in a box in my trailer. He was in a car accident"—I almost choke out the rest—"bad enough to put him in a coma."

"I don't know what to say," he whispers into my hair. "It must've been a shock to you. Like reliving what your brother is going through."

I wiggle my arm free and jiggle my wrist. "He gave her this bracelet. And I found this in the box." I point out the gold heart charm. "He died before he could give it to her," I say as I hold back a throatful of tears. "She must have been so heartbroken and scared."

Dalton squeezes my hand. "And desperate enough to make a wish?"

Only deep desperation must have fueled Alice's wish . . . no, not Alice, but Bernice. A woman related to me who lost her brother and went through something terrible. And for that, I'll find a way to expose them all—Hawkins, Mack, even Dalton.

WE PULL UP to the hotel and let Stella's engine rumble to a quiet purr. Dalton's hand inches toward mine, and it takes everything in me to not yank it away. But out of fear, I let him slip his fingers between mine. I'll keep up the charade until I have more to go on.

"Do you mind if I leave my bag here one more night?" Dalton nods toward the hotel out the window. "I have another long night ahead of me, last-minute stuff, but I promise I can stay over tomorrow."

"Yeah." I level my voice to hide the tremor in it. "That's fine."

It feels too awkward to just get out of the car and walk into the hotel, so I drum up something believable, something unsuspecting. Keep your enemies closer, right?

"Mr. Flynn is hosting a wrap party at his home tomorrow night. I think it's a press junket but . . . would you like to go with me?" It's a sneaky way to keep an eye on all of them under the same roof, and I plan on pulling an Isadora and soaking up as much gossip as I can. About Alice. About Eleanor. And maybe with enough luck I can warn a few people about what's been going on under their noses and put a stop to it.

"Are you sure you wouldn't rather have some dreamy actor escort you to this big bash?"

I shake my head and force a smile onto my face. "Nope. You'll do. Oh, but it is black tie. Is that a problem?" With money being tight, I doubt Dalton even owns a tux.

Dalton's own smile is more genuine than mine. He bobs his head up and down, saying, "Are you kidding? We happen to have an extensive tuxedo aisle in the costume warehouse. I'll just borrow one, so consider it a date."

Headlights illuminate the car as a newspaper delivery truck pulls up behind us. A few feet away, the valet in the booth waves his hand at us, prompting Dalton to start the engine and inch the car forward.

I turn in my seat and watch out the back window as the delivery man walks around to the back of his truck, bringing out stacks of papers on a dolly. Through my open window I hear him call out, "Early delivery, Joe—hot off the press!"

The delivery man hands the valet a clipboard, then approaches Dalton's car. He knocks at the window. "You'll have to move up more, son. Can't get my dolly through."

Dalton gives a nod to the man, then looks at me. "I guess that's my cue." He starts the engine, watching the man return to his delivery in the rearview mirror. "I promise I'll look like a proper gentleman tomorrow night," Dalton assures me, and he leans over to kiss me good night.

But I am still watching the delivery man out the back of the car. The truck's lights send a brilliant beam across Stella's back seat, drawing my gaze to a pair of work gloves and a tarp splattered with dark specks.

My heart races furiously as I turn my head toward Dalton, his lips hovering next to my cheek as if they're still waiting for their kiss. "What is that?" I point to what's in the back seat.

He looks at me for a moment that feels too long.

"Oh that," Dalton says slowly. "Just an old tarp. Remember that stack of scripts back at the studio? I've been putting off the last one in the pile. It calls for a pair of boots to be stuck in mud, and well, Mack won't order anything remotely authentic, so I've got to collect it myself."

A tingle of warning prickles across the back of my neck. "Where would you find mud around here?"

"Well, considering LA hasn't had any rain lately, I've been going to the tar pits, but I don't think I got enough to make the right sound. The things we do for cinematic greatness." He sighs and reaches behind my seat. The clang of metal fills the car as he lifts a bucket so I can see it. "Just me and a bucket of goo," he says with a grin that looks forced.

The delivery man is growing impatient. He honks his horn as the sickly glow of his truck's headlights splash light on the muddy tarp.

My entire body feels alarmed. My decision to not trust Dalton comes tumbling over me in waves. My head starts to spin as I think of the mud—in his car, on the shoes, on the tiara.

I swallow the terrible feeling welling up inside me, telling me that Dalton hasn't been working on creating authentic sound for the film. Instead, he's been to the tar pits to get rid of someone. And if he's buried Eleanor there, then maybe he buried Alice too.

CHAPTER THIRTY-ONE

THE SOUND OF THE MORNING paper thrown outside my door wakes me. I sit up too quickly and rub my forehead, the confusion of last night rushing back to me.

The mud in the back of Dalton's car upset me so much that I had to do some real acting to hide my suspicion while saying goodbye to him. I went straight to bed, but I could only toss and turn, replaying everything in my head until I'd finally succumbed to exhaustion.

But not even sleep could comfort me. My dreams became nightmares of missing girls, tinkling charms on their wrists, as I lay in a hospital bed unable to open my eyes and help them.

Another soft thud sounds from the hallway. I roll out of bed and pad my way to the door and open it. The paper's headline, in its bold black ink, stands out to me:

MISSING STARLET FOUND

My first thought is of Alice and my gaze immediately dips to the sub-headline.

La Brea Tar Pits Relinquish Gruesome Find

Beneath the menacing words is a black-and-white photo of Eleanor. I reach down and pick up the paper, its oversized pages crinkling in my trembling hands. "Eleanor Dunn," I choke out. *No, no, no . . .*

My throat tightens, constricting against the tears. I retreat into the room and sink down onto the end of the bed, forcing myself to read the article, which describes with enthusiastic terror how Eleanor's body has been found.

> *According to Detective Wayne Banks, an anonymous phone call alerted the Los Angeles Police Department to the Rancho La Brea Tar Pits, located on the corner of Wilshire Boulevard and South Curson Avenue, where officers spotted an elbow protruding from the murky tar along the main pond's west end. County forensics enlisted the aid of Harvey Donahue, a diver and six-year veteran of the LAPD, who successfully retrieved the remains. The body has been identified as Eleanor Dunn as per a Flynn Studios identification card found in the victim's pocket.*
>
> *Miss Eleanor Dunn, formerly of Ditmas Park, Brooklyn, New York, was employed by Flynn Studios and was wrapping up the film AMONG THE STARS, co-starring James Dean and newcomer Alice Montgomery. According to sources at Flynn Studios, and friends of the deceased, Miss Dunn had been missing for days. The LAPD continues to investigate this case.*

I try not to read the article again, but I find myself pulled in, skimming it over. The mention of Eleanor's body submerged in the tar is horrifying. It makes me imagine how she must have looked, her dead body blackened by sticky pitch . . . Eleanor's soft hair matted in thick clumps. The hope I've been holding on to—that she'd rushed back home to New York for a family emergency or something—crumbles.

And then a terrible thought hits me. That Alice has been beneath the murky depths of the tar pits this whole time.

My heart is heavy as I press my sweaty palm to my throat. Dalton had a muddy tarp in his car. He admitted he's been going to the tar pits.

A sourness suddenly creeps into my throat. I race to the bathroom and hover over the sink, splashing cool water on my face. When I look into the mirror, my face is pale and sickly. My arms are too weak to hold me up because the thought forming inside my head is one I can't bear. It leaves me terrified that since placing my trust in the wrong person this entire time—I could be next.

THE PHONE RINGS and rings but I won't answer it. I'm sure it's Dalton, checking in with me about tonight, but I don't want to talk to him. Not after reading about Eleanor being found in the tar pits and knowing he was recently there, collecting his mud. A gnawing ache forms in the pit of my stomach.

I nearly reach my breaking point when I ask the operator to connect me to the police department, but I chicken out. That nagging fear that Dalton had a hand in Eleanor's disappearance keeps rearing its ugly head, and my brain is twisting things that he'll get away with, since his uncle is a detective.

This is too much. I don't want to be here anymore. I push my hair back from my sweaty forehead and try to calm down. But the tears keep coming, filling my heart with a dread so strong it equals how I felt the night of Ryan's accident. "I just want to go home," I cry to myself, hiccupping the words. "Mom, please . . . help me come back to you!"

Alice's life is consuming me. I thought figuring out where and why she disappeared would be my way home—that if I could just find out what happened to her, it would open a magic portal and send me back into the arms of my mom, who would comfort me, or into the chair at Ryan's bedside. But now everything is speeding along like a freight train down a dark track. I have no control of what is going to happen.

For all I know, I could be stuck here for the rest of my life and never see my family again. And then what? Wind up missing, like Alice? Or worse—dead, like Eleanor?

I pick up the phone again and dial the studio. Through thick tears I manage to tell the woman on the other end of the line to give Judy a message—that I won't be going to the party tonight. I hang up quickly. I don't want to give a reason why. All my excuses have built up into one large panic attack.

Within half an hour, Judy is at my door. I let her in, greeting her with a handful of crumpled, damp tissues. My fingers leave smears of newsprint on the door. I haven't stopped reading the article about Eleanor. Judy gives me the once-over then walks into the bathroom, returning with a damp cloth. "Now you just sit down here and take a deep breath." She motions to the foot of the bed and hands me the cloth.

I lay it over my eyes and press hard, hoping to push my remaining tears out of my eye sockets.

"Now what is this all about?" she asks. "What's this nonsense about not going tonight?"

I can't see her from beneath the towel over my eyes, but I feel her staring at me. "I can't do it," I mumble. "Eleanor's dead."

I hear Judy sigh, then feel the bed sink as she sits next to me.

"Yes, I saw the paper," she replies. She plucks the damp tissue from my trembling fingers and replaces it with a dry one. "It's a terrible, terrible tragedy," Judy says. "We'll just leave it to the police to figure things out. So, before things get very busy for you these next several months, you should go to Mack's party."

"It's just a party," I say sourly.

Judy shifts her position beside me on the bed. I hear her intake of breath before she lets it out. "Yes, it's a lavish wrap party hosted by our generous employer, but it's also a media event. It's your first opportunity to give press interviews, to show them who you are, talk up the film. Besides, you are expected to be there." Judy sounds firm and I imagine her lips to form her signature straight line. She's not sweetening this to convince me, but rather giving me an order that it's my job and I have no choice in the matter.

"Tonight is the kickoff to a fabulous career, Alice. Enjoy it." Judy removes the cloth from my eyes, forcing me to look at her. "Do you have any idea what goes into making a film?" She looks at me as if I'm a child. "We've only just wrapped. Once the studio edits and cuts the film, it duplicates and distributes it to theaters. You and I have a lot of work ahead of us—promotional opportunities, interviews, you name it. Trust me, Alice, you're going to be swamped. Tonight's party might be the only event you'll be able to breathe at for a long while."

I take a hard swallow at the forcefulness of her words. But this still isn't right. Eleanor was part of the film, no matter how small her role was. In my opinion, the party should be postponed—or canceled altogether.

"Eleanor would have loved a party like this. Considering what's happened, I don't think any of us should be celebrating," I say with a croaking voice that is more angry than mournful. "How can anyone at the studio attend a party when one of our own has been *murdered*?"

Judy gives me an awkward pat on the knee. She rises to her feet and steps away to look out the window, the harsh sunlight making my eyes squint as she pulls the curtain to the side. "To be perfectly honest," Judy says slowly, "Eleanor probably placed herself in an unpleasant position for such a tragedy to happen."

What? My hand freezes on the towel I've been twisting as anger boils inside me at her words. "You can't mean that."

"Sadly, I do," Judy says matter-of-factly and turns to face me. "Her resume showed that in the span of three years she'd only ever been cast as an extra. She wanted more, and I'm sure she was stupid enough to go looking for it."

"So what? That doesn't excuse what happened to her! She was murdered!"

Even if Eleanor was flirtatious and ambitious, she shouldn't have ended up dead.

My throat is so tight, holding back the scream I want to unleash on Judy, but I can't. I'm not 100 percent sure about her involvement with Mack and Hawkins. My skin crawls with an unwelcome itch as I remember how I felt in Hawkins's office. Like a frightened rabbit in a cage with a wolf. And if Judy knows what's going on, telling me to go and have a good time tonight while turning a blind eye toward the casting couch, then she's just as bad as the wolf.

"The world is an ugly place, Alice. I'm sure you know that already. You're a smart girl."

Judy steps away from the window and plants herself in front of me. "My point is that sometimes a girl, a certain sort of girl who has gumption and dreams, wants what the average girl doesn't, and she'll go to great lengths to get it. Los Angeles is a seedy town. Maybe Eleanor wasn't careful enough."

"Careful enough?"

Judy pauses at my tone but shrugs. "It's a sad fact, but starlets are a dime a dozen in this town. When one disappears, another takes her place. This is how Hollywood runs. The well never runs dry." She reaches for her purse and a pair of white gloves, tugging on them as if eager to inflict pain on the tiny threads holding them together. "Simply put, there's an endless supply of girls willing to do anything to make it big in this town. Those are the girls who become legends."

But women shouldn't disappear because of it. They shouldn't lose their lives because they want to succeed. Where I come from, people stand up for this. They fight against men like Hawkins and Mack.

I watch through teary eyes as Judy opens the door. She lingers before stepping out into the hallway.

"You can be *that* girl, Alice." Through her tough veneer an encouraging smile spreads across Judy's lips. "Now, wash your face and put on that beautiful dress and heels I sent over. You have an obligation to the studio to be at this party. It's in your contract to attend every function that has to do with the film."

Judy steps out into the hallway. "I'll see you there."

She closes the door behind her, leaving me rattled and alone. If I can find a way to expose Hawkins and Mack—maybe I can convince Judy to help me. I'm still raging mad at her beliefs, at what she said about Eleanor, but I have to remember Judy's a woman of this decade, not mine. I'm sure she's seen her share of what goes on, but maybe I can be the strength she needs to stand against it. I just have to do it in a way that doesn't reveal I'm not Alice. Because if anyone finds out the truth, I'll be suspect number one in her disappearance.

CHAPTER THIRTY-TWO

I DRIED MY TEARS, MUSTERED my courage, and asked the concierge to call Judy, who arranged for a studio car to pick me up. If Dalton calls, I won't be here.

During the entire ride through the winding, narrow streets in the Hollywood Hills, I think of the mess I'm in—of Dalton's splattered tarp in his back seat and Eleanor's mud-splattered tiara in his prop bin.

Of the shoes in the trailer . . . Did a workman leave them behind? Did Dalton hide them, or did someone else? I need to find my way home because the walls of Alice's world are dangerously closing in on me.

I chew on my fingernail as the car climbs a steep hill and turns off into a narrow driveway. Mack Flynn's home is nestled deep into the mountainside, not far from where I grew up. It seems a lifetime ago that I'd ever wondered who lived in the stately homes on this road—the 1920s Spanish Tudors and bungalows whose white walls and red-tile rooftops sprout from the trees just feet below the Hollywood sign.

The limousine slows as it pulls up to the white stucco mansion. Enormous double doors stand wide open, spilling light onto the colorful porch tiles. The chauffeur opens my door and I step onto the gravel drive. Jazz music greets me through the open doors and windows of the sprawling house. The smell of sweet roses and hothouse gardenias fills the air. As I reach the top step, the smell of flowers becomes overpowered by cigarette smoke, and James steps out from the shadows.

"You surprised me!" I press my hand to my chest, feeling my heart beat out of control. "What are you doing out here?"

James gives me a crooked smile. "Waiting for you." He stubs out his cigarette on the banister and tosses it over the side. "Dry season," he motions. "You can never be too careful with an ember." Then he pulls a comb from the interior pocket of his jacket and runs it through his hair, as if it needs perfecting.

He tugs at his collar and thrusts one of his hands into his pocket now that it's no longer occupied with a cigarette. His discomfort mirrors my own. I don't want to be here—not after the news about Eleanor, not after Judy told me I have no choice, and especially not now that I suspect Hawkins and Dalton are more dangerous than I first thought. Alice's life has sent me down a tunnel so dark I fear I'll never see light again.

I whip up a smile as I take in James's ebony tuxedo. "You look very dashing."

"And you." James reaches for my hand and twirls me fully around. He looks over my shoulder, scanning the driveway full of cars. "No date?"

I shake my head. "It didn't work out."

"Sorry. Shall we make our grand entrance then?" James extends his elbow.

Everyone notices as we step into the foyer. Party guests stop to stare, some inching closer, hanging on every word and laugh we utter. If only Ryan could see this. James is polite and gracious to everyone who approaches us. The small of my back warms beneath the gentle pressure of his hand as we weave past the guests and further inside.

The house has been so transformed for the gathering that it no longer resembles a residence. The furniture, except for a few strategically placed love seats, has been removed to allow room for tiny round tables elaborately set with cocktails.

Every corner is aglow with candlelight and crystal and tall vases of white-and-green flowers. The champagne flows, and elegantly dressed waitstaff go from room to room passing sparkling goblets to partygoers.

The party reminds me of the hotel's cocktail soiree but on a much more impressive scale. That was the first night I had pretended to be Alice among these people. Tonight, though, feels very different. I don't want to pretend anymore. I want this to be over. It's as if the entire universe has shifted since I found the obituary in Alice's box, filling me with an overwhelming dread. I breathe in through my nose and try to focus on the music surrounding me. I even try imagining Ryan is here with me at the party. This is just like the lavish Hollywood parties he'd told me he read about.

"Champagne, miss?" A waiter appears next to me offering flutes on a silver tray.

I accept the glass and make a silent toast to Eleanor . . . and Alice. They deserve to be here, and yet not a single person has said anything about the headline in this morning's paper. I haven't heard a single whisper about Eleanor's cruel death or a question about how, why . . . who could have done this to her. It breaks my heart.

Just then the room vibrates with the sound of clapping. Mack Flynn stands at the top of the staircase and lifts a glass of champagne.

He descends the stairs, smiling as he shakes hands with those closest to him. My manager, Geoffrey, is one of the first to greet him, pumping Mr. Flynn's arm in a firm handshake. Isadora is beside him, sparkling from head to toe in a shimmering silver dress. She wears a tiny tiara on top of her raven-colored hair that reminds me of Eleanor.

Sadness creeps its way into my heart. I take another sip, and the cool champagne becomes warm in my stomach, numbing the pain away.

Everywhere I turn I am greeted with air kisses and compliments—how beautiful I look tonight, how I have stunned everyone with my performance, and how wonderful it will look on the silver screen.

"Congratulations!" Someone I can't put a name to raises their glass from across the room, our eyes meeting over the haze of smoke.

A small orchestra is set up in the corner of the grand parlor, transforming the crowded space into a ballroom. Smooth chords of jazz draw people to the center of the room. I waltz with men I've never met before and spin until I believe for sure I'll fly straight out the French doors and off the balcony—another star catapulted into the night.

James has disappeared but I don't mind, and when a hand taps my shoulder, I turn with a smile.

Everything around me slows as I stare into Hawkins's smug face.

He leans in close.

"You look positively lovely this evening," he whispers against my ear. His hand finds my back, his other hand clasping mine firmly as he spins me out onto the dance floor.

"You're the last person I want to dance with." I force my body away from his, but he only pulls tighter, drawing me close to lean against his chest as if we are dancing.

He reeks of alcohol.

He tilts his face to my ear. "There, there, pretty girl. We don't want to cause a scene now, do we? After all, all eyes are on you. This is your night. All of this is for you."

I am suddenly aware of how everyone watches us. "This isn't for me."

"Ah, but it is. All of it." His voice purrs like a contented cat. He sweeps me past a table for two, where an older gentleman and his wife smile with adoration at the both of us.

I pull away, but Hawkins holds his arm firmly behind my back. My fingers are locked with his—aching to be free. The guests around us drink their champagne, laugh, dance—never suspecting I am being held prisoner during a waltz.

I frantically scan the room hoping to spot James, but I can't find him.

Another smile illuminates Hawkins's face. "You're Mr. Flynn's beacon of hope. Did you know the studio is under the threat of bankruptcy?"

I arch my back, leaning away from his whiskey breath.

"It's true. You're his golden ticket out of debt. The star everyone will flock to the cinemas to see." He lets out a deep laugh. "The star that will pad his bank account—and mine, after convincing Mack that you didn't need the . . . *usual* audition."

With a shove, I propel myself out of his arms and glare at him.

Hawkins draws me close again and sets his lips against my temple as he twirls me around in a dizzying circle. His hot breath makes me sick, a swell of nausea creeping into my throat. Then suddenly he leads me through the crowd, down an empty hall away from the party.

Judy rounds the corner. I nearly weep at the sight of her.

"Judy!" I call out, wrenching myself from Hawkins's grip. "You've got to help . . ."

"There you are." Judy saunters closer.

Oh, thank God!

But her eyes aren't on me, they are on Hawkins, and rather than glaring at him and ushering me someplace safe, Judy sidles up to him.

To my absolute horror, she links her arm around his, leans up, and plants a kiss on his lips.

CHAPTER THIRTY-THREE

My limbs feel frozen in place. Judy warned me about Hawkins and told me to stay far away from him. But it's obvious she's closer to him than I ever imagined.

I notice the sparkle dangling from her earlobes—Egyptian gold ovals encrusted with rubies and emeralds. The same earrings she showed me in the costume warehouse after I chose the gray dress.

Hawkins follows my gaze. "Are you crazy?" He reaches over and clutches Judy's jaw, turning her head as he examines the baubles she's wearing. "I told you to never wear these. Eleanor wore them for the photo shoot. Someone might recognize them."

"So destroy the photos. It's not like anyone here will ever know who wore them last." Her gloved hand reaches up to caress her ear. "Besides, they're way too pretty to sit in a vault."

Horror seizes my heart as I gawk at the earrings dangling against Judy's neck. "Judy . . ." But my words are cut short as my disbelief chokes me.

Judy's hand reaches out to me, but I yank my arm away. She purses her lips as if I've offended her and then shifts her gaze to Hawkins and tilts her head. "I think our girl is having a breakdown."

Hawkins lets out an exasperated breath, but he seems distracted. He keeps watching the other end of the hallway.

I follow his gaze. The party is in full swing in the other room—the blaring music, the erupting laughter. I need to reach the end of the hall, where I'll be safe, then slip away to find a phone, call the police. My entire body is shaking. Every atom inside me buzzes, telling me I am in danger. But I also need to find answers—it's what I've been searching for all along.

What really happened to Alice? Is her disappearance linked to Eleanor? Maybe it's smarter to run, get back to people. I'm torn as I look down the hallway again.

Judy situates herself between me and my way back to safety. She studies me for a moment, her beautifully made-up face twisting with curiosity. "You really bumped your head hard, didn't you? I thought it was all an act that day we saw you stumbling onto the set, but you really don't remember, do you?"

"What don't I remember?" I inch a tiny step forward. Whatever happened to Alice must be a secret Judy has been keeping all along. And whatever it is, I am going to find out.

A bitter smile forms across Judy's pretty face. "You didn't think I would find out, did you? You figured I was too busy with my career, managing *your* career, to notice."

"Enough, Judy," Hawkins hisses.

"Maybe this will jog your memory," Judy continues. "You weren't supposed to come down off that mountain. I was such a good friend, taking you up there after filming wrapped for the day so you could mourn your brother. But then you had too much to drink, and you told me everything, like it was a goddamned confession. As if you hoped I'd help you."

She inches closer to me. The smell of something stronger than champagne lingers on her breath, and her mascara is smeared around her eyes. She looks wrecked, but there's a fire in her eyes that wasn't there a second ago.

"I thought you were crying over your brother, but you were only crying for yourself. You were worried your career would be over if you exposed what was happening at the studio, so I helped end it for you. A bottle of bubbly, a clumsy slip. It was perfect. Until you wandered back onto the set and everyone was back to adoring you."

I narrow my eyes at her. "You left Al . . . *me* for dead in Griffith Park?"

"And *you*," Judy redirects her fire at Hawkins. "I was the connection you needed—to introduce her to Mack, set her up with Geoffrey, get the pretty girl a job at the studio, that's how it's always been, right—after you've had your fun?"

"Baby, you're making this bigger than it has to be." Hawkins steps closer to Judy, attempting to put his arm around her to soothe her. "Do you even know how many dames throw themselves at me for the slightest chance at making it big? Dozens. Hundreds. It's all an act to make them believe they've got what it takes, and if the act gets a little too realistic, then hell, maybe *my* name should be on a marquee in lights."

"No," Judy spits back. "*She* was different." Her eyes dart between the two of us as her finger jabs at Hawkins's chest. "She didn't go through the channels like the others. You thought I'd never find out that you were in love with her. You were willing to risk it even after she promised to ruin us."

Every inch of my skin tingles as if I am standing next to an exposed wire, ready to burst into flame. Judy is going to explode, bringing everyone down with her—everyone in Alice's sick, twisted world. But it's too late to stop asking questions.

And now I know the truth. Alice knew what was happening. She was going to expose them. But Judy didn't give her the chance. "You killed Eleanor, didn't you?" I turn on her. "Because you suspected she was getting too close to Hawkins? Because she was my friend, and you were afraid she'd have the same agenda?" I showed up after Judy thought Alice was gone for good, but she must have thought Eleanor would be easier to get rid of. I push further—I need to know. I need to know what they did to that poor woman. "What did you do, Judy?" An image of Eleanor covered in muddy tar flashes through my head like an assault. It's all too horrifying.

We've stepped farther away from the music and laughter in the other room and are now inches from an open door. A balcony just outside hovers over the dark canyon. My senses snap, driving me into a panic as Judy edges closer, her face full of rage. It's fight or flight now that her alcohol-fueled confession has placed me in her crosshairs.

Judy staggers up to me, her eyes dark and raging with madness. "I didn't kill anyone. *You* did."

CHAPTER THIRTY-FOUR

IT FEELS AS IF THE floor is sinking beneath my feet as both tears and terror swell inside me. "Eleanor was my friend," I say, my voice squeaking. "I'd never do anything to hurt her!"

Judy's hand latches onto my shoulder and shoves me past Hawkins, pulling me with her out onto the balcony. There is a warm breeze blowing down from the mountain that shadows the house, but it chills me. I don't feel safe here. I need to get back inside the house.

"I have to admit my first attempt to get rid of you wasn't planned out very well," Judy says calmly as she leans against the railing. It's as if we're having a normal conversation and the topic is the weather, not murder. "It was *your* body the police were supposed to find in the tar a month ago, but I couldn't figure out how to lure you there. That's when I knew I could capitalize on your grief. You were so distraught that night I took you to the sign." She glares at me with a sick gleam in her eyes.

"As soon as you were gone, our man Hawkins set his sights on Eleanor. Then you came back. That's when the light bulb went off. That's when I knew I could make *both* of you disappear. I just had to wait for the right time."

I glare at Judy. "You're crazy. Let me go!" I desperately try to pull out of her grip, but her hand holds me too tight. Hawkins just stands there, watching the scene unravel around him.

I spare a second to look at Hawkins. "You didn't have to kill Eleanor; she was never a threat to you."

Judy lets out a laugh that sounds too loud. "Everyone's a threat, sweet Alice. Don't you know that by now? This is Hollywood—home to scandal and revenge. It's all a matter of going after what you want, and how long you can get away with it."

"Well, if it's him you want," I nod toward Hawkins, "you can have him. He's all yours. Maybe you should consider putting a leash on him."

Anger burns in Hawkins's eyes. He leans into the space between us and growls, "You mean nothing to me. Just another pathetic starlet trying to make it big, that's all you are. And you are so gullible, too, thinking I loved you."

The thought of Alice feeling something for Hawkins makes this even more disgusting. Thank goodness she figured out something was off about him, because the very idea of the two of them together is nearly as twisted as Judy's jealousy.

Judy shakes her head as she studies Hawkins. "You can lie all you want, but I've known for a long time she means more to you than the others." Judy gives him a hard shove in the center of his chest, enough to make him sway with the impact. "I was doing you a favor by getting rid of her, you bastard."

A flash of lightning illuminates the sky, followed by a crack of thunder. The wind picks up and suddenly the open air around us feels entirely too dangerous.

If Judy wants to be rid of Alice once and for all, she only has to shove me over the railing.

As if reading my thoughts, Judy edges closer, grinning. "Oh, I've thought of everything, Alice. My plan is much better now. See, you were jealous that Eleanor was getting close to that Foley artist you've been spending so much time with." She sways a little as she speaks, and she reaches out to grab the railing. "She couldn't have both men in your life, so you convinced that little studio rat of yours to get rid of Eleanor. She was annoying and petty anyway. If Dalton did the dirty work, then Eleanor would be gone. The police would arrest him for murder, and he'd be out of the picture without a substantial story to back him up."

"Judy," Hawkins hisses. "Keep your mouth shut!"

But Judy ignores him and continues her rant. "When the police find your body on the ground below, they'll call it a suicide over your boyfriend killing your friend. And Hawkins and I will be long gone."

The dark sky lurches closer and all the sounds from within the house sound muffled and too far away amid the approach of the storm. "You're sick, you know that? Dalton's uncle is on the force. He'll believe Dalton when he tells him your ridiculous plan to frame me."

"We've got that covered too," Hawkins chimes in. "Evidence speaks louder than words."

The headband. The shoes. They weren't covered in dried mud. It was tar. And Judy is the only one with full access to my trailer. That's why she took notice of Dalton's coat. It wasn't because she was concerned for me, or worried about my reputation. She was plotting.

"You won't get away with this," I warn. "I'll tell the police everything I know."

"You won't if you're dead." Judy smirks. Even though Judy is drunk, she's wired with energy. She lurches forward, pinning my body between her and the iron railing separating me from the house and the darkness below. She presses her lips to my ear. "I walked away from that sign knowing you were lying at the bottom of it, but you fooled us all and disappeared," she seethes. "But then you were back before anyone could wonder if something terrible had happened to you. I admit, I was worried your memory would come back and you'd spill everything that happened. But I promise you; I'll get rid of you for good now."

I shove hard against her, pushing her away. But Judy is unbelievably strong. She has me bent backward over the railing. All it will take is one more shove, and I'll be over the top of the balcony. I let out a scream. Hawkins reaches out to cover my mouth, but he stumbles, allowing me to slip under his arm.

I bolt down the hallway, far away from the balcony and the two people who want Alice—me—dead. I run as fast as I can toward the archway that opens to the party. When I reach the room full of people, the orchestra's jubilant tune comes to a slow pause. My heart is beating with a fierceness I can barely contain—my fear rushing to my cheeks for everyone to see. I thought getting away from Judy and Hawkins would make me feel safe, but now that I've made it back to the party, I feel trapped.

"It's time for a toast!" Mack's voice rings out.

The waitstaff rolls a pyramid of champagne glasses onto the dance floor. A cork pops, and the guests roar with enthusiasm. Mack pours an open bottle of Dom Perignon over the top of the pyramid, creating a stunning, golden fountain.

"Everyone, raise a glass!" he announces. "To our Golden Girl!"

All eyes turn toward me and the guests in the room clap. Someone shoves a champagne flute into my hand.

Isadora stands across from me, smiling, her mouth open and wide as if she's intent on inhaling the entire room. Our eyes meet. Isadora raises her glass.

And then I notice Dalton standing in the doorway, his face earnestly seeking mine over the top of everyone's heads. I hand my full glass to a man standing next to me and break into a run, pushing past everyone who stands shoulder to shoulder. I ignore the stares, the shock, and hurl myself into his arms.

"Oh, thank God," Dalton says, holding me tight. "I called your room, but you never picked up. I was beginning to think the worst." He holds me close and continues to whisper, "I should have stayed with you last night. I've been beating myself up that I left you alone and something happened."

I wrap my arms around his neck and cling to him, not caring that behind me whispers gather like locusts. All I care about in this moment is he's innocent. He didn't team up with Hawkins or Mack or . . . "Something bad did happen, Dalton. We need to leave. Now."

The music is too loud for him to hear me over the lump in my throat. He grabs my hand and begins pushing his way toward the foyer, leading me behind him.

All around us people start talking again. The orchestra strikes up, sending waves of chords throughout the room. Between the champagne and the terror, my mind is playing tricks on me. The music sounds as if it is growing insanely louder by the minute, competing with the rolling thunder outside. I shouldn't have had so much to drink. I took it for granted that I wouldn't need my wits about me tonight.

A smiling man blocking our path to the door asks where we are going. There is no time to explain. I need to get out. Only then will I be able to breathe easier.

A clumsy guest bumps into Dalton, pushing him closer to me. Dalton's lips press against my ear. "God, you're beautiful. I'm so sorry I was late. But listen, there's something important I need to tell you."

"Dalton." Dread pulses inside me. I've had enough of Alice's life. We're wasting time. "You have to get me out of here." I turn to look over my shoulder. "Please hurry . . . Hawkins and Judy . . ."

Dalton takes my hand again and leads me toward the foyer. "They're just outside," he tells me, looking back over his shoulder.

"Who?" I shout, but he doesn't hear me. "Wait, who?" I pull on his arm.

And then the nerves hit. Does he mean Judy and Hawkins?

I freeze as his hand tugs on mine, trying to pull me forward with him. But I can't move. The room is too hot, blurring with smoke and laughter and leaving me seasick. Another crack of thunder hits, shaking the entire house. The lights flicker and someone bumps into Dalton's arm, causing him to sever his hold on me. A button on his jacket comes loose and a stack of photographs spills to the floor.

Photos of Alice. Of me to anyone who lays eyes on them.

There is skin. Lots of it.

Dalton's eyes meet mine.

He scrambles to the floor to collect them. I watch, horrified, as it feels like he moves in slow motion, his fingers taking forever to reach each one, as if he means to torture me to pieces.

"Grace, I . . ." He grabs another photo. "I can explain . . ."

It's too late. It doesn't matter that the girl in the photos isn't *really* me. She might as well be, right down to the little beauty mark.

But what practically kills me inside is that *he* has them.

Dalton and I stare at one another for what feels like forever, the photographs still scattered across the floor. The party slowly ebbs its way back to my senses—and to my horror, I become acutely aware of the other people in the room.

The man who'd bumped him has staggered off. A kind woman leans down to help Dalton pick up a photograph he's missed. Her face blanches at the picture she holds in her hands. Rather than giving it back to him, she reaches out and offers it to me.

I back away. I can't touch it. There is no way to erase these photos for Alice. No way to fix the problems she created for herself. Alice left them all behind when she slipped from the sign, leaving me to deal with it all.

And I can't.

I spin around and shove my way through the elite crowd I am supposed to be part of—past Isadora, who turns her head to call to me, past Mack—that terrible man—who smiles as if I've approached to talk to him. On the other side of the room is a terrace and a small spiral staircase that leads down to a garden and an illuminated swimming pool of clear, crystal blue. The lights flicker again, this time plunging the entire room into darkness, only candlelight flickering in tandem with the bolts of light that streak across the sky. Panic erupts around me, but I race past it all and into the windswept night. Above me hangs the empty balcony where I struggled with Judy and Hawkins. I look up, relieved to see they are no longer there.

There is a gate at the far end of the yard. I yank at the latch, leaving it to swing open behind me, and pick my way up the side of the hill as fast as I can, my feet on autopilot as if they know the way. The party soon fades behind my back—the laughter, the music, the look on Dalton's face as I turned and ran away from him. I've left behind Judy's jealousy and hate, Alice's dreams and heartache, as I race toward the hillside aglow in the building storm.

The sign is a beacon reminding me who I am and where I've come from. It is constant and strong, firmly rooted into the ground. I pause to look at it.

Hello, old friend.

The thinly worn footpath I take brings me alongside the letter *Y* in the middle of the sign. The letters don't seem so tall and imposing now. I've conquered this beast before. Slowly, I meander past each one in search of the *H*. When I reach it, I gaze up; it's just a plain, unimpressive sheet of metal that no longer intimidates me. An uncomfortable thickness fills my head, and I swear I hear someone call my name. For a moment, the world feels like a dream, as if the party never happened. As if Alice had never existed. It is just me—alone.

Footsteps sound through the thick brush below me, and a voice calls out—that familiar voice that once set my heart on fire.

"Grace! Where are you?"

I press my back against the metal, making myself as small as I possibly can, but the twigs snap louder. The footsteps come closer.

I tell myself it's the wind, but I have to get away, and the only way is up.

The ladder hangs over my right shoulder, just within reach. I turn and grab it, pulling the metal ladder down its track toward me, cringing at how it squeaks. I lift my skirt and place the toe of my shoe on the rung, then hoist myself upward. Arm over arm, higher.

Each rung I climb reminds me of that night I wanted to help Ryan. But now I know—this sign has to be cursed—no one's wishes ever come true. None of ours did.

I climb higher, the picture of Ryan fading in my head. The world around me turns to haze, confusing me, bombarding me with other memories that aren't my own—strange memories of Hawkins kissing me, of wanting to capture the world, then flashes of camera lights and voices telling me to smile for them.

The grass rustles along the hillside as a dark figure moves its way up the mountain, closer to the sign. My heart beats furiously as I recognize Dalton's hair.

He has found me.

CHAPTER THIRTY-FIVE

DALTON REACHES THE PATCH OF dark brush and shrubs beneath the ladder, his face angled upward, staring at me; his hands are on top of his head protecting his face as the wind and rain lash at him, as if he can't believe I have already climbed so far up despite the elements.

"Grace! Come down, please! This is insane!" he calls up to me.

I cling fast to the ladder, refusing to come down. This is the only place I need to be right now to clear my head. If my home doesn't exist, then this is all I have.

"Listen to me, please! It isn't what you think!" Dalton sounds out of breath. He leans forward, his hands on his knees.

I turn my head, ignoring him, and focus on how much higher I need to climb to create distance between us.

"Fine." Dalton throws his hands up in the air.

"What are you doing?" I call down to him.

He grabs onto the bottom rung. "I'm coming after you."

"Just leave me alone, Dalton." I hang for a beat, steeling myself against the onslaught of rain, and then slowly resume my climb, the clang of his shoes on the ladder below fueling me to stay out of his reach.

"No," he calls up hoarsely. "Not until you hear the whole story."

There is a strain in his voice, but it doesn't stop me. I press on. The top is only a few feet away.

"You were right about everything," he yells below me. "Hawkins was recruiting actresses. He took photos of them and passed them on to Judy, who made sure they landed on Mack's desk. Once the studio hired them, they took a cut." Dalton pauses on the ladder below me and looks up. "It was Hawkins who decided on the nudes. He invited the women and some underage girls back for more photos, promising them screen tests for a phony film. Most of those photographs you saw in his office never even went to Mack—just the ones Hawkins thought he'd like. He'd pass them on to Judy and she would set up the auditions."

A swimmy feeling of disgust sweeps over me but also a peculiar sense of clarity, as if I can see everything Dalton is telling me from a distance. I see Alice falling straight into a trap—and Eleanor too.

Dalton is on the opposite side of the ladder, facing me. In a soothing voice, he tells me, "Steady there."

My chest heaves as if I've just run up the hill alongside him. But Dalton grabs my hand and holds it tight.

I watch his Adam's apple move as he swallows and catches his breath. "Why did you run?"

I close my eyes. Too much has happened tonight for me to think straight.

"Grace, the pictures aren't you. I know that." His voice pleads with me. "They're Alice." He takes another breath. "I know the pictures are embarrassing but . . . why'd you run like that?"

The metal of the ladder is cold and wet but sure in my hands. It keeps me grounded, clearing away the rest of the champagne in my system. "I wasn't embarrassed, I was scared. You said they were outside." I sneak a look at his face.

"Yeah, my uncle and a few officers from the precinct." Dalton looks confused. "Why would that make you run? Who did you think I meant?"

"Hawkins and Judy," I whisper. "I thought you were about to hand me over to them to finish what they'd started." My body starts shaking uncontrollably.

His fingers press over mine so I don't fall. Either that, or so I won't climb higher to get away from him.

"I know what they did," he says, breathing heavily. "I know everything. That's why I tried calling you to warn you. I was late tonight because I was helping my uncle piece everything together," he says in a rush. "I told you in the car last night that I'd gone to the tar pits the other day. That's why the tarp and the bucket were on the back seat. While I was there, a couple of squad cars pulled up. I saw my uncle, so I went over to see what was going on."

He looks into my eyes with urgency. "I know I seemed a little distant last night. It's because . . . because I've never seen a dead body before."

His words still the blood in my veins.

"You saw Eleanor?" Dalton's face blurs behind my tears.

He nods. "My uncle told me to leave, but I looked anyway. I thought it was a branch sticking up out of the tar." He closes his eyes as if trying to make the memory go away. "It was an elbow. Thank God my uncle was working that night," Dalton goes on. "Otherwise, I wouldn't have been able to enter the crime-scene area."

Dalton's expression is full of worry, but I am sure it is no match for how I am feeling. He saw Eleanor. Saw her body.

"Why didn't you tell me?"

"My uncle told me I couldn't. Not until they figured out what happened. Someone reported her missing," he continues, still holding onto my hand like a lifeline. "Then someone tipped off the cops, like they knew I'd be there. The call came from Mack's office, but the officers said the caller was a woman."

"Judy," I breathe out. "She and Hawkins tried to set you up to get rid of me. They planted Eleanor's tiara in your prop bin and a pair of muddy shoes in my trailer."

Dalton looks away for a moment as a crease begins to form between his eyebrows. "So that's why the guys at the station kept talking about a pair of shoes. They found footprints in the mud. I let them compare them to mine but they didn't match," he says. "That's how they knew it wasn't me."

The next crack of thunder is earsplitting, and Dalton's hand leaves mine and his arm encircles me through the rungs, holding me firmly against the ladder.

"I stayed at the station all night going over the evidence with my uncle, and we talked about Hawkins." His voice strains against the storm as he speaks. "Another detective pulled a team together from the precinct and they raided his office. The guy was sloppy enough to leave spare clothing in a closet there. The pair of shoes from there matched the prints found in the mud. They also found correspondence between him and Judy. Apparently, his ditzy receptionist was supposed to keep their connection hidden, but she slipped up. That's when my uncle figured out that Judy must have made the call, pointing them to the tar pits while I was collecting that stupid mud."

Dalton leans into the ladder. It's the closest thing to a hug as we stand on the same narrow rung. Deep down I know he couldn't have been involved in what Hawkins or Judy had been doing. I hate myself for not trusting him. My brain can't wrap itself around what Judy told me.

"Judy admitted everything to me. She was drunk, but she came out with it that she and Hawkins killed Eleanor," I choke out. The reality of it is still incomprehensible. The fear has built up so much inside me that I can barely hold on to the ladder. "And Judy admitted that she tried to kill Alice." I tell him what happened on the balcony and that Judy pushed Alice off this very sign to make it look like suicide, or at the very least, an accident.

Now I know Judy was the one to sabotage me on set. The near misses, the forklift. All failed attempts to get rid of Alice after my appearance told her the first plan failed.

"The shoes the police are looking for are in my trailer. They were on the floor near your coat, but I hid them in the closet."

Dalton watches me carefully as he listens, then exhales a deep breath. "It's okay, Grace. They aren't my size. The cops know it wasn't me."

"I still can't believe it," I say shakily. "I knew Hawkins was responsible for something. I just never pieced it together that he was working with Judy. That she was the mastermind to get rid of Alice, and Eleanor." What Judy had planned—what she's done—is a million times worse than those files of photos Hawkins took.

I give Dalton a questioning look. "Why did you have those pictures?"

"My uncle had a bunch of stuff that was confiscated from Hawkins's office. I happened to notice Alice's folder and I stole the photos so I could give them to you, so they'd be safe in *your* hands," Dalton reassures me. "You know, my uncle told me that Alice visited him about a month ago." He nods. "She was scared. Apparently, Hawkins was pressuring her into a film she didn't want to do, something, well . . . let's say it isn't the sort of flick a reputable studio would want to be associated with. There were accidents happening on set. Strange things. She didn't feel safe. And after what you've just told me, I'm guessing those accidents were set up by Judy."

I nod.

"You were the one who got away, Grace."

I don't feel as lucky as I probably should. I give Dalton a long, weary look. "But did Alice? Where is she?"

Dalton eyes darken. "Apparently someone did report her missing. An anonymous call. I saw the report. It said not to alert the press. Probably to prevent the reporters from showing up at the studio and the media looking into it. And then you showed up."

I wonder who it was. A concerned coworker from the studio? There's a tickle in my brain that makes me wonder if Alice may have called in her own disappearance—deliberately leading the police to Hawkins and Judy. Oh, I hope so.

He reaches over and brushes my windblown hair away from my eyes. We should start climbing down where it's safer, but I am still so rattled by what's happened, my feet feel glued to the ladder. I've seen enough Lifetime movies to know someone could kill out of jealousy, but I never thought I'd ever be this close to it. "Hawkins knew Judy pushed Alice from the sign. He was supposedly in love with Alice. How could he have been okay with that?"

"Men like him don't love people like Alice—or Eleanor. Not even people like Judy," Dalton tells me. "He uses them because he loves money and opportunity."

I shake my head, still trying to piece it all together. "He told me the studio is going under. Alice could have helped keep it afloat."

A sad look shadows his eyes. "Fame grows posthumously."

"You mean . . ."

"Once filming finished," Dalton says grimly, "the studio would profit from Alice even more if she were dead."

CHAPTER THIRTY-SIX

"WHY DID YOU COME TO the sign, Grace?" Dalton asks. "You could have gone back to the hotel or left town—you could have run anywhere after you left the party."

"Because I feel scared and confused," I admit. "I've felt this way the entire time I've been Alice's stand-in, but the last time I felt this desperate was right here on this stupid letter." I never should have gone to the sign in the first place the night I made my wish.

Look where it got me. I thought figuring out what happened to Alice would fix things.

That it would send me home.

I look into Dalton's eyes. "I'm afraid I've done nothing to help Alice—that being here has only messed things up."

"Are you kidding?" he says with real surprise. "You got Hawkins and Judy to confess, and you found out Mack runs a shady business. Meeting me and trusting me with your secret connected you to my uncle, who's on his way to Mack's house right now to take the three of them down to the station. Wherever Alice is, if she comes back, she won't have to be afraid of them anymore."

He loops his arm tighter around the rung of the ladder. "And don't forget, before all of this, you tried to fix things back home by being selfless and making a wish for your brother, even if it meant you would fall from this sign." His hand covers mine. "I'm sorry, so sorry all this happened. But I'm not sorry you came into my life."

Dalton fishes around his breast pocket. "I have the photos, but I guess it's not the right time to give them to you." He tears his gaze from me to look at the sky, which looks angry and dangerous.

I cast a glance upward, then give him a lopsided smile. "My dress doesn't have pockets anyway."

"I guess that could be a problem." Dalton chuckles. "Tell you what, I'll hold on to them for you, just until we get back down." He looks at the ground beneath us. It really is a long way down. Then his hand reaches out and caresses my cheek. "Your brother would be proud of you. You're the bravest woman I know."

Just then, the distant sound of police sirens wafts up the mountain. The glow of red and blue flashing lights illuminates the surrounding trees. Dalton's mouth stretches into a full grin as he says, "Right on time."

"This is all so crazy." I nod toward the lights below. "The last time I climbed this sign I was so scared of the police catching me. Now it's a relief to see their lights, knowing Judy and Hawkins won't hurt anyone again."

We watch the squad cars pull up to the front of Mack's house. "It'll make a great story one day."

"Maybe you'll write about it." I laugh at how ridiculous it all sounds.

But Dalton's expression registers seriousness. "Yes, maybe I will, and I'll send it off to Rod Serling and become famous."

A brilliant streak of lightning flashes just above us. The wind whips my dress, the rain coming sideways now, plastering my skirt to my legs. The storm is getting worse, but Dalton's hand reaches out, tucking another tendril of my hair behind my ear. "You're my muse, Grace Brighton. And I promise you; you will get your happy ending."

I am tipsy, but it's no longer from the champagne. It's because of Dalton. I am 100 percent over the moon for him. I lean in, misjudging the angle of our faces and bumping his nose with my forehead. Feeling foolish, I laugh, my voice suddenly halted by an enormous crack of thunder. The storm is directly over us, the sky heavy with clouds and raging. It reminds me of the night I came to the sign. The night I fell.

"We have to get out of here." Dalton's voice is whisked away in the onslaught. He lowers himself to the rung below us and I move to follow him when the hem of my gigantic skirt catches beneath my shoe, slipping on the wet metal and yanking me down. I gasp as I lose my grip on the ladder and scramble for footing. The only thing to grab onto is the sleeve of Dalton's jacket as he leans around the side of the ladder to catch me.

"Hold on!" Dalton cries out.

I clutch desperately, but my fingers are losing their grip on the soaked fabric. I can't hold on much longer. With my other hand I frantically reach up, but his arm is too high. There is only air and the relentless wind. The next horizontal bar beneath me is too far to step onto, the ladder out of reach.

"Give me your hand. I'll try to pull you up!" Dalton shouts.

I look down. The ground is so far away. "I c-c-can't!"

"Okay, I'm going to try and swing you over. See if you can grab onto the side." Dalton's voice sounds strained as he holds my weight. It's only a matter of time before he loses the strength in his arm to give me a full enough swing.

I pump my legs to help him, inching my body closer to the edge of the *H*, but my dress is soaked to the point that I am weighing us both down.

"Give one more try," he urges as he leans farther over, placing himself in a precarious position.

If either of us makes one wrong move, he could fall along with me. I can't allow that to happen. I've been so scared that I've already lost Ryan to this monster of a hill. I won't lose Dalton too. If I have to choose, it will be for me to lose my grip, to fall to the ground below—not him.

I try to swing again, forcing my body to lunge sideways, knowing I am a dead weight on his arm. Closer . . . closer . . . There is a clang.

Something catches. My bracelet has looped itself onto a piece of metal jutting up from the scaffolding.

My hands never reach the other side. Dalton leans as far as his body will allow him as momentum and gravity works against us. I am slipping from his grasp.

"Dalton," I cry up to him. "I need you to let me go."

There is a look on his face I've never seen before. "No! I'm going to pull you up!" He tries to anchor himself for a better grip.

I watch him struggle. The determination on his face crushes me, but I have to convince him. It's time for me to go home.

"God, Grace!" he calls out. "You're slipping!"

The ground is so far below me. I fight the urge to look down. "I don't belong here, Dalton. I need to go home—to my parents, my brother. You have to let me go."

Disbelief is etched across his face. "No! How do you know you're not going to fall and die?"

"Because I've done this before," I tell him. "Because I'm in the same spot I was when I made that wish for my brother. The same place Alice grieved for hers. I just need to make a wish." My voice sounds strained, but my words are sure and strong. "That I go home. It's what I want, Dalton. Please understand that."

Wetness splatters my cheek. Dalton is crying.

There is no time. If I truly believe it will work, then I need to act fast. I made that wish for Ryan because I didn't want him to die. But if I stay, just to be with Dalton, there is no telling what might happen. My own life is literally hanging in the balance.

My fingers ache as they clutch Dalton's arm. I have only seconds before his strength and mine give out. My breath comes in ragged heaves, my tears choking me. I close my eyes tight and picture Alice long ago, making her own wish, knowing that the truth of what Judy and Hawkins had done would change things for her. Dalton's uncle will make sure they're locked up for a long time. He'll make sure Mack is exposed for what he's done. And Ryan . . . I picture Ryan waking up to my parents' smiling faces.

"Please," I beg. "Please send me home. I've done all I can here, but I need my life back. *My life*. My heart is yours, Dalton, but I'll never fit in here . . . and I can't give up what I believe in to stay with you."

Dalton's arm feels tense as I still hold on to the edge of his sleeve. I hear a whisper, heavy with heartache: "*Love you.*"

I make my wish over and over until my heart beats to the sound of it. My fingers unclench, his sleeve no longer between them. I hear a gasp from above me.

Lightning, too close this time, zaps the next letter over. A scream erupts from my throat as sparks burst from the impact. Thunder rolls then unleashes its fury, the boom so forceful, it rattles and shakes the sign. For a split second, only the bracelet holds me in place, until that, too, gives way . . . sending me falling in a rush through the air.

CHAPTER THIRTY-SEVEN

THE WORLD GOES WHITE—A stark contrast to the darkness surrounding the mountain. It's as if time has slowed, prolonging the impact I know will eventually come. As the ground yawns closer, Dalton's face grows smaller until he is nothing more than a tiny dot, then is gone completely.

It's as if my own world is made up of soundless black-and-white, like Dalton's movies before he adds a sense of reality to them. Then something chimes in the distance—a hollow, tinkling sound. Below me, someone walks along the hill, stopping at the foot of the *H*. They move as if fluid, full of light and shadow, a flash of gold on their wrist. Then they turn and face me.

I know it's Alice. In a flash everything becomes tinted with vibrant color. She stretches her hand out to me and as soon as we touch, her memories and emotions flood me. So real—so heart-wrenchingly tragic. Hawkins's selfishness. Judy's cruelty. I absorb the sting of betrayal and the devastation of her loss—her parents, her brother, the life she wanted and ultimately lost—as it all rushes through my veins.

Through time and space, Alice's hand is entwined with mine as I fall toward the ground. The air around me slows. The mountain, the trees . . . all still as if holding a collective breath. I am pulled to the ground—the parched dirt, the dusty hillside, the swaying shrubs. And then something shifts. Inside me is a peace I've never known before.

There is a noise, like an electrical snap, and Alice is gone.

"Dalton?" I look around me. But I am alone.

The storm is gone, and the lights of the city twinkle far below. My heart pounds in my ears, drowning out the other sounds around me. Finally, the drumming inside my chest slows, allowing the rest of the world in. The rustle of the leaves in the breeze. The hoot of an owl. A party somewhere off in the distance. I listen for the telltale sounds of a tuba, a saxophone, but instead all I hear is bass, something techno, something familiar.

I sit up, disoriented and shocked to see my hoodie, my leggings, not the elegant dress I was wearing just a moment ago. I pat down my legs, my arms, and take a deep breath, drawing the cool night air into my lungs. Confused, I gaze up at the giant letter *H*. There is no dark-haired man perched on the ladder looking at me with relief, telling me he loves me. My chest is tight, my heart crushing over having left him behind.

But I am alive. I survived the fall.

A few feet away, a rectangular bright light flashes. I crawl over to it, feeling the crunch of the earth beneath my knees. My phone's screen is in perfect condition, as if it never fell from the top of the sign. It lights up again. I scoop it off the ground and stare at the screen, scrolling through notification after notification of missed texts and phone calls from my parents. My heart thuds erratically. It feels like forever ago that I hated this—their coddling concern—but now I soak it in as if I've been in a desert without water, feeling the love my parents have for me through their words on my screen.

Grace? Where are you?

We're at the hospital.

Why aren't you answering your phone?

Your dad woke up and you weren't in your room.

Call me as soon as you get this. It's urgent.

I can tell there is panic in my mom's texts. I look intently at my phone, suddenly unsure of what to do. My heart is feeling so many emotions right now. Along with my mother's digital hysteria there are three missed calls from my dad.

I've been gone so long, yet . . . the messages are as if I haven't been gone at all. Is it possible it's the same night I snuck out of the house to make my wish for Ryan? The thought makes me scan the hillside just behind the Hollywood sign. There are no police officers waiting for me, no flashing lights on the service road beyond the fence.

The sky is still full of dark clouds but not as threatening as when I scaled the sign. I seek out the small cameras positioned on the letters, their eyes blank and dark, and I know I'm still invisible to their detection, the power not yet restored.

I scramble to my feet, making my way down the hillside to the boulder along the fence. Walking and texting is difficult, and I have to stop a couple of times to correct a few words. My thumb hovers over the screen to tap my voice mail when it rings.

"Mom?"

"Oh honey, you picked up!" My mom's voice comes through the speaker. "I've been trying to reach you. Can you get to the hospital?"

I suddenly feel sick. This is it. The moment I've dreaded.

"Grace? You still there?"

"Yeah, I'm here, Mom." I swallow the lump in my throat and pick up my pace.

"Ryan is . . ." Her voice cuts out. This spot on Mount Lee Drive is always sketchy with service.

Fear tears through me.

"Mom? Can you hear me?" Oh God. She has news about Ryan. I break into a sprint, desperate to reach home. But first I have to get down the service road and through the gate. The storm is passing, and when it does, the cameras will come back on, catching me. And if those cops are back . . .

"He's going to be okay!" My mother's voice breaks through the scratchy, fragmented connection.

I stop. *What?*

"Wait, say that again . . ."

"I said Ryan's showing signs of waking. You want to be here when he opens his eyes, don't you?"

Of course I do. I've prayed for weeks that he'll wake from his coma. This is more than I've ever hoped possible.

"Oh my God, Mom." I bend over my knees as her words sink in. "This is . . . Are you sure? He's going to be all right?"

"Yes! Now get on over here. I can't promise he'll be awake when you get here, but the doctor said he's shown a sudden improvement and his eyelids twitched about ten minutes ago."

Ending the call, I turn around to look up the hillside at the big letters of the sign. I shake my head, still not believing what my mom has just told me. Ryan is waking up. He is going to be okay. "Thank you," I whisper . . . to the sign, to Alice, to Dalton. To whatever power made this possible.

The ground beneath my feet feels solid as the world around me shifts back into bizarre familiarity. The lights of the city glow brighter than ever as I run the rest of the way home.

CHAPTER THIRTY-EIGHT

THE DOOR TO MY BROTHER'S ICU room is wide open. Cheerful, hopeful voices stream out into the hallway. I could burst into the room—I'm surprised I don't—but I take a second to listen as I will my pulse to slow down from racing over here. My parents are talking to the doctor. And then my mother starts to cry.

That's what nearly unravels me.

What if the news that my brother is finally waking is a false alarm?

I steady myself, placing my hand on the doorframe for support, and then I find the courage to walk in.

My parents stop and turn toward me.

Tears feel hot and violent as they swell in my eyes as I prepare myself for the news all over again—the accident, the coma. I can't bring myself to look at Ryan lying in the bed. I focus only on my mom's eyes, trying to gauge what is going on before anyone says anything.

Mom's face softens. "Hey, what's the matter?"

"I just . . ." God, I've missed her. "I'm just not ready for this." I press the backs of my hands over my eyes, holding the tears in. "I've been trying and trying to get back. Just to sit with him one more time. And now it's . . . he's . . ."

"Whoa, wait a minute." Dad steps closer, pulling me into a hug. "What are you talking about? Ryan's going to be all right. It's only a matter of time now before he opens his eyes and comes back to us. Isn't that right, doc?"

I lift my tear-streaked face. The doctor is standing alongside Ryan's bed, checking his vitals. He lifts Ryan's wrist and presses his fingers to it. When he finishes, he gently lowers Ryan's hand to rest at his side. "That's right. Any day now. Maybe today, even. But don't get your hopes up. These things take time, but this young man here has shown a remarkable improvement over the last few hours." The doctor shakes his head. "I'd say it's almost as if some powerful forces are at work here."

"See, honey, it's all going to be fine." Mom places her arm around my shoulders and gives me a reassuring squeeze.

I nod at my mom's affection and the doctor's words. But Ryan is still very quiet, lying there on the bed with just as many tubes in his arm as the morning I visited before the audition.

"Where were you?" Dad asks me. "I woke up and you weren't in your room."

I tear my gaze away from my brother and look at my dad. "Sorry, I needed some air and to . . . uh . . . well, I went to the sign to make a wish for Ryan."

A quizzical look spreads across the doctor's face. "Like I said. Powerful forces. I'd say whoever you wished to made good on it." He winks at me. "If you'll excuse me, I have some rounds to do, but I'll be back to check on him soon." He motions toward my brother as he drapes his stethoscope around his neck. "If he wakes up, call for the nurse right away. I'll make sure I get here as soon as I can for the big moment."

The doctor hurries off, leaving my parents and I alone with my brother.

"In this weather? You can't hike to the Hollywood sign in a storm, that's . . ." My mom's eyes are wide with concern, but she doesn't finish her sentence. I slip my hand into hers, letting her know I'm fine, and the simple touch seems to settle her. My father pulls three chairs around the bed, and together we begin the wait, hoping it will be sooner than later.

"What's that?" Mom points to my wrist where the charm bracelet dangles. "I've seen that before. Wait . . . is that what I think it is?"

I raise my arm so she can get a better look.

"I haven't seen this in years. Didn't it have more charms on it?" she asks.

Just like when I spent my time as Alice, the bracelet holds three charms. The race car, the ladybug, and the newest addition, the heart.

"Isn't that the funniest thing?" Mom says, as she touches the heart charm. "I was in the gift shop downstairs to pass some time, and they sell the same charm. I even looked at this very one, thinking it would be nice to add to the bracelet your dad's Aunt Bernice once owned. I passed it along to you when you were a little girl, but I haven't seen you wear it since . . . what? Middle school?"

"Aunt Bernice?" My thoughts fly back to the file I'd discovered in the costume warehouse. Bernice Brighton. She's my dad's aunt? Later to adopt the name Alice Montgomery?

"Well, she'd be your great-aunt," Dad opens his eyes and adds to the conversation. He is clearly exhausted from the lack of sleep these last few weeks, and the excitement of Ryan's imminent waking.

"I found it in my jewelry box. I don't know what happened to the other charms." They don't have to know I climbed the Hollywood sign and lost them somewhere between now and 1953. That would sound insane.

"I wish you could have met her," Mom says with a flash of remembrance as she continues to admire the bracelet. "Did I ever tell you that you look like a younger version of her?"

"Is she . . . still alive?" It feels weird asking about Alice. After spending what felt like weeks impersonating her, she is still very much a part of me. I still wish I could know what happened to her. If she found her way back to Hollywood, or if she moved on and found something better. I hope she managed to get far away from the cruel people who tried to hurt her.

"Oh no, she's gone," Dad says quietly, his eyes closing once again. "She died several years ago. For a while no one knew where she was. Some say she ran off and became a movie star, but I never saw her in any movies, so that may just be a rumor."

Mom places her hand on Dad's arm. "Yes, I remember that. Ryan tried to prove that she filmed a movie with James Dean, but it was denied for years. The film was scrapped and never made it to the screen. In fact, Ryan was adamant that the film was on location at the Hollywood sign, just near our house. Can you imagine? Aunt Bernice and James Dean?"

"I think Ryan invented that story," Dad pipes in, "just to say someone in our family knew his man crush."

I look back and forth at my parents. If they only knew.

"He even has a picture. You know the one, right, Glenn?"

My dad nods.

My heart quickens at the mention of the photo. That's what started this whole mess in the first place. Sneaking into Ryan's room, finding that picture on his phone . . .

"How come he never showed me?" I ask.

Mom shrugs. "Probably slipped his mind. He's been so busy with finishing school and his film." Her gaze meanders off to watch him lying beside us. At least she's speaking of him in present tense. And she doesn't seem to know that I bailed on Ryan's film. I suppose it's time to come clean.

As if on cue, my dad asks, "How was the audition, kiddo?"

I force myself to look at them both rather than down at the floor. I'm going to be strong. I'm going to tell them I didn't do it because it's not what I want. That I need to be my own person, be an adult, and—

"It's okay, Grace," Dad says. "Your mom and I know you didn't show up."

My mouth is open to defend myself, but nothing comes out.

"Ryan's classmates have been keeping me posted on what they're doing for the senior project while he's been . . ." He steals a peek at my brother. "They called today to say you didn't make your time slot."

But instead of disappointment, Dad's face is full of understanding. Mom's too, as she places her hand on my arm.

"We know it's not what you want," she says softly. "But you always said yes to Ryan to help him, because that's who you are."

I feel like I'm going to cry again. This whole time I've spent worrying they'd be furious I let Ryan down. That I'd be responsible for his film failing, for ruining his chance to graduate with proof he can make it in the film industry. I have no words to explain myself. And it doesn't matter. They already know. My parents understand.

And then it happens. Movement, like a faint swish. Ryan's foot jerks.

Waiting with bated breath, the three of us stand up and quietly hover around the bed. It starts with a flutter beneath his eyelids. The slight roll of his eyes beneath them, as if he's dreaming.

His chest expands with a deep breath, and seconds later, my brother opens his eyes.

CHAPTER THIRTY-NINE

"WE'RE HERE," MOM SAYS SOFTLY. Her hand reaches out to cradle my brother's. The moment his fingers flex and grasp hers, though weakly, feels dreamlike. We've been waiting for this for so long.

His blond hair frames his worried face like he has no idea he's been in a coma. But as soon as he recognizes me and my parents, my heart leaps.

Ryan's tongue licks his dry lips, and he swallows a few times before attempting to speak. All that comes out is a crackly, "Mom?"

"Yeah, honey. You're going to be okay. We're all here," she says, tearfully.

Dad leans over so Ryan can see him better without turning his head. "Just take your time. Don't feel like you have to talk right now, okay, son?"

It's the slightest nod, but Ryan bobs his head against the pillow. His eyes are wide as he begins to focus on the room.

"You were in an accident and you're just now waking up," Dad tells him.

"How long?" Ryan croaks.

Mom clutches his hand to hers. "Long enough, sweetie. We've all been waiting for you. Glenn, why don't you let the doctor know?"

As soon as my dad leaves the room to hurry down the hall to the nurses' station, Ryan looks at me. I can't help myself and lean over to hug him.

"Geez, Grace." He hesitantly wraps his arms around me, weakly returning my fierce hug. "It's like you haven't seen me in years."

"It feels like it," I murmur into his shoulder. Ryan squirms, but it only makes me cling tighter. He lets me hug him a little longer, and then I feel his head move above mine, as if he's looking beyond at my mom, probably rolling his eyes.

The moment I pull away, he says, "You're crazy, you know." Ryan gives me a funny look now that I'm not smushing my face into his chest.

My heart has never felt so full. "That's a compliment, right?"

"Yeah," he acknowledges. "It is." I stare in joyous disbelief that my brother is finally awake—and alive.

Dad returns to the room with several nurses behind him. The doctor arrives moments afterward, checking Ryan's vitals and asking lots of questions.

He is officially out of the woods, but he'll have to spend a few more weeks in the hospital for tests. Once he's cleared for release, he'll begin the long and arduous task of rehabilitation to get the use of his legs back. It's going to take one day at a time, but at least he's going to make it.

I don't want to leave, but my parents insist that I head home to rest while they stay at the hospital a little longer. They assure me he'll be fine. There is so much commotion anyway that I feel like I'm in the way.

The moment I get home I text Beth, telling her that Ryan has woken from his coma. After gushing over the good news, I tell her what I've wanted to suggest for a long time now.

You know, rent is cheaper when it's split.

Beth's reply comes in: *I couldn't agree more. Does this mean what I think it does?*

Time to start looking, I text.

The reply dots bounce up and down as I wait for her to answer, and when she does, it's an emphatic, excited parade of emojis followed by: *Already have the websites up. Starting the search tonight!*

It instantly hits me how much I've missed her.

Now, as the cicadas fill the night with their song, I look out my window into the distant hills. The letters of the Hollywood sign stretch across the mountain. I spent weeks missing my brother. Praying he'd be all right. And now that those prayers have been answered, my heart aches with a new emptiness.

Opening my laptop, I Google Dalton's name but quickly exit the search.

A part of me is scared to know what became of his life, to know if he fell in love with someone, if he married—if he is still alive.

I want him to be happy. And even though his last words to me were that he loved me, I love him back enough to want his life to be wonderful, even with someone else.

But I don't think my heart can take it if I find out he's no longer alive.

Instead, I spend the next hour reading articles about Old Hollywood and how casting-couch accusations eventually exposed the questionable happenings at Flynn Studios, which ultimately closed in financial ruin after several women came forth with their own "me too" moments. I hope it was the women in the photographs. I hope they found justice. Finally, after some digging, I stumble across the newspaper article about Eleanor's death. The one I had read that morning in the Chateau Marmont. It leads me to another article about the two individuals arrested for her murder—a Judith Flannery and a seedy-sounding man named F. W. Hawkins, whose real name was Archibald Harper. Then I find:

> *A Jane Doe, admitted to Los Angeles County General Hospital in early September, with broken bones and severe memory loss, has been identified as Bernice Brighton. Brighton, who bears a resemblance to actress Alice Montgomery, denies any such association to the missing starlet.*
>
> *She has been released after a full recovery.*
>
> *Alice Montgomery was reported missing from Mack Flynn's Hollywood Hills estate on September 20. The investigation is still ongoing. Authorities have stated the actress had attended Mr. Flynn's home for a celebratory evening marking the upcoming film, AMONG THE STARS. Montgomery was to co-star with James Dean.*
>
> *Alice Montgomery is the second actress associated with Flynn Studios to go missing. Miss Eleanor Dunn, also cast in AMONG THE STARS, was reported missing and later found deceased in the La Brea Tar Pits. A hearing has been set for Judith Flannery and Archibald Harper, AKA F. W. Hawkins, in association with her death.*
>
> *Further investigation has been conducted into the similarities between Montgomery and Brighton, after rumors of a stage name came to light. Findings were ruled inconclusive.*
>
> *Flynn Studios has since shuttered, shortly after filing for bankruptcy.*
>
> *Detectives for the LAPD investigated employee files, most of which were found destroyed or removed from the studio premises following several accusations of company scandal.*
>
> *Mr. Flynn, studio chairman, has declined to comment.*

I feel satisfied. Sort of. Maybe my presence really has affected everything. Reaching from 1953 until now. So many actresses, and many other normal, ordinary people, have come forth with their personal experiences about predators and what goes on behind closed doors. I finally Google the name Alice Montgomery. An article stating her disappearance from the premiere party pops up.

STARLET REPORTED MISSING
Hollywood Party Scene of Disappearance
Los Angeles—

Alice Montgomery, an up-and-coming Hollywood starlet, disappeared from Mack Flynn's estate early this morning. Flynn, chairman of Flynn Studios located in downtown Los Angeles, had opened his Hollywood home for a lavish star-studded extravaganza celebrating the studio's latest blockbuster wrap.

Montgomery, a newcomer to the industry, was reported missing shortly after midnight. She is described as a petite, attractive blonde, wearing a black-and-white evening gown. "Miss Montgomery is a rare, beguiling talent," says Geoffrey Mullins, Miss Montgomery's manager. "The uncertainty as to her whereabouts is truly disconcerting." Despite rumors that Flynn Studios is in financial distress, Mr. Flynn and his guests enjoyed an evening of sumptuous gaiety. In attendance was Mr. James Dean, slated to co-star with Miss Montgomery on the studio's latest film, AMONG THE STARS, as well as Hollywood's beloved Jane Powell, Rock Hudson, and Gregory Peck.

The Los Angeles Police Department has opened a missing persons investigation.

There is nothing else substantial. Nothing to prove she'd been a starlet with big dreams and high hopes, or that she'd ever starred with James Dean. Despite this article, it's as if she was erased from the history of the Golden Age.

But I do find information on Bernice Brighton. She lived a quiet life in Northern California on a small vineyard, passing away years ago at the age of eighty-six.

I close my eyes for a beat and feel thankful. Aunt Bernice had a good life after all she'd been through—once she was no longer Alice Montgomery.

Finally, I summon the courage to type in the name Dalton Banks.

A slew of hits pops up.

FROM FOLEY ARTIST TO SCI-FI EXTRAORDINAIRE

DALTON BANKS SIGNS CONTRACT TO WRITE FOR ROD SERLING ON LATEST UFO EPISODE

It is the last one that tugs at my heart:

TIME TRAVEL: REAL OR MYTH? A TALE OF LOST LOVE

With an almost feverish agenda, I search for anything and everything on the newly famous Dalton Banks. I finally come across an online interview in an old issue of *Galaxy* magazine, stating he was inspired by a true event and would never marry so long as he continued to believe time travel was possible. There is also the mention of him constantly searching for "the one that got away."

I look out the window at the big, white *H*. It seems almost impossible that I have been there with Dalton. While my time in the past feels strangely fuzzy and lost—like remembering something that feels real but has never happened at all—I can still feel his fingers holding on to me.

I don't want to lose the feeling. Ever.

CHAPTER FORTY

I PULL THE PACKING TAPE across the last box as my parents' car drives down the street. They're heading to the hospital, but this time it's without the weight of worry in their hearts. Ryan has improved so much since waking from his coma two weeks ago that he's been given the green light to begin physical therapy. Aside from his being in a coma, his left leg was shattered in three places after being pinned beneath the steering wheel of his car. It's going to be a long recovery, but at least he's alive. That night on the road beneath the Hollywood sign could have ended much differently.

Between my visits to the hospital and shifts at the library, Beth and I have been apartment hunting with a vengeance. Just days after Ryan woke up, she called to tell me a small apartment was available for immediate occupancy down on Sixth Street.

It's a block down from the apartment Dalton lived in and while it hurts my heart to think of him, I fell in love with the place the moment I stepped inside. It's affordable and safe, and my mom can check in on us regularly—which I don't seem to mind as much anymore.

There's something I need to do before I leave home, so I set off down the street, following the same route I took that night it stormed and my panic drove me to the wild hillside overlooking Beachwood Canyon. It's the middle of the day and the sun is out. The officers in the police car at the end of the road barely notice as my sneakers hit the pavement.

I walk through the pedestrian entrance at the gate, past others heading up the narrow path and even more heading down. The hike is long but not nearly as long as it felt that night, when I'd stop every few feet to listen if anyone was following me. I pass all the signs that remind me I'm being monitored on camera. I have no doubt they're all working now.

And there it is. The Hollywood sign draws closer, mighty and strong on the top of Mount Lee. I don't climb the fence. Don't use the boulder to launch myself into the dried patch of shrubbery to approach from below. I continue walking until I round the communications center, until I'm at the chain-link fence overlooking the back of the sign.

There are people on the rise of dirt behind me, taking pictures and posing with the infamous letters in the background of their shots. A helicopter flies overhead and they tilt their phones to the sky and take photos of that too. *Tourists*, I think, as I shake my head.

I can't explain what happened to me on top of this sign. I don't know for sure if I was ever *really* in Alice's time, but the feeling I still carry with me is enough for me to believe it truly happened. It's as if Alice's entire life exploded, and I was sent to make things right.

That's what I wished for that night I climbed the sign. *To go back and make things right.*

I thought my wish was for Ryan, for what I couldn't do for him.

But it was about Alice—*for Alice.*

Now, even though I am grateful to be home, my heart aches with an unbelievable emptiness. I miss Dalton. I miss his laugh and the way his eyes lit up when he talked about his futuristic screenplay and how he believed anything was possible. Most of all, I miss the way he held me close—the way he believed in me unconditionally and saved me from meeting a fate similar to what Alice could have experienced.

The top of the *H* towers over the sundrenched hillside in front of me. If I look hard enough, I can still see him up there—that young man with pitch-black hair, eyes the color of an ocean—and I hope that, just for an instant, I really was there with him.

The people behind me leave one by one, and soon it's just me and the sign. I push away from the fence and turn to head home, when a prickling feeling touches my back. I swing around. There is nothing but a line of letters and the breeze fanning the California holly growing near the poles supporting the *H*. The breeze carries a far-off tune. It's something I've heard before, something I danced to in the arms of the young man I now miss. I look for where it could be coming from. It sounds as if it's all around me. And then, suddenly, it's gone.

Something lands at my feet just inside the fence. I kneel and reach through the links, parting the sparse blades of weeds to pinch the tiny thing between my fingers. It's when I bring my hand back and open it that I see it's a charm. A tiny spaceship.

A rustling sound comes from the base of the sign. It might be the wind, but the music starts again, sounding louder the more I concentrate on it. Dalton is somewhere, waiting for me. I smile to myself as thoughts of time and space—and a wish for a love stronger than either of those—takes shape in my brain.

ACKNOWLEDGMENTS

WORDS CAN'T EXPRESS HOW GRATEFUL I am that *When I Was Alice* found its way into the world. This book took years and many drafts to shape it into what it is today—and it was worth every minute. My heart is full that it's landed in the right hands, with the right team who share equal vision and passion as I have for this story.

Thank you, Sue Arroyo, for that email and phone call that changed my life.

A huge thank-you to Helga Schier—I swear the universe knew what it was doing when it chose you as my editor. Your knowledge of Hollywood and the film industry has made all the difference. Thank you for pushing this book to reach higher stakes and for untangling the muddled draft that landed on your desk.

To the entire CamCat team, you are the best, especially Maryann Appel for creating such a stunning cover that perfectly captures this story. Champagne to you all!

Thank you, Cyn Balog, for always cheering me on and for those writing sprints! Cheryl Rainfield, you were there at the very beginning of this story—thank you for helping me lay the groundwork. Thank you to Lisa Amowitz for your very, very early read and suggestions on how to make this world come alive. And thank you, Marlo Berliner, for your insight and passion to see this book one day find a home.

Of course, I never could have done this without the love and patience of my family. My son, Christian, who helped birth the idea of a fifties time-travel novel, and for researching the right music for the story. My daughter, Megan, whose love for books is nearly as insane as mine. You are the best brainstorming partner ever! My husband, Chris . . . Had we never met, I surely would travel to the end of time to find you.

ABOUT THE AUTHOR

JENNIFER MURGIA WRITES MOODY FICTION—especially with a little mystery. Her books have been published in the United States, Germany, Poland, Hungary, and the Netherlands. She is a 2014 Moonbeam Children's Literature Award Winner. Jennifer is also a freelance editor for YA, MG, and adult fiction. She currently resides in Bel Air, Maryland.

For more information about her books, visit
www.jennifermurgia.com.

If you enjoyed
Jennifer Murgia's *When I Was Alice*,
please consider leaving a review
to help our authors.
And check out
Laura Wetsel's *Burnt Ends.*
A Mystery
BURNT ENDS
Laura Wetsel
MURDER TASTES SWEETER WITH A SIDE OF BBQ SAUCE
BURNT ENDS
Laura Wetsel

CHAPTER ONE

THERE IT WAS—SMOKING MEAT, the sweet stench of my childhood. Hickory, molasses, tomato, brown sugar. Kansas City's love letter to everyone but me. Darnell, my best friend from our early rehab days, drove us into the parking lot of Rocky's BBQ Smokehouse, and I gagged on the meat-laced air. *Don't toss your waffles, Tori.* The giant statue of Rocky the Pig—"Rocky the Cannibal"—smiled down at me in his chef hat and apron, holding a platter of ribs like he enjoyed making my stomach angry.

Darnell parked his truck with a displeased grunt. "Seriously, Tor," he said, wiping the sweat from his bald head. "I said I'd help you move, not run a stakeout in a hundred degrees."

"Don't worry." I took a gulp of Topo Chico to help settle my queasy gut. "My target should be here soon. Then you can help me move into my aunt's place." I twisted the zoom lens onto my digital camera and aimed it at a family tottering out of the restaurant with sauce-splattered shirts.

"Fine, then I'm running in for some brisket," Darnell said. "At least, assuming they've got any with the meat drought they've been—"

"Hold up," I cut him off and nodded at a green sedan rolling into the lot. "That's her." I pointed my lens at the driver's door, getting ready to fire away. When a woman stepped out with crutches, I groaned.

"Guess she wasn't lying." Darnell shifted the car out of park. "The brisket will have to—"

"Wait."

Darnell hit the brakes, jerking us forward. "Now what?"

"I want to see if she uses them inside. It would be hard in a buffet line."

"You're kidding, right?" He raised his brows at me. "If you go in there with that huge camera, there's no way she's ditching her crutches."

"That wasn't what I was thinking. I only knew to come here because my target's sister posted this online." I pulled out my phone to show Darnell the selfie post of Sasha Wolf with the caption, "Waiting for @GinnyWolf. #RockysBBQ #SisterLove."

"Okay," Darnell said. "Am I supposed to be seeing something here?"

I tapped on Sasha's photo, zooming in on her sunlit head. "See that sunlight shining on her ponytail?"

"Yeah, and?"

"She's under an atrium, which means I'd have a great shot from the roof."

"The roof? You're not seriously thinking of climbing Rocky's, are you?"

"Why not?" I said, tying my blond curls into a fist of a ponytail. "You've seen me scale walls and trees before. I'm a nimble little freak."

"I meant about trespassing." Darnell pointed to his police badge like he might arrest me.

"You know we private eyes don't have to follow your rules." I gave him a reassuring smile. "Just have a smoke, and I'll be back before you've even put your butt out."

"One cig, Tor," Darnell warned, tapping a pack of Marlboro Lights on the face of his watch. "Otherwise, have fun moving by yourself."

For a recovering addict, Darnell was a horrible liar. I knew he'd never abandon me, not for anything. Hanging my camera around my neck, I hopped out of the truck into the afternoon sun, where I already felt like I was sucking meat-flavored steam through a cocktail straw. I'd just have to deal with the nausea. I hustled toward the black and orange pavilion, noting its unclimbable plastic siding and security cameras mounted at the entrance. Maybe I'd have better luck in the back. I circled around and found luck in the form of a supply truck parked right beside the restaurant. No driver, no cameras, no people. This was my way up.

I hoisted myself onto the hood and made my way up the windshield to the top of the truck. The gap between the truck and building was only two feet, so I made the easy jump. Soon as I hit the roof though, my phone started buzzing in my pocket. This wasn't an ideal time to take calls, so I let it ring out while I got on my hands and knees to crawl toward the atrium.

When I got to the glass, I peered down below at a buffet hall where six dozen carnivores were dressed for the upcoming Fourth of July weekend and savagely stuffing their smeared, sticky faces with brisket, thighs, and ribs. My stomach kicked at this familiar scene. I'd been avoiding the barbecue world for nearly fifteen years, and now that I was looking down on it like some divine creature, I remembered why I'd stayed away. Barbecue didn't just make my stomach mad. From my head to my chest to my teeth, it made me mad everywhere. But I didn't want to think about why. Not after what I'd done last night.

As I searched the crowd of meat-eaters, I found Ginny, my target, at a table with her sister, her crutches against the wall. I raised my camera to my eye and focused on Ginny's face. She was teasing Sasha, lifting her brows and puckering her lips, and as she stuck out her tongue, a memory flashed in my head—I was a fourteen-year-old again in an inflatable pool of barbecue sauce with my cousin Annie. My hands shook, releasing the camera, but I jolted my neck back before the camera hit the roof.

That memory was another reminder why I should avoid smoking meat, but it made sense why the past was on my mind when Annie was the reason I was on this stakeout. She had filed her case to investigate Ms. Wolf with my agency yesterday afternoon. I had no idea though who this Ginny Wolf was to Annie as I placed the burning hot camera back on my face and snapped pictures of Ginny, her crutches, her gold pendant and butterfly tattoo, all material things identifying her.

When she stood up for the buffet, leaving her crutches behind, I videoed the fraudster walking free and easy without them. As I'd thought, another liar.

My evidence secured, I returned to the restaurant's edge and jumped onto the supply truck. I wasn't loud, but I must have made noise inside the truck because the driver's door opened. When I saw who stepped out, I knew an apology wasn't cutting it. This was the largest man I'd ever seen. Not only was he around seven feet tall with brisket-sized arms and an ugly blond bowl cut, his steely blue eyes were fixed on me like he wanted to rip my throat out.

"Hey," his tuba voice bellowed. "You taking pictures of me?"

"No," I said, but my answer didn't put him at ease because he jumped onto the hood to come after me. I didn't think it wise trying to fight a guy triple my size, so I rolled to the back of the truck, caught its back edge, let myself dangle, and released my grip. Soon as I hit the pavement, I sprinted.

I had a head start on the driver, but I'd only gone a few strides before I heard his monster feet slapping the ground behind me. Around my neck, my camera thumped like a heart against my chest. I tried to call out for Darnell, but the heat mixed with the running filled my lungs with hot air, making me choke.

Behind me, the slapping feet were only getting closer. You're not gonna make it.

And as I had this thought, my ponytail got yanked, and I was thrown to the pavement. I tried pushing myself up fast, but a boot crushed down on my spine first.

"Get off me," I gasped.

I strained to push up again, but the heel only dug deeper between my shoulder blades to cut off my breath. "I'll teach you not to spy on people," the voice said before my camera strap was snatched off my neck. "This is mine now. Better not see you here again." The boot then lifted, and the thug ran off.

I turned over and snapped my mouth open for air. "Darnell," I wheezed, choking to breathe.

Darnell heard me this time and opened his door. "Tori?" he called out. "Are you okay?" He ran over and helped me up.

"Yeah, thanks," I said, patting my chest.

Darnell's lip curled in distress at my arm. "Damn, what happened?"

I looked at where he was staring and saw my arm bleeding. Not the worst cut I'd had, maybe an inch long, but I could barely feel any pain. "That truck driver over there stole my camera." I pointed at the troll, now on the other side of the lot. "I'm getting it back." As I took a step forward, Darnell grabbed me by the shoulders.

"I don't think so," he said like he was my dad. "You see the size of that guy? You're lucky he didn't crush your skull."

I tried to shake loose, but I was weak in Darnell's grip. "Please," I begged him, "my camera's priceless."

"Tor, your life's priceless." Darnell opened my door. "Now get in. I got something for your arm." I obeyed and climbed inside, where Darnell wrapped my wound with paper towels. "That should help with the bleeding. Now you stay put while I charge that man with assault and theft."

I cleared my throat with protest. "You can't do that," I said.

"Excuse me?" Darnell's eyebrow ticked up at me. "Why not?"

"I was trespassing. If you charge him, he'll report me."

"So what? He's dangerous." Darnell opened his door, and I grabbed his arm with my uninjured hand.

"Do it and I'll lose my license."

His eyes widened with fury as he sucked on his teeth. "The things I do for you."

In case I didn't know Darnell was mad, he slammed his door and peeled out of the parking lot so fast my backpack flew to the floor of the car, spilling open at my feet. I couldn't blame him for getting angry about this situation when I was even angrier. As I bent over to gather my stuff, my seat belt tight across my body, my teeth were grinding hard.

That asshole stole your camera.

Darnell lit his fifth cigarette of the hour, and my phone buzzed in my pocket again. This time I pulled it out to check. "Great," I said. "My boss."

"Good, you can tell him how your assignment almost got you killed by an ogre."

I answered the call. "Hey Kev."

"Hi Tori, got a minute?" Kevin sounded nervous or drunk.

"Sure, what's wrong?"

"Nothing," Kevin lied. "We got a case request last night about an accidental death case. The widow's saying it wasn't an accident and specifically requested you, but I can give it to someone else if you'd still rather stick to fraud cases. Thought I'd ask you first."

"Why is she asking for me?" I said, my stomach hardening to prepare for a punch, though I knew the answer to my own question.

"I think it has to do with your last name. Aren't you related to Kansas City's Favorite Uncle?" Hearing that nickname made me gag like I'd smelled bacon. "Tori?" Kevin called out.

"Yeah, he's my uncle."

"Well, Luis Mendoza was a cook at the Uncle Charlie's location in Leawood. His widow claims she's getting death threats and that the police aren't looking into it..." Kevin's voice whirred beneath the buh-dump of my heartbeat. Turned out getting my camera stolen wasn't the worst part of my day. I just needed to stop hearing about this case before I smashed something.

"Don't want it," I said before hanging up and shoving the phone in my pocket. Darnell stayed quiet while I took staccato breaths. *You're fine. You're fine. You're fine.*

It wasn't until we reached Victory House, the sober house I was leaving for my aunt's, that Darnell turned to me and broke the silence. "So what did your boss say to get you so worked up?"

I was still in disbelief at my hysterical reaction that the words came out like I wasn't the one saying them. "He asked if I wanted a case at Uncle Charlie's."

"Uncle Charlie's? Man, good call turning that down. Your family's your worst trigger, and you've only been clean two years." Darnell reached into the back seat for a fresh Topo Chico, which though warm, was still a Topo Chico. He handed me the bottle.

"Thanks," I said. With the black bottle opener ring I wore on my thumb, I popped off the cap and started chugging down the prickly bubbles. It wasn't a drug, but the sparkling water did calm me down.

"Was it about Luis Mendoza?" Darnell asked. I nodded while swallowing. "I remember that case," he said. "Memorial Day. Guy was on heroin, fell, hit his head, passed out in the cooker. Ruled an accident."

I sipped the bottle with more restraint. "Sounds like his widow doesn't agree with that story."

"Denial's the first stage of grief." Darnell smashed his cigarette into the ashtray he'd taped to the dashboard. "Guess she's stuck there."

"Yeah, you don't got to tell me about grief."

"You know," Darnell said, nodding at my bottle of water, "you shouldn't drink that so fast. You'll give yourself indigestion with all that carbonation."

"Don't worry, I've got my resources." From my bag, I pulled out an orange bottle and pointed to the label for my anti-narcotic prescription.

Darnell gave me an incredulous glance. "That stuff treats heartburn too?"

"What can I say?" I chased down two pills with a gulp of water. "It's a miracle drug."

As I chugged the bottle down to its bottom, my mind returned to Kevin's call and my foggy memory of what I'd done last night. It was after I'd read Annie's case request that I got so upset I stole oxies from the girl next door and relapsed hard. In consequence, I became even more boiling angry, looked up my treacherous extended family online, discovered Luis Mendoza's suspicious death at the drive-in only a month ago, and saw an opportunity to finally get revenge. That was why I'd submitted a case request to myself as Luis's widow. My plan was to investigate Uncle Charlie and bring him down. But last night I was wildly high, and in my present mildly drugged-up state, I could see the danger in my vision. Because even if my gut knew Luis didn't die by accident, it also knew with more clarity now that I couldn't investigate the truth. Like Darnell said, my family was my worst trigger. And seeing as I was already hiding my recent relapse from him and my aunt, I didn't need to make my situation any worse.

CHAPTER TWO

I OFFERED TO GIVE DARNELL a hand moving my stuff into his truck, but he wouldn't hear none of it. Not with my bloody arm. So I cooled off in the AC instead and rode the warm wave of those two oxies I'd taken while reassuring Rebus in his cat carrier. "Don't worry, Reebs," I said in my mothering voice. "We're going back to Aunt Kat's. Remember? You grew up there as a kitten."

He didn't care what I had to say though. In fact, he scowled at me with his mismatched eyes—one yellow, one blue—and once we hit the road, his grumbling escalated to a growl that didn't let up until Darnell pulled into the driveway of the canary-yellow house with the dark purple door.

"Man." Darnell blinked at the house. "Your aunt sure likes purple."

"That's an understatement," I said.

I looked at the porch with its lilacs, dream catchers, and windchimes, and a lump sprang up in my throat. Though I visited Aunt Kat all the time, I hadn't lived here since she took me in as an orphaned teenager. Now I was back, broke, and desperate after Victory House gave me the boot for relapsing, and I had to make sure my aunt never found that out. Otherwise, she'd definitely send me back to rehab, and I really didn't need to go through that drama again. Anyway, I was planning on resetting myself and throwing the rest of the pills down the toilet tonight. I just wanted to escape myself a little while longer.

The purple door opened, and my purple-haired aunt hopped onto the porch in her paint-smattered smock. "Tori," she shouted, waving her hands. "You and your friend can set your things on the porch. Nobody inside but you."

I nodded, and she went back into the house. "Sorry," I said to Darnell. "She smokes weed all day for her back pain and gets paranoid around cops."

"I get it, but you gonna be okay around her pot?"

"Yeah, never did like the smell."

After Darnell unloaded my stuff on the porch and left, I took a seat on a box of books while the fan overhead tickled my neck hairs. This occasion called for another Topo Chico, and I reached over to grab a new one, popping its cap off with my thumb ring. It was one of those days when I might drink the whole crate.

"He gone?" Aunt Kat called out from behind the screen door.

"Yeah, you're safe."

Aunt Kat came out onto the porch barefoot, her arms open and ready to squeeze me until her bloodshot eyes bulged at my arm gash. "Holy cow, you're bleeding."

"Yeah," I sighed, "but I think it's stopped." I patted the blood-soaked wad of paper towels. "Took a spill moving stuff."

"You need to disinfect that immediately."

"Probably."

I downed the rest of my water and picked up Rebus in his carrier to follow my spindly aunt into the lavender living room stinking of citrus skunk. When I unlocked the cat cage, Rebus darted under the plum couch to cry. Aunt Kat dropped to the ground to comfort him.

"Poor kitty," she said, tapping the hardwood floor with her violet nails. "I've got some grass-fed raw beef if that'll cheer him up."

"Nah, he'll be on a hunger strike until he feels like hunting."

"Well, he's not going outside while he's a guest in this house. I don't want him bringing any of those pests in here like he used to do."

"He can't go outside anyway right now since he'd only run back to Victory House."

"Right." Aunt Kat gave a nod. "Cats do have that homing instinct, don't they."

I looked around the living room to see if anything had changed. There was the purple couch, the purple rug, the purple table with the purple pipe, vape, and bong. But the display case was empty, meaning my aunt's American Girl doll collection was missing. Guess I couldn't be offended she'd hidden them when I'd appeared on her doorstep with only one day's notice and had actually relapsed. I'd told her Victory House wanted me out because they needed my room for someone else and thought I was ready to be on my own. Clearly, Aunt Kat suspected I could be lying.

"Is that supposed to be a Scottish cow?" I gestured to her new painting of a long-horned, shaggy cow in a kilt playing bagpipes, its strokes of violet, magenta, and cyan so thick the paint could be yarn.

"Yeah, I was commissioned to do a Highland Cow with bagpipes," Aunt Kat said. "It's fun, don't you think? Thought I'd hang it in here a few days before sending it to the buyer."

There was a knock at the door, and my aunt jumped to her feet. "Tori," Darnell shouted. "You left your mail in the truck."

"I did?" I rummaged through my backpack. Only two envelopes. "Mustn't have scooped everything off the floor."

"Feed it through the mail slot," Aunt Kat instructed. Three envelopes plopped into a basket beside the front door.

"Thanks for helping me pay my bills," I said.

"Anytime."

Aunt Kat grabbed the mail and held up a star-spangled, glittery envelope without a stamp. "Going to a party?" She handed it to me with an elfish twinkle in her eye.

"Yeah, must be a social thing for N.A. that someone threw in my mailbox."

But I already knew what was in the envelope when I ripped it open, and as I pulled out a card written in my attempt at florid handwriting, my face flushed hot. Aunt Kat leaned over my shoulder, and I shoved the invitation back into the envelope before she could read it and worry.

"What is it?" she asked.

"You're right. It's an invitation."

"From who?"

"A friend you don't know."

"No, I saw your reaction." She shook her head at me. "You're hiding something, I can tell."

"Fine," I said since I knew she'd only pester me until she got her answer. "Go ahead and find out." I handed her the envelope. "But don't say I didn't warn you."

"I'm sure it's nothing—" Aunt Kat pulled out the card, and it leapt from her hands like it was cursed. "My gosh," she shrieked. "Why on earth is Charlie inviting you to his Fourth of July Barbecue tomorrow?"

"Technically, you don't know it came from him. There's no return address or postage."

"Then who sent it?"

"How should I know?" I plopped down on the couch to consider how to best deal with my aunt's curiosity. If she knew I'd invited myself, she'd be suspicious and would probably consider that I was using again. "You know," I began, cracking open another bottle of Topo Chico with my thumb ring, "my boss just offered me an accidental death case at Uncle Charlie's. The widow requested I investigate what happened to her dead husband."

"What? Why would she want you?" Aunt Kat reached for the overstuffed ashtray. "And why are you getting this invitation at the same time? That can't be a coincidence."

"Exactly," I said, taking a swig of water. "I don't have any online presence saying I'm a PI with my agency, so I don't know how the widow knew my name. As for the invitation, I have no idea how it got to Victory House either. Maybe someone in the family's been watching me."

"Watching you? Tori, don't you give me a panic attack with that kind of talk. Please tell me you turned that case down."

"I did. Thought it would be a bad idea getting involved with the family."

"Of course it's a bad idea." Aunt Kat flicked her lighter at a joint. "It's been years since Charlie screwed you over. He's nothing but trouble." She took a drag.

"Yeah, maybe the widow's working with whoever invited me," I said. "If Luis didn't die by accident—"

"Like he was murdered?" Aunt Kat's forehead puckered up. "Then even better you turned it down. You know you're not supposed to be working murders anymore, especially ones involving Charlie."

"That's why I was good and turned it down," I reassured her. "But I wouldn't be surprised if Uncle Charlie did murder this guy. You know I've always suspected he had a hand in Dad's death to steal the drive-in."

"I know," Aunt Kat sighed. "And I want to be honest with you right now. I don't think you're wrong about that either."

I leaned forward. "What?" I said.

"Well, I've always kept my thoughts on this subject to myself, but seeing that you're doing so well managing your addiction and anger issues, I think I owe it to you to tell you my theory."

"Your theory on what?" I exclaimed, my pulse shooting up. "That Uncle Charlie killed Dad?"

"I'm sorry, are you okay to hear this? I really don't want to set off your temper."

I took a deep breath. "Yes," I said, more composed, "go on."

"You were too young to remember, thank goodness," Aunt Kat continued, "but Charlie and I saw what happened to Billy when your mom left and how he turned to heroin. Probably would have killed himself if not for you, and he was clean for a long while, but Charlie understood Billy's addictive nature. What I think happened is Charlie got so jealous of Billy's success that he deliberately got Billy hooked on drugs again."

My face was fever hot. "What do you mean?" I pressed her. "How did Uncle Charlie get Dad addicted to heroin again?"

"This is making you upset, I can see it in your face—"

"Tell me."

Aunt Kat sighed again. "I don't think it was an accident, what happened with that scalding sauce falling off the barbecue cooker onto Billy's hands. My hunch is Charlie planted it there on purpose because he wanted Billy addicted to painkillers."

"Oxies," I stated as if I wasn't on them now.

"Right, and you know better than anyone how addictive they are. Billy tore through his first bottle in a blink, and that's when Charlie began dropping off heroin baggies in Billy's mailbox. I wouldn't be surprised if Charlie cut that stuff with something deadly either, if only to be sure he'd got the job done."

I strangled the Topo Chico bottle as if it was my uncle's neck. "What do you mean he dropped off baggies in the mailbox?"

"I saw Charlie's car at the mailbox and found a baggie of heroin inside after he'd gone. I told Billy about it, but by then he was hooked and didn't care. Then he overdosed soon after that. The way I see it, Billy poisoned himself to death, but Charlie gave him the poison."

"So he could steal the drive-in," I said under my breath.

I thought back to that Fourth of July weekend, half my life ago, when Swenson's Barbecue became the most popular joint in KC, with cars lining up for hours to get a taste of that smoky, sweet brisket. Weeks later, Dad was dead, and when his will turned up, revised days before his death, it blew all our minds because it said Uncle Charlie was the heir to the barbecue business. Aunt Kat argued in court it couldn't be right, claiming there was a different will that said I was supposed to inherit my dad's business when I came of age, but with my uncle's connections in high places, he got away with his scheme. So Uncle Charlie cut me out of the business and he got super rich off my inheritance. His role in my dad's relapse, though, was a new twist to the tale.

Now my chest was heaving, especially with those two oxies I'd taken. Though opioids were supposed to calm you down and make you feel all cozy warm inside, they could also incite rage when the situation called for it. This situation called for it. Everything in me was at a boiling point—my heart rate, my blood pressure, my breath. I needed to release the pressure. A shrill scream cut my lungs, and I swung my water bottle on the coffee table. Water and glass sprayed everywhere.

"Oh my God, Tori," Aunt Kat said. "Are you okay?"

I was still panting with short breaths as I looked up from the mess to my aunt's terrified blue eyes. "Sorry," I muttered, "I'll clean this up later." I got up and made for the door.